Guardians of the Golden Urns

KL VanderJagt

Soriano Ragazzo Publishing

Published by Soriano Ragazzo Publishing, 2620 Clarke Dr, Lake Havasu City, Arizona
86403, Contact: Sorianoragazzopublishing@outlook.com

ISBN: 979-8-89890-000-7

LCCN: 2026901227

Cover design and interior layout by Soriano Ragazzo Publishing, Tina Harden

Contents

Prologue

SEPTEMBER 21, 1949

Chang Bin Han ran down the hall, his face contorted with anger and fear. When he entered the council room, he saw the family elders seated on cushions surrounding a low table where tea awaited the thirsty.

"Chairman Mao made the declaration at the First Plenary Conference," he shouted to the room. "What shall we do now?" Bin Han referred to the Chinese People's Political conference being held in Peking.

His father rose and walked to the fervent young man. "We've planned for this, my son."

When the eldest spoke up, all turned to listen. "We have the urns secured and the families selected that will carry them to their new home. Chiang Kai Shek cannot remain on the mainland. He plans to join his army on Taiwan. The airlift is ongoing."

"When do you plan to leave?" Chang Ailun asked. "My son is still on a mission. He is undercover with one of Mao's security teams gathering information. I need to get word to him so he can return."

"Inform your son, Zi Bo, that we leave next Monday," the eldest Chang said rising. "Taiwan will be our new home."

With the meeting over, the elders left to prepare their families. Chang Bin Han arrived back at his parents' home to find it in a state of organized chaos. His mother directed the packing and his father and brothers carried the chests down to a small truck. He watched for a moment, his heart heavy. *Will I ever see my home again?*

Hong Shi ran down the steps and up to Bin Han. She placed her hand on her fiancé's cheek. "Please, try not to be too sad. We will start a new life in Taiwan where we don't have to worry about what the Admiral said."

"Do you really think China will become what the residents are saying?" Bin Han's arms encircled Hong Shi's small waist. "I wanted to stay."

"The Admiral knows men, and they all know our history. How can you doubt them? Do you not know what Lenin and Stalin have done."

"No one can know the future."

"I understand how you feel, but the elders have decided. We must follow. Are you worried about your cousin?"

"How can I not? Chang Zi Bo is still with Mao's security force. His father already said he needed to get word to him so he can get back in time. He's been undercover for so long, how can I not worry that he'll get away in time."

"Have faith in his skills. He trained well and volunteered for that mission." Hong Shi kissed Bin Han's cheek. "Let's finish bringing down my things. Since I can't bring everything, I only packed what was most precious to me."

The two went back upstairs to get her chest. When everything was lashed down, the truck left for the warehouse where the larger trucks waited. The caravan would then head for Shanghai.

The next few days passed in a whirl of activity. News spread of this skirmish and that battle. The Kuomintang army was in disarray. Many of Chiang Kai Shek's Nationalist soldiers were either captured or surrendered en masse to their communist adversaries. Waves of fleeing soldiers, some of them child soldiers who'd been kidnapped in order to fight, were joined by civilians as they fought their way to escape and survive.

Chang Bin Han reported to the main house on Monday morning for a final update. He was surprised to see the gathering present. The atmosphere was tense as the guardians tried to say their goodbyes until they would be reunited in Taiwan. Bin Han heard a murmur spread through the group and looked up to see his cousin Chang Zi Bo standing in the doorway. With a smile, he started forward to greet him only to be stopped by the look on his friend's face. What followed he'd remember for decades to come.

Chang Zi Bo's face contorted as he yelled, "Gong he." The communist cry of "work hard" echoed down the hall and was followed by the sound of pounding soldier's feet.

Stunned, Chang Bin Han froze at the sight of his beloved cousin leading an attack against his own family. When a shot dropped a cousin standing beside him, Bin Han snapped out of it and leapt into action.

Weapons appeared from inside shirts, from out of boots and from back knife guards. A few warlord pistols were pulled out and shots rang throughout the building as the fight raged room by room. There was a definite drive forward as the soldiers pushed towards the stairs leading up to the urn room. The mission was obvious—capture the urns.

Outnumbered and outgunned, the guardians fell one by one, but made the soldiers pay a heavy price for every step. Hatred pulsed through Chang Bin Han's body as he watched his family die. All he could think of now was making Zi Bo pay for his betrayal. He fought like a madman, and in after accounts of the fight, Mao's soldiers spoke in awe of the fighter who wouldn't fall despite his many wounds.

Blood pouring from face, neck and shoulder, Bin Han reached Zi Bo and the two faced off knife-to-knife since bullets were already spent. Zi Bo may have been taller, but Bin Han was known for his prowess with a blade. They crashed through the door to the library with its relics and treasures.

Zi Bo rolled away from Han's slash and came up near a jian from a century past. Pulling it out, he slashed in return. Spinning away, Bin Han grabbed a long blade of his own and the two faced each other again.

"Why?" Bin Han cried out. "Why would you do this?"

"Mao's voice is the voice of the future. One China, one people. He will rid us of these corrupt and greedy leaders. He will put an end to these forever wars. Can't you see that?"

"All I see is an oath-breaker who murders his own family. Judas hung himself, I won't give you the chance!"

The next minutes blurred as sword struck sword to the grunts of enraged adversaries. Zi Bo's blade sliced Bin Han's side causing him to stagger back and fall against a bookshelf. With a grim face, Zi Bo swung his blade high, then paused for a brief moment. Bin Han pulled his back-up stiletto from his boot, and with a flick, sent it flying towards his cousin.

A look of surprise froze on Zi Bo's face as he stood over his intended prey. A knife handle protruded from his chest, a small red circle blossoming around it.

"You cheated," Zi Bo gasped their childhood complaint as he fell.

Chang Bin Han staggered to his feet and looked down at Zi Bo's body. Tears gathered.

"This wasn't a game," he murmured.

Bin Han took out a handkerchief, pressed it against his wound binding it as best he could. He ran to the back of the library, opened a hidden door and raced up the steps inside. At the top, he opened another door to enter the urn room. Hong Shi and two of his uncles were in the room, placing the urns inside their case. Only the Admiral remained corporeal. He stood tall with his beloved jian in his hand to face the threat. Outside the locked door they could hear the sound of intense fighting.

"Hurry," Bin Han said and grabbed Hong Shi's hand pulling her back towards the secret passageway as the door to the room shook with blows.

"You two go," one of his uncles yelled. "We'll delay them as long as we are able."

"Admiral," one uncle turned to the warrior, "You must go."

"I will fight."

"No," the other spoke up. "We have a duty to do. Please allow us our honor."

"I WILL FIGHT."

The two uncles looked at each other and nodded. One picked up the Admiral's urn and faced the Admiral. The Admiral's face flush with anger. "Don't you dare!" he shouted.

"Fachu hui jia!" uncle commanded giving the Admiral the command to "go home."

With a roar, the Admiral became incorporeal and his form was sucked back into the urn. The lid snapped shut. Uncle put the last urn into the case, then ran to Chang Bin Han. "Take it," he handed the precious cargo to the wounded man, shoved some yuan into Bin Han's pocket, then pushed the two through the passageway and sealed it from behind.

Through the wall they heard the room door shatter when the soldiers came through. Hong Shi cried as she ran down the stairs. All that mattered now was saving the urns.

In the back kitchen, Hong Shi put the case in a large laundry basket then covered it with rags. Looking around, she found the aunt's two newborn Shih Tzu puppies and their mother. Placing them on top of the rags, she covered them with some small towels. Carrying the basket between them, the two lovers ran out into the chaos on the streets.

People ran up and down the roads in panic as soldiers battled and pushed their way into houses. Some soldiers looted, some just shot wildly. One officer came up to them and pointed his gun.

"What are carrying away?" he demanded.

Hong Shi burst into tears. "Please sir, you can take everything in our house, just let me keep my dogs."

The officer pulled back the towel to look. Sensing danger, the bitch growled and barked. The man pulled his arm back as if he would strike out, but stopped at Hong Shi's plea.

"Please, sir, she's a new mama. She's only trying to protect her babies. Please understand! Didn't you ever love a pet?"

The man hesitated and flushed with embarrassment. "Go," he said through gritted teeth and motioned his soldiers to let them through.

Bin Han and Hong Shi headed for the warehouse only to find that it had already fallen to the soldiers. Zi Bo's betrayal had been complete. Thinking of alternatives, Han led them to an old friend who owed the family a favor. A fisherman by trade, a smuggler by talent, the old man hid the two until the fighting quieted down.

"We have to leave as quickly as possible," Chang Bin Han said to the fisherman.

Nodding, the old man pushed his nets aside. "Wear these clothes," he commanded pulling out pants and shirts from his dirty basket.

Hong Shi held her nose as she put the fishy smelling shirt over her blouse and pulled up the pants under her skirt before slipping the skirt off. She put the skirt over the dogs.

"Here," the old man said, "feed the dogs." He gave her small pieces of dried fish to hand feed the mother. Then told them to take some for themselves. "We'll need bribery money. You got any?"

Chang Bin Han emptied what was in his pocket. "I have less than five thousand yuan."

"I think I can work with that."

"Please, that's all we have."

The fisherman paused. "Let me have the dogs. I can sell them."

With their nod, the man left. Hong Shi collapsed. "Are we all alone?" she asked weeping. "Are they all dead?"

"I don't know. I'm hoping the others who escape will join us in Taiwan." Chang Bin Han tried to sound confident, but his gut knotted with fear. Remember the oath, focus on the mission. He collapsed to the floor.

A few hours passed. Hong Shi tended to Bin Han's wounds as best she could, then her eyes drooped as she leaned up against his shoulder to rest. The fisherman returned to announce they'd be leaving now. A woman followed him into the room, dropped a small package and without a word, reached for the basket.

"Wait, our case." Hong Shi slipped the case out from under the dogs. With a quick pat goodbye and a "sorry," they watched the dogs be carried away.

The urns were wrapped up in more fishy old rags and transferred to a large backpack. Hong Shi's stomach roiled at the pungent odor, but the odor made passersby give them a wide berth as the exited their hiding place and walked to the end of the docks. They boarded a dilapidated dhow that only frightened her more.

"Are you sure this is safe?" Hong Shi whispered to Bin Han.

"She's the best," the fisherman said with pride. "She may not look fancy, but she's taken everything the sea has thrown at her and kept me afloat. We'll get you there. My wife put together some things to treat your wounds."

"Thank you," Hong Shi said smiling as they boarded the boat. The exhausted couple went to the stern where Hong Shi bandaged her fiancé's wounds again grimacing as she did. "Are you in pain?"

Bin Han smiled at her concern. "I'm fine. Our family are warriors."

The next ten hours were a nightmare for Hong Shi. Waves thrashed them about and her stomach protested. Chang Bin Han, although green most of the voyage, stood watch and tried his best to care for his lover. They dozed whenever they were able. By sunrise they could see Taiwan on the horizon and Hong Shi wept with relief.

Upon disembarking, the two said their thanks and headed to the location where they hoped to meet other family members.

When they arrived however, the house had been ransacked and only an old servant who had been badly beaten remained.

"Some men came looking for you," the old man gasped painfully. "They were dressed in black and demanded to know where the Changs were hiding. I said I knew nothing. I'm just the caretaker. They finally believed me and let me live. It's not safe here. You must go."

"We don't know where to go," Chang Bin Han said. "Did anyone leave any messages?"

"I've seen no one but you." The old man took a sip of the water that Hong Shi offered him.

"We must take you to get help," she said.

"There is no time. They could return at any moment. I will return to my family now that I've seen you and told you what happened. Go, please!"

"We don't have enough money to catch another ship," Chang Bin Han said with despair. "Where should we go?"

"I cannot know that," the man said. "If I do not know, I cannot betray you." The old man stood, shakily, but he walked to the far wall. Kneeling, he pried up the floor board and pulled out a small pouch. "Emergency yuan," he gave a small bitter laugh. "This seems like an emergency."

"We've lost everything," Chang Bin Han mourned. "Our family, our history!"

"Oh, wait," the old man said. "There's a chest here that was sent over by the elders." He stood and motioned for the couple to follow him. In the next room, the man slid open a section of the wall to reveal the chest. Chang Bin Han opened it to find some books of Guardian history. He bowed his head in thanks for this small fortune—not all of their history would be lost.

Taking the money and chest, the two headed back to the docks. There they were able to barter passage to Luzon. The captain married them at sea. In the Philippines, Chang Bin Han managed to get falsified documents under the name of Chen Bin Han. With their new identity, they worked their way to Hawaii and then to San Francisco. By the time they arrived, they were exhausted, and Hong Shi became ill.

The doctor said she needed to go to the hospital, so she was admitted to St. Mary's Medical Center under their new name of Chen. While in the hospital, Hong Shi shared a room with an older Chinese woman. The two became good friends and since the woman was an American citizen, she agreed to sponsor the young couple.

With their sponsor's help and guidance, the young couple were finally able to settle down and breathe. Chen Bin Han worked as an accountant at the old woman's store in Chinatown while Hong Shi worked as her companion. She cared for the woman until her death five years later. When the will was read, the couple were surprised to learn that their benefactor had bequeathed that business to them. Fate had taken their family, but fortune had provided.

Cast of Characters

<u>Residents: In ancient China surnames go first:</u>

Admiral Zheng He

Physician: Ming Chou Ho

Yang Ho Chengli: Mayor

Yang An Jin: Gambler

Song Lin Ji: Courtesan

Wei Zan: a Huli Jing or Mythical Nine-tailed Fox

<u>Cast of Character: name definitions:</u>

Jianyu (building the universe) Jonny Chen, youngest brother

Bolin (rain) Chen: eldest brother,

Min (quick, clever) Chen: second brother

Han (victory) Chen: father

Lei (thunder) Chen: mother

Ting Wang: elderly shop assistant nicknamed Ting-a-Ling

Bella: Jonny's sometimes girlfriend

Wu Zhang: Shaman Madam Zin

<u>Villains:</u>

Frankie Liu: Head of gambling syndicate for Chinatown

Kang: MSS agent (Ministry of State Security)

Jackie Ling: Frankie's Lieutenant

Chapter 1

How many ways can I screw things up? Jonny Chen paced his room sweating even though San Francisco in February was anything but warm. Frankie Liu would be looking for him and demanding payment. Payment Jonny didn't have. Jonny looked down at his hands and feet and wondered what he'd lose if he didn't come up with the money.

"Frankie Liu isn't known for his patience," Jonny spoke into the mirror in his room. His face looked back but didn't supply him with any answers. "I can't believe I lost that hand. A queen high flush shoulda been unbeatable." Jonny still saw the four aces being laid down one by one and the pot going to the smart-ass smiling winner. He had seventy-two hours remaining to come up with the rest of the money to make good on the IOU to Frankie.

His ruminating was interrupted by his mother's voice calling from the kitchen.

"Jonny, come for breakfast. We need to get started and have to give you the keys. Hurry up!" Lei Chen's voice sang out almost like a melody even when frustrated by her wayward and irresponsible son. Her other two sons had finished eating and sat packed and ready to go.

"Bolin, Min, did you remember extra socks and thermals? It's very cold up there?" Lei reminded her boys again until she noticed their grins. "I know, I know. Silly mothers."

Han Chen walked in and gave a weak laugh. "Leave the boys be, mother. They are grown men, now."

"Can we help you, Father?" Bolin asked only to be waved away.

"I am fine. Where's Jianyu?"

"I'm here, Dad." Jonny entered the room. "And you know I want to be called Jonny."

Han Chen's jaw clenched, but he held his temper. This was not the day to fight the ongoing battle. Han reached into his pocket and pulled out the store keys. "The store is now in your hands. We are trusting you to handle it for this long weekend. We shall return on Tuesday. Ting Wang will be in later today to help you, but please remember his advanced years and do not take advantage."

The family then loaded up the Enclave and headed out leaving a perplexed and resentful third son behind. Jonny muttered and slammed around the upstairs apartment before it was finally time to go downstairs to open up the store. The cold and foggy morning didn't promise much business and that proved to be a self-fulfilling prophecy. Even when Ting Wang, or Ting-a-Ling, as Jonny liked to call him, showed up, the Thursday morning dragged on.

At lunchtime, Jonny ordered Ting's favorite noodles from down the block and had them delivered. Then, he took the old man's favorite cushion from the chair by the cash register and put it in the break room.

"Hey, Ting-a-Ling," Jonny called out, "come get lunch."

Ting walked in and sat down with a sigh. "These old bones appreciate the break."

Jonny smiled and presented the noodles with a flourish. "Your favorite." Jonny said placing the bowl down then pretending to give a loud sneeze. Covering his nose, he then withdrew two long chopsticks. "Ta da." He handed the chopsticks to Ting. "Enjoy your lunch."

The old man began to laugh, slowly at first, then it built till his belly rolled. "You...you...foolish boy," the old man gasped.

"Ah," Jonny smiled, "but you love me."

"Indeed, I do. Go watch the register."

"Yes, sir."

The rest of the day continued like the morning and there was only so much stock re-shelving a person could do. Jonny finally told Ting-a-Ling go home early.

Jonny ate some noodles delivered from across the street and took a Tsingtao beer from his brother's stash. Closing time finally arrived and just as Jonny was locking the glass front door, two large muscular men appeared, pushed the door open and stepped through.

"Mr. Chen?" one man spoke in a voice that demanded attention. "Mr. Jonny Chen?"

"Y-yes."

"Mr. Frankie has asked us to pay a small visit to see how you're doing."

"Uh-um-uh, I'm fine." Jonny felt like his knees were turning to rubber. Both these men had arms bigger than his thighs. Their smiles never reached their eyes and chilled him right down to his bones.

"Good. That's good. Glad to hear that. Mr. Frankie sure does like you. In fact, he was saying just the other day how much he enjoys your company. You always make him laugh. He sincerely wishes that you continue to do so." The man's smile continued as he nodded.

"I have two more days left. Please tell Frankie I won't disappoint him." Jonny returned the smile until he thought his face would crack. "I'll make the delivery in person." As soon as the words came out of his mouth Jonny began to curse himself. *Deliver, deliver what? Nezha, God of gamblers save me.*

"That's good to hear. Frankie will be pleased. So, we will expect you the day after tomorrow. Frankie is looking forward to it. Perhaps you will have one of your new tricks to show him? He has been in a bad mood lately so he needs a good laugh. Yes?" Laughing, the two men turned to leave and one looked back. "You don't want to disappoint us or you'll get a visit from Jackie and he's not a nice as we are."

"Nor as pretty," the other man said.

When they left, Jonny locked the door falling back against it. *I definitely don't want to meet Frankie's enforcer.*

Bang! Bang! The door shook from the force of the knocking. Jonny let out a scream and fell forward scrambling away on hands and knees.

"Jonny, you idiot, open the door," screamed a high-pitched female voice. "What'sa matter with you?"

Gasping, Jonny looked up to see Bella, his sometimes girlfriend, standing with arms akimbo and glaring down at him from the front door. Her foot started to tap. It always tapped when she was kept waiting, and she pounded on the door again.

"Hurry up, it's cold out here." Bella pulled her jacket collar around her as Jonny jumped up to open the door. His heart slowed it's its erratic beat and his breathing returned to normal.

Bella pushed passed him and walked to the chair by the counter, sitting down and crossing her legs being sure to show them off to their best advantage. Cold or no, she always showed them to their best advantage. With a toss of her long coal black hair she sighed, tilted her head and announced, "I had no plans for tonight, so I thought I'd let you take me to dinner."

Jonny thought of his empty wallet, his looming debt, and Bella's very expensive taste. "Um, sorry, Bella, I gotta work tonight."

Bella's pretty pout appeared as she slid off the chair and approached with her slinkiest walk. Jonny closed his eyes a moment because he did have a weakness for her slinky walk and she knew it.

"Oh, c'mon baby. Are you really going to leave me all alone tonight?" Her hand slid down his chest.

"I-I really have to stay here, Bella. Y-You can stay with me. I can cook us up some of my mom's rice soup or noodles."

Bella's mood turned sour. "Really? Noodles? That sounds like a real good time. Maybe I should just go over the club and see what's cooking there. I bet someone there might be willing to take a girl to dinner." Bella pushed at him and started to turn away.

"Ah, c'mon, Bella, don't be like that. I promised my family I wouldn't leave this weekend. They already think I'm a screw-up. I gotta do right this one weekend at least. Please, baby." Jonny grabbed at her hand and brought it to his lips. "Besides, you know if any guy looks at you, I'd have to turn him into a toad." Jonny tilted his head and gave Bella his silliest smile. He knew he'd won when she laughed.

"You're such a jerk. I don't know what I see in you," Bella said but there was no sting in the words. "Okay, let's go have your noodles, but you owe me big time."

After a quiet dinner and some energetic couch wrestling, Bella announced she had to head home leaving Jonny frustrated and energized. What to do for the rest of the evening. He sat on the couch and pondered his dilemma, his fear increasing now that Bella was no longer here to divert his short attention span.

"There has to be something here that I can hock for some serious cash," Jonny spoke to himself. "Dad keeps the good stuff locked up." The rule was no one went into the locked attic room without Dad. Saying that, Jonny dug the keys out of his pocket and swore when he noticed the key to the locked room was missing. "Damn."

Angry now that his father didn't trust him and feeling somehow justified, Jonny thought about his lock picks. At first, he'd just played around with them for fun and as part of his learning some of his magic tricks, but now, he'd put them to good use.

He ran to his room, grabbed the lock picks and went up to the third floor where the locked room was at the end of the short corridor. The lock challenged his abilities, but he finally succeeded and with a mental "screw you dad", Jonny opened the door and turned on the lights.

Jonny started to look around for something valuable enough to cover his considerable debt to Frankie. His family-owned eclectic store of antiques, collectibles and pawnshop brought in a multitude of items to choose from. A dragon sculpture caught his eye. That was a possibility, but when he looked for the maker's mark, he noted it was a forgery...a good one...but a forgery. That could get him killed if Frankie thought he was trying to swindle him. A few other items caught his eye. Maybe he'd need two or three items to cover his debt. His desperation increased. Multiple items missing would be harder to cover for.

As he kept looking, his second time around he noticed a dusty old squat Buddha clay figurine. He'd passed over it the first time. Now something about it pulled at him. There didn't seem to be anything special about figure. No exceptional craftsmanship, no gold or silver, but now it made him curious. He reached to pick it up, but it wouldn't move. He tried again, and this time when he tugged, it started to turn so he continued the movement until it rotated around and faced front again. To his surprise, the wall opened with a soft click. "What the..."

Stunned, Jonny slid the door open and walked into an unexpectedly large room. There were multiple chairs arranged to face a top-of-the-line large screen TV. In one corner, a small fridge and microwave sat in a small wall cabinet. A large display cabinet dominated the back wall with book shelves on either side. The walls of the room were painted with symbols Jonny didn't understand being the lackluster student he had been. He noticed two up-to-date computer set ups he would've killed to have.

"What the heck?" Jonny exclaimed. This could only be for his brothers. They had their own hangout. Of course, they did! *And Jonny is not included!* Pain threatened to choke him, but he swallowed it. He fought to calm his breathing. He wasn't sure how long he stood there before his attention went to the back cabinet with the cushions in front. Walking over to the cabinet, he noted the rich cherry wood and fine craftsmanship.

"Now we're getting somewhere," Jonny said. "This has to be where the really good stuff is." He tried the door. "Huh, it isn't even locked." When the door opened, what he saw took his breath away. *Gold! They were gold!* Jonny took a deep breath. They looked like urns. There were five golden urns inside the cabinet! One had an arrowhead dangling from a red cord wrapped around the neck of the urn. Jonny shrugged. What on earth was his father doing with five urns? What did this mean? They had to be worth a fortune! Jonny picked one up and looked it over. He had an eye for value and he knew this was priceless. This would not only pay his debt, but would give him credit for a long time to come.

Frankie would owe him!

Jonny did a little dance around the room. When he was done, he got curious enough to wonder what was inside the vessels. He hoped it was nothing creepy like actual ashes from someone's ancestor. That would cause serious problems. Frankie was very superstitious, especially about the dead. Jonny tried to open the lid but it refused to move despite multiple attempts. But ashes or not, it was still gold.

"It must be soldered shut." Jonny looked at the lid but couldn't tell. He shrugged. "Guy did a great job." After looking over the urns, Jonny selected the least ornate to give to Frankie. He began to prepare his negotiation for his future credit line as he left the room. He never gave a thought to how he'd explain the theft to his father nor did he pay attention to the pile of books laying on the bottom shelf of the cabinet.

As for his brothers, SCREW YOU!

Chapter 2

Jonny and Ting-a-Ling sailed through the following day and if Ting-a-Ling noticed Jonny's change in demeanor, he kept it to himself. Jonny amused the customers with his sleight-of-hand card tricks and pulling quarters from the ears of children causing them to giggle and then letting them buy candy with their magic quarters. Sales were good.

"You can be charming when you choose to be," Ting-a-Ling said smiling.

"I'm always charming," Jonny quipped. "As long as Dad's not around. He's like one big wet blanket."

As they closed up the store for the day, Jonny began to get nervous. He started to practice what he was going to say to Frankie and what he would demand for his credit line. Maybe he should negotiate that before he showed Frankie the urn otherwise, he'd lose his bargaining power. *Yeah, that's good. After all, tomorrow was the official deadline, right? I'll take a picture to show him I've got the goods. Yeah, good idea.* With his new found plan and wobbly-kneed courage, Jonny headed to Frankie Liu's casino outside the city limits.

Upon arrival, Jonny asked to see Frankie and was escorted up to the third-floor office suite and frisked for weapons before being ushered into Frankie's inner office.

"Come in, come in, my boy," Frankie said with a broad smile as Jonny entered, "Look at this, boys. He's even here ahead of schedule. I told you he was no welsher, didn't I? Jonny, my boy, I'm very proud of you. Okay, let's have it. Where's my money?"

Frankie, you know me so well. I think you will be particularly happy with what I've got for you. But I need to show it to you in private." Jonny smiled.

"Private? What is this?" Frankie's head jerked up and he frowned.

"It's a bit delicate and I would consider it a huge favor. I'm looking out for your best interests, Frankie. Please believe me."

Intrigued, Frankie shooed his men from the room. "This had better be good."

Jonny took a deep breath. "I found an item that I think will not only clear my debt, but will give me a real nice line of credit I can work with here at the casino. So, I'd like us to figure something out before I bring you the item."

"You want to negotiate with me?" Frankie's face began to flush, "You think you can negotiate with me?"

"Please, Frankie, when you see the item, you'll understand." Jonny rushed to reach into his pocket and pulled out his phone. The picture of the urn glowed in all its golden splendor. "See?"

Frankie's rapid breathing began to calm as he reached for the phone. He gazed at the urn for a long moment. "That's real gold?" Frankie's eyes glittered with greed.

"Yes, sir. The workmanship is exquisite. It's very old and worth much more than my debt. I thought to sell it and pay you off, but then I thought, why not let you be the owner of something so wonderful and unique. Was I wrong? If so, I can sell it and just give you the cash."

"No! You weren't wrong. I want it." Frankie's wheels started to turn. Jonny was a gambler and not a particularly good one. He'd go through his credit even if it was a large credit. He'd make bigger and riskier bets. That's just who he was. "Let's negotiate."

After the haggling was finally over and done, Frankie called his men back into the room. "You are to escort Jonny back to his store and he will pick up an item. You will then bring him and this item back here to me. If anything happens to either of them, it better be because you're both dead. Am I understood?"

"Yes, sir."

Jonny was driven back to the store in Frankie's personal limo with two large bodyguards. "So, this is how the rich and famous live?" Jonny said smiling. They didn't smile back. The men waited by the front door while Jonny grabbed the case containing the urn and re-locked the front door. The ride back was just as silent.

Jonny placed the case on Frankie's desk and unlocked it. Frankie opened the lid and held his breath. "It's beautiful." With reverent hands he lifted the urn and turned it around to examine it. He tried to take off the lid, but again it didn't budge.

"I think it's soldered closed. I couldn't open it either. Whoever did it though is good cause I can't see a line of solder."

"It's feels empty."

"I think so." Jonny shrugged. "But, I'm not sure."

"It's smaller than I thought it would be." Frankie mused.

Jonny stayed silent. The deal had been struck and Frankie may be a hard man, but he kept his word for good and for ill. In his business, reputation was king.

"We're good?" Jonny asked after a long moment.

"Oh, yeah. You can go. The office has your credit line."

Jonny walked with a bounce in his step as he left the office. *Maybe Bella will get her fancy dinner after all!*

Chapter 3

BUSINESS WAS GOOD THAT night and kept Frankie busy down on the casino floor, but his thoughts kept circling back to the urn sitting locked in his desk cabinet. After midnight, business slowed to the point where he turned things over to his Lieutenant, Jackie Ling, and went back to his office.

After unlocking his cabinet, Frankie placed the urn on his desk and spent some moments looking at it. He noticed the markings encircling the upper third of the rim. It looked like ancient mandarin so he went online and tired tried to decipher it, but was unable to get an accurate reading. Some of the symbols didn't translate or didn't make sense.

Then he tried to look up urns and their uses. The results were always the same...human ashes. He sat at his desk and wondered. *So, did this one just not get used? Then, who was it for? Why would it be sealed if it wasn't used? But it's gold and worth a fortune. Should I care if there's someone's ashes inside?* He shuddered.

By three, Frankie was ready to drop. He pushed back his chair and rolled his shoulders to try and relax the tension. He picked up the urn to lock it back in his desk and shook his head one last time.

"What were you for, I wonder?" he mused out loud as he touched the lid. The urn grew warm in his hand. Then, with a flash of bright light, the lid popped off. Blinded, Frankie screamed and dropped the urn. A swish of wind released from the urn coalesced into a shimmering figure of a large bearded male wearing a long golden robe. "A question," the figure said.

Terrified, Frankie fell back off his chair and landed with his feet up in the air. He rolled over and scrambled away on all fours towards his door only to have the figure appear between him and the door.

"You asked a question," the figure repeated frowning.

Throwing himself to his back and staring up at the glowing figure, Frankie stammered, "Wh-what are y-you?"

"That is not a proper question. You are not a guardian." The figure began to swell in size and the glow darkened to an orange red until it filled Frankie's sight. The burning smell of sulfur rose to choke him. The very air around him seemed to crackle with an energy that made his hair stand on end.

"No-no. I-I'm sorry. I'm sorry. Wh-what the hell is a guardian?"

"How dare you defy the spirits and misuse our gift," the voice boomed.

"The spirits?" For the first time, Frankie experienced true bone deep fear. His mind whirled with it. Frankie felt his pants dampen.

"Return me immediately or face the wrath of the Guardians."

With that pronouncement, an angry swirl of wind raged around the room and re-entered the urn and the lid snapped back into place. Only then did Frankie become aware of the banging on his door.

"Boss, boss, are you alright? Open the door."

Frankie heard the pounding but was unable to stand until his bodyguards broke through the door, shattering the wood. He stumbled to his feet and leaned against his desk.

"Boss, are you alright?" his guard asked rushing forward. "We heard something weird going on in here, but we couldn't get in."

Anger surfaced now that the danger had passed. "What good are you slobs," he croaked. "What am I paying you for when someone can get in here and threaten me? In my own place!" Frankie was going to say more but he noticed his guys looking down. His face flushed a deep red. "Someone get me another drink. I spilled mine all over myself."

"Who was it, boss? How'd he get out?" his guard scanned the room, confused.

He hesitated. "I don't know. Never mind that drink. I'm going to call it a night." Frankie needed time to figure what to do. One thing for sure, he would be paying a visit to Jonny. "Tomorrow, I want you two here bright and early."

With that, Frankie walked down the corridor to his private quarters and slammed the door.

***

Jonny unlocked the shop's front door only to be brushed aside as two burly men pushed him back and a third man plus Frankie Liu entered carrying a case. Frankie nodded at two of his men who positioned themselves at the door. The third grabbed

Jonny by the throat and none-too-gently escorted him back into the break-room.

Choking and gasping, Jonny collapsed to the floor when released. Frankie strolled into the room and placed the case on the table.

"Frankie," Jonny croaked hoarsely, "what's the matter?"

"What's the matter?" Frankie said softly at first shaking his head. "What's the matter?" His voice rose an octave. "How dare you do this to me. Are you trying to curse me? Who put you up to this? The guardians? Who the hell are they...a new gang?" Frankie started to shake with rage, his fist clenched as he reached into his jacket. Jonny knew that was not a good sign.

"Frankie, I don't understand. What are you talking about?"

"The ghosts, the...the spirits..." Frankie's hands flailed about and he started to feel somewhat silly.

"What spirits?"

"The one in your damn urn." Frankie motioned to a man to open the case.

"Huh?"

There lay the urn in all its golden glory, but neither Frankie nor the man touched it. "Go ahead and pick it up," Frankie ordered and subconsciously took a step back.

Jonny picked the urn up and looked from man to man and shrugged his shoulders. "Okay. Now what?"

Frankie cleared his throat when nothing happened. "Last night a spirit came out of that thing and threatened me. Something about the wrath of the guardians. Are you a guardian?" Frankie's hand trembled as he held up his fist and shook it at Jonny. "I just want you to know that you'd better clear me with your damn evil spirits because if anything happens to me, my people will avenge me. And..., I'll see to it that your family pays the price as well. Do you understand?"

"Frankie, I don't know what you're talking about. Really! I don't know anything about any evil spirits. I'd never threatened you. Please believe me. I'm no guardian...whatever that even is." Jonny tried to placate Frankie, but the man wouldn't listen.

"So, you say." Frankie couldn't help but believe Jonny. He wasn't that good a liar. But he had to do something or he'd never hold his head up again. "I don't ever want to see you anywhere near my casinos again. I'm putting the word out on you."

"But everybody knows you've already canceled my debt."

Frankie turned red around the collar. "I'd undo that if I could, but you can forget about any line of credit." *Besides, how would I ever explain the reason. I can't ever let anyone find out about this.*

Frankie motioned to his men and they all turned and walked out.

Jonny dropped into a chair in disbelief. If someone had told him that Frankie would have put on a scene like he just witnessed, Jonny would have said it was a lie. Frankie was afraid, actually afraid. Jonny picked up the urn and looked at it again. It looked the same. Felt the same. *Huh, Frankie must be losing it.*

Ting-a-Ling came to the door of the break room and said, "What's with Godzilla and Kong?"

Jonny shrugged and closed the urn back into the case before Ting-a-Ling could catch a good look.

"You're not in trouble with them again, are you?"

"Nah. Everything's fine. Let's get to work. The family will be back in a couple days so we better be shipshape."

The two worked the rest of the day without incident and after closing, Jonny decided to call around to see if he could find a game. Turned out Frankie made good on his promise. Jonny was now persona non grata at every casino and every underground game. He was out in the cold.

Chapter 4

MEANWHILE

The ride up the mountain was beautiful and peaceful. Lei Chen gazed out the window as it frosted and couldn't help tracing pictures on its white foggy surface. She drew funny faces like when the boys were young and she'd loved making them laugh. Nowadays, they'd just smile. Only Jonny was still silly enough to laugh. She knew her husband resented his silliness sometimes, but she loved that side of her youngest.

She looked over at Han Chen and could see the faint lines of pain etched on the corners of his mouth. This trip would be hard on the boys. There would be a lot for them to handle and a lot for them to learn. The responsibilities of both the family business and the family legacy were about to be passed down. Were they ready? Was Han ready when it had been passed to him? In a time of computers, cell phones, and space travel, would they believe?

Bolin, their eldest, had always been the serious child. Thoughtful and analytical, he was a born scholar. Lei knew that Bolin had wanted to travel for further studies, but being the filial son he was, he obeyed his father's wishes and stayed home to run the business taking his courses online. How would Bolin's scientific mind make sense of what he was to learn? It would be his responsibility to lead.

Min, on the other hand, loved all things physical. Sure, he was good at his studies, especially math, so he handled all the accounting, but his passion was sports. He'd earned a black belt at both taekwondo and karate, played soccer through high school and competed in track. Now all his games were played after hours with friends and neighbors. Though competitive by nature, he was still a good sport. Min would follow his brother anywhere. He had an inner strength that Lei knew Bolin would need when the tough times came.

"How much farther?" Min asked. "I may need to make some yellow snow."

"Min," Han laughed. "Not much."

Lei laughed with her boys. How she wished they could all have been here, but Han had been adamant. He felt Jonny was neither ready, nor suitable. Her heart broke a little, but she could not change Han's mind.

The Enclave pulled up in front of an isolated private Buddhist retreat nestled high in the mountains. The buildings were surrounded by tall trees making the seclusion feel total. Lei directed the boys to gather the luggage and take it to the living quarters. Han took out the keys to unlock the small temple and brought a case to place on the altar.

"Where is everybody?" Bolin asked when he joined them in the temple. "The place looks empty."

"It is empty. We have the place to ourselves," Han told him.

"But we didn't bring any food," Min complained.

"Always thinking of your stomach," Lei laughed. "They left the kitchen stocked for us. I promise you won't starve."

"Well, speaking of food, it was a long drive," Min said placing his head on his mother's shoulder and smiling.

"Go away with you. I'll fix you something in a few minutes. Han, turn on some heat in the lodge before we freeze. I'll go check out the kitchen. You boys are going to get firewood for the fire-pit here in the temple. You may need to split some of it. I told the monks you would do it. And don't give me any of those looks." Lei laughed to herself as her sons walked out to do as she asked.

Han rested on the couch listening to his wife as she prepared their dinner. He wondered if she realized how often she sang when she cooked. Her sweet voice soothed him and somehow the pain lessened. She had her own special magic. Always did. He'd fallen in love with her the first moment he'd seen her in middle school, but she hadn't even given him a glance. Despite his many efforts to catch her attention, nothing had worked. Then one day a young boy had climbed up a jungle gym and got frightened. The older kids were laughing and teasing the boy and Han got angry. He pushed the kids away and climbed up to help the boy get down. When the boy ran back to his class, Han turned to leave and felt someone touch his sleeve. It was Lei. She'd smiled at him.

"You ready to eat?" Lei asked from the kitchen door.

"I think so."

"I'll call the boys."

"I can do that." Han started to stand.

"No," Lei said, "I'll go get them. You can set the table if you have to do something." Lei put on her coat and went out to call the boys in. She worried about her husband. Her boys seemed oblivious to the signs of strain, thank goodness, but this time together would test them a great deal. Their world was about to fall apart and be built anew. She hoped they were up to the task.

The boys came in and brushed the snow off their coats and warmed their hands for a moment before sitting down at the table.

Lei set the warmed dishes on the hot pads and everyone dug in. Conversation dwindled as they ate, but Lei noticed how little Han took. He sipped on his tea and soup and managed to eat only half of his rice.

"Father," Bolin said, "Aren't you hungry?"

"Not really, son. Got a lot on my mind. Besides, you boys eat enough for an army. I may have a snack a little later."

"If I leave you anything," Min teased taking seconds.

"What did you want to talk to us about?" Bolin asked. "Is there a problem with the business? Is that what's bothering you?" Bolin put his chopsticks down and frowned.

"No, no, son. The business is doing fine. You boys are handling yourselves very well. I'm proud of you both."

"Is it Jonny? Is he in trouble? Is that why he isn't here?" Min asked.

"No. This doesn't concern your brother." Han hesitated.

"I know you still grieve for Nana and Papa. Is there a problem with their will?" Bolin asked.

"Everything has been handled satisfactorily, but in a manner of speaking, their passing has made this necessary. You see, this is about our family legacy. You have heard me speak of this in the past...remember?"

"You mean the stories you use to tell talk about China and the old days before our family came to the States."

"Yes." Han took a deep breath. "And remember how I said that our ancestral family served the Emperor in the past and guarded a treasure for the empire over those centuries." Han paused again and looked from son to son with an intense stare.

The boys looked back at him and their brows lowered. Min responded first. "Are you trying to say that we have a... treasure somewhere?" Min said with a half laugh.

Han nodded.

"Holy shit," Min said.

"Min," Lei admonished.

"Sorry, Mom, but what the heck are you talking about Dad. What kind of treasure?"

Han looked at Bolin who had remained silent. "There needs to be two Guardians. I lost your grandfather when they had the car accident, so the time has come for me to pass the knowledge on to the next ones. That will be you, Bolin, and you, Min."

After a moment, understanding dawned on Bolin. "You're ill."

Min looked confused for a moment then said, "What do you mean?" Then he looked at his father as realization struck. His faced blanched. "You're sick?"

Han sighed. "Yes, my sons, I am. I have a cancer."

Shocked, Han's two sons stared at their father. He was their rock...a strong man who had always been there. They couldn't comprehend what he was saying. "What kind of cancer?" Bolin asked.

"Pancreatic."

"When do you start treatment?"

"There's nothing they can do for me."

"What are you talking about?" Bolin said. "You haven't had any treatment."

"I know, but I've talked to the best doctor in this world or the next," Han spoke softly and laid his hand over Lei's. "We've decided to enjoy the time we have together and not spend it on useless treatments that would only spoil the quality of my remaining time."

"Father, you have to try. What doctor told you it was too hopeless to try?" Bolin's voice rose with anger.

"You'll meet him soon." Han said. "But, for tonight, please, enough. You have had a big shock and have much to think about. We're all tired. It's late and I need to rest. Tomorrow, we have much to discuss." Han's face looked drawn and both of his sons saw his pain for the first time and felt shame that they hadn't seen it before.

Min wanted to object, but Lei's look stopped him, so with murmurs of agreement, they all went to their rooms. The night was long for the Chen family, but sleep did finally fall along with the snow.

When the family gathered the next morning at the breakfast table, the solemn faces betrayed everyone's state of mind. Lei placed the porridge before them and commanded they eat. They obeyed her like automatons.

Finally, Min broke the silence. "How long?" He asked the dreaded question.

"Long enough to be sure my sons can carry on our legacy." Han smiled. "Let's not focus on what we cannot change. Let's enjoy our time together and share our knowledge. You are in for some exciting surprises." Han took Lei's hand, then looked at his sons. "When you marry, you must choose as wisely as I did and I shall explain that to you as well. Now if you are ready to begin, we must go to the temple."

"Dress warmly. The temple is only heated by the fire-pits," Lei reminded them.

Han unlocked the temple, and the family entered the room and approached the altar where the statue of Buddha faced east and some tablets remained from a previous ceremony. A clay pot filled with sand sat before the statue to hold burning incense sticks should the family choose to light them. But they weren't here to worship —they were here to learn. Han opened up his case and pulled out a few large books. They were cloth bound together by heavy string. When Bolin opened the cover, the writing was on paper in Cantonese script. Now he understood why his father insisted they learn it.

Bolin opened another book that looked very old and gasped when he noted the date. "Father, this isn't possible! It's almost a thousand years old!"

"Why isn't it?" Han said with a raised brow.

Bolin held up the book for Min to see and Han almost laughed at the disbelief on their faces. "This is not a trick," Han said. "The dates are real. I brought the very first book started by your ancestor so you could understand our beginnings. You are both to read it tonight and I will answer your questions tomorrow."

Lei took a red velvet bag out of the case and unwrapped an urn that looked like gold and placed it on the altar. Bolin put the book down and walked over to pick it up. Looking at the markings, he said, "The markings are in Cantonese like the books. What is it?"

"This is our family's legacy. This urn and its companions are what those books are all about."

"Are our ancestors in the urns?" Min asked.

"No, son." Han said. "These urns were given to the Emperors to use as a reward and as a tool."

"By who?" Bolin asked.

"Only the Emperor may truly know. My family was never told. We were sworn to a task and accepted the pledge by blood oath. It remains unbroken."

"But we don't even live in China anymore?" Min said.

"What does that have to do with it? Our pledge remains. One day perhaps, freedom will return to China and our family will also. But that is not what we are here for today. We are getting ahead of ourselves." Han sat down on the floor and motioned everyone to sit beside him. Lei took the urn from Bolin and sat beside her husband. Han opened the case in a tent-like fashion leaving space beneath it.

"I think the time has come to show you what I am talking about. You will not understand or believe until you see."

Han took the urn that Lei offered to him and held it under the case. He smiled a smile his sons hadn't seen before and spoke, "Close your eyes." They looked at each other, then did as their father asked. They heard their father say, "Dear physician, I have a question. Can you appear?"

The brothers felt a change in the air around them almost like electricity. It startled them and they both opened their eyes.

Chapter 5

Physician Ming Chou Ho, Song Dynasty c. 960-1279

I am a humble follower of the teachings of Shennong, the Divine Farmer, and father of Chinese medicine. For many years I served my village as their physician and grew in reputation until one day an official of the Song Emperor's court came to my home. I became aware of this fact when the man walked through my door unannounced and uninvited and looked around in disdain at my cluttered surroundings.

"You are the physician known as Ming Chou Ho?" the man asked and waited for my obeisance as he brushed imaginary dust off his silk robes.

"Yes, I am," I replied bowing low. "How may I be of assistance?"

"The Emperor wishes you to come to the palace. You will gather your things and come with me."

"Is the Emperor ill? I cannot bring all my things so perhaps if you could give me an idea, I could select what I may need." I bowed again.

"The Emperor is not ill. He wishes to speak with you. Bring only your essentials. Anything else you require will be provided. Be quick." With that, the man exited my home.

I rushed to throw a few herbs, oils, cups and my needles into my bag along with a change of clothes. I paused at my shrine to say a quick prayer to Shennong and looked back at my home. Sadly, I had no wife to take leave of. Many years ago, despite all my skills, I could not save her nor our young son from the pestilence of bad water.

The ride was quiet since my escort felt no need to speak with an underling of my rank. I looked at the view out of my window and marveled at the change of scenery. We traveled the remainder of the day and stopped for the night at a lovely inn. My escort, who never spoke his name to me, was shown up the stairs, and I was led to a small room in the back of the house.

Dinner, consisting of white rice and vegetables, was served in the kitchen. I saw a fine tray with a small roasted chicken taken upstairs and to my embarrassment, my stomach grumbled. The hostess glared at me for my lack of manners. I bowed in apology.

Despite my poor surroundings, I slept well and woke early. I was given a hard-boiled egg to eat and a small apple. My escort walked down the stairs and motioned for me to follow.

The scenery continued to change as we drew closer to the city. The streets bustled with passersby, all taking care not to come too close to our cart. A few brave souls offered delicacies at the windows, but were waved away. I would have loved another bite, but was not asked. The smells of the city entered the window with the scent of animals, unwashed humans and garbage. My escort raised a scented silk cloth to his nose making me hide my smile. This man seldom left the palace nor spent time among us commoners.

Once we passed the outskirts, the narrow streets widened and I saw beautiful gardens and colorful homes with sweeping roofs to ward off the rain as well as the evil spirits. Fine silks in all colors of the rainbow fluttered in the breeze. Flowers bloomed and the fragrance made me forget that which I had just passed through.

The cart came to a stop at the palace gates. The guards looked inside, and with a bow, we were allowed through. At last, the cart stopped and the door opened. My escort got out and said, "Follow me. Bring your medicine bag."

I did as he instructed and he led me through the palace allowing no time for me to wonder at my surroundings. We walked past a blur of dazzling silks, porcelain vases and cloisonne or jade sculptures.

My escort stopped in front of large black, red and gold double doors. He turned to me. "Your head must touch the floor during your kowtow. Your head must never be higher than the Emperor's. Say nothing unless asked. No direct eye contact is permitted."

"I am aware."

He nodded to the guards and they opened the doors. My strength of will was tested not to look up as I studiously stared at the floor while following the escort. When he stopped, I dropped to my knees and touched my head to the floor, staying there until a voice said, "Rise."

When I stood, I did not fear my head being above His Imperial Majesty for his dais was up a few steps and I am a small old man. I waited to be apprised of the purpose for my summons. After a moment, a calm quiet voice spoke.

"Physician Ming Chou Ho, news of your achievements has reached our ears. Your supreme service to your village and those surrounding it are to be commended. I wish for you to examine my son."

"I would be honored." I bowed again.

"Come with me." The rustle of His Majesty's robes let me know to follow before the escort could nudge me forward. We walked to a side door then down a long corridor past ornate doors and more art. Another door opened and the three of us entered a large room where a raised dais held a young man in obvious distress. Without thought, I went to the boy and heard the gasp of the escort before the Emperor silenced him.

Feeling the boy's brow, I could feel the fire of his fever. Sweat covered him and I smelled the odor of corruption. I looked up to the woman at his bedside. "Are his bowels loose?" She nodded. "For how many days?" She held up four fingers. I knew then that the Emperor had dispatched his envoy right away. Turning towards the Emperor, I said, "Have others been sick?"

"Yes."

"When and how?"

"My son went hunting with his guards and a few friends. They camped outside the palace walls for two days. When two guards became sick, they returned. That was six days ago."

"And the guards?"

"The physician has been unable to help them. They cling to life only because they are young and strong." I could hear the sadness in the Emperor's voice. He cared not only for his son, but for his subjects. "Do you know what ails my son?"

"I fear it is a pestilence that comes from bad water."

"My physician agrees. He said you have studied this a great deal because of your wife and son. He told me of your efforts to teach your people how to keep their water safe. He says if anyone knows how to help, it would be you. Can you?"

"I shall try my best, Your Imperial Majesty. I will need a few things that I haven't brought with me. If someone could obtain them for me as quickly as possible, I can make my medicine."

"It shall be done."

The next two days I spent containing the young man's body fluids by decreasing the fever and administering small but frequent sips of tea filled with my herbs to increase his body's defenses as well as fight against the foulness I believed he'd ingested. My esteemed colleague, the Imperial court physician, continued to work with the other guards, however one joined his ancestors. The other victim's chi was stronger and he began to recover.

On the third day, the fever broke and the young man opened his eyes, smiling weakly at his mother who'd never left his side. Tears flowed down her porcelain cheeks as she kissed his forehead. She turned to me and smiled. "We are in your debt, good physician. We must think of an appropriate reward."

"No reward is needed, Your Imperial Majesty. I am honored to serve my Emperor."

But she had other plans.

The next morning after he had checked on his patient, Ho was summoned to the Emperor's chambers. After he arrived and performed his kowtow, His Imperial Majesty spoke. "Physician Ming Chou Ho, her Imperial Majesty and I feel that your services would be best applied here. You will be given suitable rooms for your use and any supplies you wish will be provided."

Ming Chou Ho began to tremble. All his memories, all his things were back in his village. He looked up for a moment and the Emperor saw his eyes before Ho remembered to look down.

"You are not pleased by this?" The Emperor frowned.

"Your Imperial Majesty, I am honored beyond words, but my home is back at my village. My memories dwell there. And what of the Imperial Physician?" Ming Chou Ho fell silent, afraid his honesty offended the Emperor.

"You are concerned for your colleague, which does you credit. He has agreed to this knowing you would serve us well. His health declines and he wishes to retire. His children and grandchildren will care for him as he has cared for us all these years. As for your home and all those things you say you desire, they shall be brought to you. What say you to this?"

Physician Ho could only say he was honored.

"You are henceforth the Imperial Physician."

***

For the next ten years, Ming Chou Ho cared for the royal court. His calm demeanor and gentle ways endeared him to most. He remained apart from the court intrigues and the number of miscarriages and poisonings dropped dramatically. Some within the court would have hated him for this, but they found they could not. Their own security increased because he was incorruptible.

The Crown Prince had a special fondness for the physician and was fascinated by his medical knowledge. They enjoyed each other's company and often debated the finer points of ethics and moral judgments. They also shared a love of Xiangqui or Chinese chess. The court would, on occasion, have competitions. The

Crown Prince, who studied strategy, often won, but Physician Ho was still stiff competition.

The provinces benefited from Physician Ho's knowledge and ongoing studies of impure water. If there were any outbreaks that he suspected were caused by impure water, he'd have the villages add some of his herbs and boil all their drinking water. Therefore, the number of deaths dropped dramatically.

One morning, while drinking his tea, the physician felt a pain in his gut that sent him to the floor where his servant found him. A physician from outside the palace walls was brought in and after his exam, gave Ming Chou Ho the news that he felt a large growth within his abdomen. Breathless, he nodded his head in agreement knowing this fact already.

The Empress came to his room accompanied by the First Eunuch. "What can we do to make you well?" she asked. "The Crown Prince cannot lose his mentor and friend."

"Your Imperial Majesty, I'm afraid my time has come. As we all have come into this world, we all know we must leave."

The Empress's eyes filled with tears. "Surely my Lord Buddha will have you cross over the Golden Bridge to reach nirvana for no one has been as good as you."

"You are very kind, but I do not wish that."

"Do you wish for the Silver Bridge? The Jade Emperor who rules there could surely use another god such as you to help in the cosmos."

"I'm afraid I don't wish for that either. I wish to be reborn. I wish another chance to have a family, to watch a son grow to manhood, to play with a daughter, to once again feel the love of a good woman. So, I ask for my body to be cremated. One of my souls will stay with my body, and another will go to the Ten Courts of

Judgment where I hope to be given the honor of eventually being reborn. My third soul has no ancestral tablet to remain with as I am the last of my family, so I know not where it will go."

"You give up too soon. I command you to get well!" The Empress's tears slid down her white cheeks. Her grief was profound as her love for this old man was deep. She owed her son's life to him, a debt she could never repay.

"You know I would obey you if I could," Physician Ho smiled then grimaced as another attack of pain burned through his body.

"I have sent for the Crown Prince. He would be devastated if he weren't here to say goodbye. You must stay with us till he can return."

"I will try, Your Majesty. I will try."

***

The Crown Prince was touring a village in the mountains and was surprised when an elderly shaman approached. The shaman bowed low and the Prince returned it with a slight bow of respect which caused the shaman to smile in return.

"What do you seek from me, Honorable Father?" the Crown Prince asked.

"I have heard good things of you and your father, the Emperor. You have served your people well. The spirits have directed me to give you a gift." The shaman motioned to his servant who brought forth a small chest and placed it before the Crown Prince.

"Inside you will find special gifts that are for you and your successors. These are to be granted to those you feel have been of great service to China."

"What do they do?" The Crown Prince asked.

"They are for eternity."

"I don't understand. What do you mean?"

The shaman's eyes glazed for a moment. "You need to return to the palace immediately."

At that moment, a rider galloped into the camp and the Crown Prince turned away to take the offered message. When he turned back to the shaman, he had disappeared.

"Where's the shaman?" he demanded.

"What shaman?" his men asked.

"The shaman I was just speaking to? The one who left this chest." The Crown Prince pointed to the chest sitting on the ground, but his men looked confused. He lifted the lid and inside were six distinctive golden urns of beautiful, if simple, craftsmanship. He lifted the lids, but they were all empty. Remembering the note, he opened and read the message. Shouting to his men, he called for his horse, and they began the long journey back to the palace at a gallop.

The Prince rushed to his mentor's quarters to find him unable to speak. The cancer had drained the last of his strength. The Emperor and Empress had already said their last goodbyes and left to allow their son this time alone with his friend.

"Honored father," the Crown Prince said," I know you have no family, but know that I will be your family. That I will care for you. I take on the filial duty for the love I bear you."

The old physician managed a smile as his chi passed. As the Crown Prince mourned by his mentor's bedside, a vision came upon him and he understood the purpose of the gift. He rushed from the room. When he returned, he carried one of the small golden urns and approached the eunuch. "This urn is for the ashes of Ming Chou Ho. Please see that they are placed within and bring me the urn when the task is finished."

"It shall be done," the eunuch bowed.

"Old friend," the Crown Prince bowed to the body of his friend, "I shall honor my promise."

And so it was that physician Ming Chou Ho's resting place came to be. The first urn was placed in a special carved cabinet. Often over the years to come, the Crown Prince, now Emperor, spoke to his friend when he sought wisdom. Sometimes, behind those closed doors, his courtiers believed they heard an answer.

Chapter 6

THE DAY DRAGGED TO a close and even the weather echoed Jonny's foul mood. The gloomy gray skies, the intermittent rain and fog were a perfect match for how he felt. After Ting-a-Ling left, he locked the door and went upstairs to the empty apartment. *What to do? I can't find a game. The club won't let me in. Damn. Frankie did a number on me.*

His cell rang and he saw Bella's name. "Hey, I'm downstairs. Come down here and let me in," Bella commanded.

When Jonny did as ordered Bella walked in and went back to the office to perch on his desk. She crossed her long legs to flash her thighs and taunted, "How come you're not at Frankie's?"

Jonny shrugged and shuffled his feet.

"Word is you got shunned."

"Want to go get some dinner?" *Diversion tactic 101. No harm in trying.*

"Aren't you going to tell me what's going on?"

"Don't wanna. Truth is...I haven't a clue what Frankie's problem is. I think he's lost his mind or something. He's talking crazy."

"Frankie may be a lot of things, but he ain't crazy. A mean son of a bitch for sure, but not crazy. You did something 'cause he's real pissed." Bella paused, tilted her head and frowned. "But, one thing I will say, I tried to talk to him about you and he acted really strange—kinda nervous. I've never seen him that way." She leaned forward and stared at Jonny. "I want to know what you did."

"I'm telling you I didn't do anything to Frankie. You know me. I'm a coward by nature." Jonny threw up his hands.

Bella nodded. "That's true."

His manhood shrunk to a new low at how fast she'd agreed with him. "Ah, c'mon, Bella, have a heart. Let's get out of here and get some dinner. I've had a lousy day." Jonny tried hard not to sound desperate.

Bella looked at him for a moment and he knew that he'd failed miserably. "Not tonight. I gotta go home and wash my hair." With that, Bella stood up and slinked her way out of the store. Jonny sunk down onto his chair and hung his head. *I'm pathetic.*

With lumbering steps, Jonny walked back upstairs and made himself some ramen noodles and watched reruns of *Blue Bloods.* After a couple episodes, he looked at the urn and thought about his brothers' room upstairs. His jaw clenched. Picking up the urn, he started up the stairs.

The clay Buddha did his job and the door slid open. Jonny felt the same resentment when he entered the room for the second time. He stood looking around and chose a large comfortable chair directly in front of the big screen. Setting the urn on the coffee table in front of him, he sat gazing at it in thought. *What was Frankie talking about?*

Jonny stood, walked to the fridge, pulled out a beer, opened it, then downed half the bottle in one long swallow. He opened the cupboard and swore when he noted it was fully-stocked. *Bastards!* He finished the first beer, took two more, then grabbing a bag of chips, he stomped back to his chair and plopped down, sulking. The second, third, and then a fourth beer disappeared as quickly as the first while Jonny's brain began to circle around the thought of how he could get even with his brothers.

Plots were formed and dismissed. The alcohol worked on his empty stomach to no good effect. He picked up the urn and stared at it as if it would give him inspiration.

"What the hell am I going to do?" The urn began to warm in his hand and the lid rattled. Startled, Jonny jumped up and dropped the urn, but the lid flew up into his hand as a bright white light flashed. Blinded for a moment, Jonny fell back into the chair, and threw the lid across the room in a panic.

A figure coalesced from a mass of vapors until it looked solid. And large. It spoke. "A question."

"What the..." Blinking and rubbing his eyes, Jonny looked up to see the figure through his watery eyes and pressed himself into the chair so hard the chair began to slide backward. He found he couldn't look away. It felt like his eyes were being pulled from his skull. *This couldn't be real. This couldn't be happening. I drank bad booze. It was drugged! That's it! I'm hallucinating! That's why this room is hidden! My brothers are dope fiends! All this time I thought they were goody two shoes. This isn't real. This isn't real! Right?*

Taking a deep breath, Jonny tried to gather himself together. *What do you do when you have a hallucination? Ignore it? Right?* Jonny stood up, turned his back on the apparition and ran over to the sink to wash and dry his face. He took a couple more deep breaths to calm himself. Then, sure that this would do the trick, he turned around to verify that the hallucination would be gone.

It wasn't.

It spoke, "You asked a question. You are Jonny, the Guardian's youngest son."

"How do you know my...what a minute...guardian...what guardian?" Jonny's brow furrowed with confusion. Frankie talked about a guardian. Frankie talked about evil spirits! *Shit!* "Are...are you an evil sp-spirit?" Jonny stammered and started to sweat. *My brothers are into evil spirits?*

The figure boomed with laughter, his large abdomen rolling with his mirth. "No."

"Then who are y-you?"

"I am Admiral Zheng He, and I know all about you." The imposing figure bowed with his introduction.

"What are you?" Jonny blurted out.

"I am a spirit from the Golden Urn."

"A w-what?"

The spirit sighed. "A spirit from the Golden Urn. I am here to answer a question."

"A question?" Jonny's muddled brain started to spin. *A genie? My own genie! Oh, boy, lucky me!* "I can ask any question I wish?"

The figure sighed. "Yes. The search for wisdom is never-ending."

Jonny ran over to the table and grabbed a paper and pen. "Oh-boy, oh-boy. What are the winning lottery numbers for the power-ball?"

The figure swelled in size. "Jianyu, your name means 'builder of the universe'. This is a cosmic joke. You are a fool. I am not a fortune teller. You waste my wisdom on a quest for riches. Han Chen must be devastated."

With those words, the figure dissolved into a mass of blue smoke that reentered the urn as the lid flew back and slammed the urn shut.

Frankie sat at his desk ruminating on the whole golden urn debacle. He felt that his men looked at him in a different way. He'd shown fear. No one dared to mention his wet pants, but he knew they didn't believe he'd spilled his drink. He'd lost face. How could he regain it?

He thought about the golden urn...he still wanted it...but the thought of the demon within terrified him. He remembered his grandmother, that superstitious old witch. She'd believed in all things supernatural, so it was all her fault that he'd reacted that way. He'd grown up on her stories. He reacted that way because of her! He thought he'd grown out of it, that his disbelief was real. Could she have been right all along?

"What should I have done?" Frankie said to the room at large.

"Boss?" the guard at the door asked. "You say something?"

"Yeah, I did. Find me a shaman. A good one. One that specializes in exorcising evil spirits."

"Boss?"

"Just shut up and do it."

In a dull gray office somewhere in Beijing, an officer entered with a report. Snapping to attention, he waited to be acknowledged. His superior looked up, sighed, and leaned back. "What?"

"Sir, we've gotten readings from an old satellite, frankly, one we thought was nonfunctional." He handed a notice to his superior.

"What made them think the satellite wasn't functioning?"

"We've never had any readings from it."

"I see. And what do these readings tell us?"

"I'm not sure, sir. I'm not aware of the purpose of the satellite. It's classified. I was just ordered to bring the information to you."

"Very well. Dismissed." Captain Ye looked at the missive and wondered what it meant. However, he was smart enough to know that if a satellite was dedicated to something, national security was involved, so he donned his cap and headed to the Ministry of State Security. At MSS, he was escorted to General Shen. The man's craggy stone-face gave Captain Ye no clue as to the importance of the missive.

"When was this received and from where?"

"We received the transmission at 1100 Friday and it appears to be from the San Francisco, California area. That would make it about 0300 local time. The signal was too brief to pinpoint with any more accuracy. The technology of the satellite is too old."

"I see."

"What does it mean, sir?"

"Dismissed."

After the captain had left, General Shen opened up his safe and took out a paper file. One copy existed and he had it. No computer record was kept, this information would always be a threat and the old guard still didn't trust the new ways.

The file had been passed down to him by his father, a great hero of the revolution. He felt a little in awe of the fact that he finally would get to open it. His father had made him swear an oath to keep it sealed unless certain conditions had been met, and one of them just had.

As he read, his brow furrowed, first in confusion, then in disbelief. He looked through the gathered data, then read the testimony of witnesses, both voluntary and involuntary. Even if none of what was in this file were true, these criminals had stolen priceless historical treasures and deserved to be punished. Shen closed the file and picked up his cell. "Get me Kang."

Chapter 7

Back at the Monastery

Bolin and Min sat stunned as they looked up at the old man standing in front of them. When he bowed, their mother rose and greeted him with obvious affection offering him a seat around the fire-pit.

"My sons," Han said, "May I present Physician Ming Chou Ho, the first resident of a Golden Urn and my dear friend. Physician Ho, this is my elder son, Bolin, and my second son, Min."

"I am honored," Physician Ho said as he bowed once again and took his seat.

The two brothers sat staring and both thought, "we're sitting on top of a mountain...around a fire...with a ghost!"

"I am sure you both have many question questions you wish to ask of me," Physician Ho said. "Please feel free to begin."

Bolin was the first to gather his thoughts. "Are you the physician my father spoke of when he said he couldn't be saved?"

"I am."

"What kind of physician tells his patients to give up all hope and not to try." Bolin's face flushed with anger.

Han began to speak, but Physician Ho raised his hand to silence him. "You are a good son. I did not tell your father not to try.

I told your father all the choices of treatments and the likelihood of success. He made his choice."

Bolin struggled for a moment then lashed out again. "Why didn't you catch this back when he could have been saved? What good is having all your supposed wisdom and knowledge if you can't save anyone?"

"You have answered your own question. I have knowledge and wisdom. I am not a fortune teller. I cannot predict the future. Sometimes I have seen things coming simply because I have lived long enough to have seen the pattern before, but I have no power to prevent them from occurring.

"I wish I could have known sooner of your father's illness, but he had no symptoms that he told me of until the disease was quite far along. Metastasis had already occurred."

"Bolin," Han interrupted, "you disrespect and blame the wrong person. If you wish to be angry, be angry with me. I was the one who ignored early symptoms, feeling they were nothing. These are things that cannot be changed. So, stop this. We have much to do this weekend. Please focus on the business at hand."

"You tell us you're dying and wish us to talk about business," Min said. "How fast do you expect us to adjust. We just lost our grandparents, now you tell us we're going to lose you, and to top it off, you tell us about some crazy family blood oath thing and show us a ghost! Yes, indeed, it's all about business!"

"Min," Lei said shocked at her son's angry sarcastic words. This meeting was not going as she'd expected. Both boys were obedient sons. What was happening?

Physician Ho raised his hands and bowed his head. "Forgive me. This is not a time for us to talk about the urns or the spirit world. Your family is in the midst of grief and you all need to take a moment. Han, you ask too much of your sons. Tonight, be together. I will go.”

With that, the blue mist swallowed him up and returned to the urn. The lid slammed tight.

Han looked at his sons as the tears gathered in all their eyes. “I'm so sorry.”

The family began to crumble as they huddled together and mourned.

***

A subdued family sat around the fire-pit the next morning when Han called up Physician Ho. He joined them bowed his greetings and waited for them to speak.

“I am sorry for my disrespect, elder,” Bolin began, “please forgive me.”

“All is forgiven. We are family here. Please, say no more.”

Lei poured some tea and passed it around the circle and the brothers were surprised when Physician Ho took a cup and smiled in appreciation.

“Um...you're a spirit, so how can you drink?” Min asked.

“In corporeal form, we have special pleasures. When we are ethereal, we all just pretend.”

“I have a question,” Bolin asked. “How can you have knowledge of modern medicine when you lived so long ago? I mean, they didn't know anything back then.”

"You're right. I knew nothing about bacteria, but I guessed there was something bad in the water that made people sick. We knew nothing about antibiotics, but we had herbal medicines that were precursors for the drugs you have now. One of the jobs the Guardians have is to help us grow in wisdom and knowledge. I continue to study all things medical because that is my interest. However, I also love music. The Lady and I have wonderful sessions discussing music and listening to new artists."

"The Lady?"

"The Lady Ji. You will meet her on your return."

"Can you do surgery?"

"I'm afraid not. While I've watched many videos and learned the technical aspects, I have no practical experience. So, I would not dare. Plus, to make myself solid enough to hold instruments takes a great deal of energy. It would have to be a short surgery." Physician Ho smiled. "You wouldn't want your physician to dissipate halfway through your operation, would you?"

"I started reading the first journal last night," Min said. "How was our family selected to be the Guardians?"

"Your ancestor grew up with the Crown Prince. In fact, when I was called to the palace to save him, there were three men ill, your ancestor was one of them. He survived because he was very strong. Later, he became one of the Crown Prince's personal bodyguards.

"When I died, the Crown Prince took on the filial responsibilities for me. I believed I would be able to cross the bridge and one day reincarnate. Imagine my surprise later when I found myself facing the Crown Prince once again. He explained to me that a shaman had presented him with these golden urns that would allow those chosen to serve as advisers to the emperors. He chose me. He was so excited and happy to see me." The physician paused looking sad for a moment, then he smiled. "And so, here I am.

"Then, a few years after the Crown Prince became Emperor, a rumor circulated that his success and power was due to a special talisman...a golden urn. A rival prince attempted to steal me and tried to assassinate him. He failed because your ancestor discovered the plot and sequestered me away to a safe place while the personal guards killed the assassins. The Emperor decided his friend, Captain Chang Han Bolin, would be named Guardian of all the urns and that your family would take a blood oath to protect them for the future."

"Am I named after him, father?" Bolin said smiling.

"Yes." Han smiled in return. "You will find many sons named Bolin in our family tree."

"What about me, father?" Min asked.

"Sorry, son. You were named after you mother's grandfather. He was a fine man, but he wasn't a Guardian." Han laughed at his son's pout and reached over to ruffle his hair. "He was a great sportsman in everything that he tried. From archery to shooting to riding, there was nothing that he didn't excel at."

Mollified, Min smiled. "How about Jianyu? Where did that name come from?"

"We'll talk about that later. Right now, I'd like to get on with what we need to cover."

"But, father," Min persisted, "shouldn't Jonny be here, too?"

Han sighed. "I have my reasons. For right now, let's say he's too irresponsible. We've decided that he's not ready to be a Guardian. We expect you to abide by our decision." Han looked at each of his sons until they both nodded in obedience.

Han cleared his thoughts and began to speak again. "There are five more urns back home that will be in your care. You will be responsible for seeing that each get the time they need outside of their urns to grow in knowledge of the outside world. Except for Physician Ho, they cannot leave their urns without our assistance. I will teach you the ritual. They can reenter on their own, or if they are endangered, there is a spell you can cast to push them back inside. They can stay out for long intervals now, but if they stay out too long, they can lose cohesion, dissipate and be lost. So, take care.

"Sometimes, your mother and I have accompanied them for short excursions, but we must be careful not to be discovered."

"I bet," Min laughed. "I can imagine what someone would think if they saw one of them coming in or going out of an urn."

"It's not just witnesses we must be careful of, Min. When the People's Republic took over China, your great grandparents escaped during the soldier's attack at great cost. Many of our family perished to ensure their escape. We may be all that is left. Unbeknownst to us, there was a traitor among us who believed in the cause of the Party. The Chinese government has been searching for us ever since. That is why the Chang family became known as the Chen family."

"How could they possibly find us here?" Bolin asked.

"There is detectable radiation released when the urns are opened, so the roof of our house is shielded. When we take an urn out, a portable shield that's within the case goes also. This system seems to be working because we've had no evidence of being spied upon."

"You mean we're being exposed to radiation? Don't we need to worry? Is this what caused your cancer?" Min shot out his questions without waiting for Han to respond.

"The radiation danger is nothing. It's similar to background radiation we all experience just being alive in this world." Han took a breath. "It had nothing to do with my cancer."

"Why didn't they just stay and serve China through the Communists?" Bolin asked changing the subject.

Han looked at Physician Ho for the first time, and the Physician spoke. "Because evil in the name of good is still evil. They may have had lofty sounds to their goals, but how they were attaining them and what we spirits foresaw coming was not what we wished to serve. Someday, they may be ready for our return and we will joyously do so."

Han took out a small chest and opened it. Inside was a scroll with a small seal and blade. "The time has come for you to sign the pledge." He unrolled the scroll and the brothers stared in awe at the number of red-stained thumbprints marking its surface. "There is more to say, but you must sign before we reveal it."

Han held up the small knife. Bolin took the blade, pierced his thumb, placed a small dab of blood on the surface of the scroll and stamped it with the family crest. Min followed suit. Han rolled up the scroll and secured the chest.

Lei spoke up. "Why don't we have some lunch, then we can talk some more. I think the boys need to rest their brains a bit." With everyone's nod, she walked over to her basket and pulled out some sandwiches and fruit. They ate in silence as each thought about what had been said.

Chapter 8

JONNY WOKE UP TO find himself in a puddle of drool on the floor, his head pounding. He propped himself up against the chair and shook himself awake. *What happened last night. That wasn't real right?* He took a couple deep breaths, got himself up and to the sink to wash his face and drink a glass of water with a couple of aspirin for his aching head.

Looking at the clock, Jonny staggered downstairs to open the store. *Thank you spirits—it's only a half day.* His stomach was roiling so he grabbed a cup of black instant coffee, but it didn't help a bit. Ting-a-Ling showed up with a smile on his face that disappeared as soon as he saw Jonny.

"Did Frankie come by again? Did he threaten you?"

"No, no, Ting. I'm fine. Just had a little too much to drink last night." Jonny tried to give his best smile. Ting pretended to believe him. The morning picked up a bit and Jonny put some effort into teasing the kids with his usual tricks. Their laughter did help a little, but his mind kept going back to wondering if he was losing it. *Imagination, hallucination, or just plain crazy.*

At noon, Ting-a-Ling told Jonny to go up and get some rest. "I'll close up."

Jonny walked up the stairs like he was walking up the guillotine steps. He made himself some ramen and sat staring at the wall.

"I won't know what the truth is unless I go up there." Jonny looked around the room as if he was expecting someone to answer him. With a deep sigh, he went up to the attic room.

The urn sat on the coffee table right where he left it. He sat down and bit his lip before picking it up and saying, "Okay, who the hell are you, really?"

The urn warmed up in his hand, Jonny closed his eyes and when he opened them, there stood the Admiral.

"Shit." Jonny dropped the urn. "You're real."

"You were hoping I wasn't?" the Admiral smiled.

"Am I crazy?"

"Would you trust me if I said no?"

"Right. So, you're not a hallucination?"

"No. How many times must I say this before you believe what you are seeing?"

"Maybe a few more."

The Admiral sat down in the chair and picked up the remote. "Do you mind if I watch the TV while you decide if you want to believe or not?"

"What?"

"Well, I've been locked up for a few days and I'm behind. I also want to watch the super bowl. Would you grab me a beer and some chips?"

"What?" Jonny repeated and shook his head. Now he was sure he was hallucinating.

"Lady Ji and I have a bet. Same with Jin, but he'll bet on anything." Zheng He had to admit he was enjoying himself.

Watching the look on this kid's face was the best fun he'd had in decades. Things had been downright boring here for years now...no palace intrigues, no rebellions, no assassination attempts. Sure, television might be fascinating, but modern times frowned on certain things. Zheng missed carrying his sword, felt almost naked without it, but Han convinced him it would garnish too much attention.

"Lady Ji? Jin?" The fact that the Admiral had used other names was just registering on Jonny. "You mean there's more of you?"

"Yes, there are. You did see the other urns, didn't you?" Zheng He's smile grew larger.

Jonny buried his face in his hands. "How many of you are there?"

"Six in all."

"Dad knows all of you?" Jonny's breathing started to increase.

"Yes. He's, our Guardian."

"Mom, too?"

"Well, yes. She's not a Guardian herself, but she's the honored wife of one."

"And my brothers?"

"By now, they do. Your father took Physician Ho with him to introduce your brothers to him." Zheng He's smile wavered and disappeared. He watched as Jonny's face flushed an angry red.

Jonny jumped up and rushed to the cabinet. Throwing open the door, he grabbed one of the urns and yelled, "Who are you?"

The urn grew warm.

Chapter 9

Lady of Talent, Song Lin Ji, Ming Dynasty c. 1368-1644

Lady Song Lin Ji sat gazing at nothing, lost in the reverie of her past. Sometimes she wished she had been a plain child. "She's such a pretty young thing," the fortune teller had said. "Too pretty for our little village. You must take her for the selection. She will do better there than to let the matchmaker choose a man for her. I see gold in her future."

Fifteen hundred girls had been chosen to begin the lengthy process of concubine selection. All had been tested for their knowledge and intelligence, then examined for any physical imperfection. After the process had whittled the number of candidates down to fifty-two, the Empress Dowager made each candidate sleep with her at night to see if any snored and to check for body odors.

The girls who passed this test were made, once again, to stand naked for examination. One girl was sent away when a tiny mole was found within her pubic hair. Ji had wondered if the girl's tears were from sadness or relief.

So, Ji entered the palace to begin her training to become a concubine for the Yuan Emperor. She was taught how to walk properly, how and when to talk, how to touch a man to pleasure him. She learned to sing, her voice a clear and light soprano. But she excelled at playing both the pipa and guqin. Her fingers slid over the string instruments with a skill that spoke of a spiritual gift. So, Song Lin Ji became a Lady of Talent, a position she felt honored to hold.

When she was deemed ready, the Empress Dowager came once again to inspect her. Lady Ji's servant girls had spent much time preparing her for this day. They had primped and pampered her, applying make-up and weaving her hair in an intricate design, then placing a carved stylus crown upon her head with jeweled beads dangling down both sides of her face. Her yellow silk robe was emblazoned with a single dragon wrapping around her body amid flaming flowers of all colors. When the concubines were presented tonight, Ji hoped she would capture the Emperor's eye.

"You look beautiful," the Empress Dowager spoke, confirming Ji's thought. "But, so do the others. Don't rely on your looks. I've heard you sing and play. My son may appreciate your talent, but you have a brain also. Beauty fades. If you wish to last at court, use that head of yours."

Surprised, Ji looked at the Empress Dowager. For once the old woman did not wear a frown. Ji bowed her head. "Thank you, your Imperial Majesty."

"You can thank me by doing well." With that the Empress Dowager left.

The parade of the concubines was a dazzling array of color and beauty. Each woman flowed forward like water over glass with only the soft swish of silk and the appreciative murmurs of the court being heard. Every now and then, the Emperor raised a finger as a lady passed, and his First Eunuch marked the woman's name. Ji noticed she was not chosen.

The women returned to their house and spent their time sewing, practicing their skills and gossiping. Time passed as they waited their turn to be called by the Emperor.

Noble Consort Bao, the current favorite, had captured the Emperor's fervor and received many gifts. She wore her favor with a jealous zeal that only grew as time passed. Whenever another concubine was summoned, Bao's vitriol, though subtle, became apparent, for soon after, that concubine would become ill and be unable to perform her duties.

One such concubine, Lady Sing Liu, conceived, and the court prepared to celebrate the news. The Emperor had yet to sire a son. His wife, the Empress, had only given birth to one daughter before the court physician declared her barren.

The Empress Dowager came to Lady Ji. "I wish for you to come to court for the celebration. I have told the Empress of your skill. You will entertain us this night. This is your chance. Please do well."

Bowing her head, Lady Ji gathered up her instruments and followed the Empress Dowager to the court where she played at the Emperor's feet, holding her audience enthralled. When she finished, he took off one of his jeweled rings and presented it to her.

"For my songbird," The Emperor said with a smile.

"Thank you, Your Imperial Majesty," Lady Ji replied glancing toward the Empress who smiled also. She backed away and joined her sisters who praised her work.

"Did you see Lady Bao?" Lady Sing Lui whispered. "She has fire in her eyes. I am afraid."

"You are wise to be so," Lady Ji said smiling at her friend. "How do you feel?"

"My stomach churns every morning. The court physician says this will pass. I pray to Buddha I will give the Emperor a fine son."

"I shall pray for this also." Lady Ji patted her friend's hand. The two had come to the palace during the same selection process and had formed a close friendship.

The rest of the evening was spent enjoying fine wine and spirits. The mood of the court was rife with anticipation.

The next morning, Lady Bao approached Lady Sing Lui. "I am told you suffer the sickness of pregnancy. Is this true?" Lady Bao smiled a sweet concerned smile.

Disarmed, Lady Sing Lui replied. "Yes, this is true, sister. Thank you for your concern. Physician says I must drink three cups of his tea every morning and the sickness will soon be gone."

"Ah, good, good. We must take extra good care of you, my sister. Please rest well." With a gentle hug, Lady Bao took her leave.

Smiling at this kindness, Lady Sing Lui went to speak with Lady Ji to tell her of the conversation. "Perhaps Lady Bao is not as harsh as we thought," Lady Sing Lui said.

Lady Ji smiled and took her friend's hand as they walked to the gardens. Her friend was always too kind, but when Lady Ji looked at the Lady Bao, she could think only of a spider spinning a web.

Two weeks later after drinking her three cups of tea, Lady Sing Lui began to have cramps. They were mild at first, but they grew until everyone knew that the baby would be lost. Then bleeding came and the court physician for all his efforts was unable to stop the flow. Lady Ji would not leave her side and wept tears of grief and suspicion.

Lady Sing Lui crossed the bridge within hours of her son.

The court mourned, none more loudly than the Noble Consort, Lady Bao.

***

The Emperor in his grief turned to his Noble Consort with increasing fervor. Lady Ji was often summoned to play and sing for that seemed to bring comfort to his grieving spirit, but he never called Lady Ji to his bed.

After four months had passed, a summons came for Lady Jang Yu, a smart and sassy concubine from the merchant class. For the next few weeks, Lady Jang Yu was called to the Emperor's bed and the women's palace began to buzz.

"Will there be a new Noble Consort?"

"Has Lady Bao fallen?"

"The spider's web is broken."

But alas, after those few weeks, Lady Jang Yu was no longer called for and Lady Bao returned. The gossip died down and the palace rhythm resumed.

Throughout this time Lady Ji played and sang.

Three months later, Lady Jang Yu whispered to Lady Ji, "Please, I need your help."

"Sister, how may I help you?"

"For our sister's Sing Lui's memory, I pray, will you keep my secret?"

Lady Ji knew then what the secret was. "You are expecting?"

"Yes. And I do not wish any to know. I fear a certain person may take action and my child and I may suffer. But I cannot do this alone and I do not know who I can trust. You were Sing Lui's friend. I am hoping I can trust you." Lady Jang Yu looked nervously about then back at Lady Ji.

Lady Ji took her hand. "I will pledge myself to you and your child. No one will harm either of you as long as I have breath. I could not save my friend. I will save you in her stead."

The two women began a friendship that grew from the necessity of protecting an unborn child. Fortune favored them as Lady Jang Yu did not suffer from the sickness of pregnancy indeed her appetite was hardy and Lady Ji found herself sneaking snacks whenever she could.

"If you do not curtail your appetites, you will soon look like a walking mountain. How can we hide you then?" Lady Ji chastised her friend. "Please control your passion for sweets."

"I know, I know. My stomach is a bottomless pit that won't be filled. I will try, sister. I will try."

Lady Ji sat practicing in the garden one morning when the First Eunuch approached and bowed.

"The Emperor wishes for you to sing this evening, Lady."

"I am honored."

First Eunuch stood for a moment and lowered his voice. "I wish to say, I may be of assistance if you need."

Startled, Lady Ji could only look up and ask, "Assistance?"

"Yes, Lady. You need only ask."

Lady Ji looked around to see that no one was close by. She realized then that little escaped First Eunuch's gaze. "Exactly what help do you think I need?"

"Not you, but the Lady Jang Yu."

"Can you help us?" Lady Ji asked as she had come up with a plan that needed much help to succeed against the Noble Consort's spies.

"What do you wish?" First Eunuch asked

"Soon we will need to remove her from the women's palace. I will need the help of the court physician to do this. We must make everyone fear a contagion so it will cause them to want to avoid us. That will allow us to be moved to another location." Lady Ji kept watch to be sure no one approached. "Can you convince him to help us?" Lady Bao walked into the garden and noticed them talking. Her gaze turned suspicious and she walked towards them.

"What time does the Emperor wish me to play?" Lady Ji asked in a loud voice stopping any further questions.

"Ah, Lady Bao," First Eunuch said with a bow. "You are here. What time would you wish Lady Ji to play this evening?"

With a brittle smile and narrowed eyes, Lady Bao replied, "Sunset."

After the two had left, Lady Ji informed Lady Jang Yu of the hastily constructed plan and the two worried over the next two weeks as they waited for the First Eunuch to confirm his ability to complete his side of the plan.

Lady Ji was returning to the women's palace one night after performing when Lady Bao appeared by her side.

"I will walk with you," Lady Bao said smiling sweet as the honey dripping down the sides of a comb.

"I am honored."

"You have become close to Lady Jang Yu, I've noticed."

"I believe so."

"I wondered why. You were not close before if my memory is correct."

Lady Ji sighed. "No, you are correct. But she was very con-soling to me after I lost my dear friend Lady Sing Lui and so our friendship grew. Is that not how friendships grow sometimes? Out of a sadness shared? Has not the loss of his unborn son brought the Emperor closer to you?"

The question seemed to catch Lady Bao by surprise. "Ah.. .indeed. Yes."

"I knew you would understand this. You are a kind and understanding soul. This must be why the Emperor cares for you so deeply." Lady Ji bowed her head so Lady Bao could not see her eyes.

"I... thank you for your gracious words. Your singing tonight was most pleasing. The Emperor has ordered some gifts to be sent to show his appreciation for the comfort you've given him." With that Lady Bao turned and left.

With a sigh of relief Lady Ji headed to her room only to find the First Eunuch outside her door.

"The court physician has prepared a potion. Both you and Lady Jang Yu are to drink it tonight. In the morning you are to eat as usual. Within an hour, you both will become ill, first with sweats and nausea, then a fever. You must call for the physician immedi-ately. He will give you another potion and a rash will appear. Then, he will say you must be sent away for the safety of the others and the Emperor. You will be sent to the isolation house, but then I have a place prepared for you that will be unknown to everyone from the palace."

So that evening Lady Ji and Lady Jang Yu drank the potion.

***

"When will this be over?" Lady Jang Yu complained rubbing her large belly.

"The physician says a few weeks yet." Lady Ji strummed on her pipa trying to soothe the spirit of her anxious friend. The last months had been tedious and confining. The First Eunuch told them the Lady Bao had sent spies everywhere in an effort to find them not believing the story of a wasting illness of the two Ladies.

"Why are they not at the isolation house?" Lady Bao had demanded. "I wish to visit my poor sisters."

"The physician has sent them to the mountains for the clear air in hopes of curing the miasma of their illness. He would not wish to risk the Noble Consort's health by allowing you to visit. The Emperor would surely punish us severely if anything were to happen to you. We will keep you well informed on their progress. Your concern does you credit, my Lady." The First Eunuch bowed deeply.

Frustrated, Lady Bao had stomped away.

Lady Jang Yu paced about the room until even Lady Ji became anxious. "Please, can't you rest."

As if on cue, Lady Jang Yu cried out as a gush of fluid poured down her legs. She doubled over and folded her arms about her abdomen. "He comes!"

Lady Ji ran to the doorway and summoned a boy to send a message to the doctor. It would be hours before he could arrive, but he had told her what to do in case, and she had stayed by Lady Sing Lui side so she had prepared herself.

The next few hours were hectic as the labor progressed faster than what the physician had predicted. The pains came one after another with little time between. Lady Jang Yu sweated and screamed despite Lady Ji's efforts to keep her calm and breathing.

When Lady Jang Yu began to push, Lady Ji knew a moment of panic. For all the preparation that she and the doctor had done, she still had never delivered a child. She still had images of her friend in her mind and feared the blood and death she had seen. What if the child died? What if her friend bled like Lady Sing Lui? She could lose both. Her hands shook. *Where was the physician!*

"Oh, Buddha, help me. I'm dying. Please Ji, help me." Lady Jang Yu wept.

Her friend's cries reached through her fear and cleared her mind. She just had to do what she had to do. Her friend pushed and Lady Ji caught a beautiful baby boy. When the baby cried a lusty cry, the two women laughed along with their tears of relief. After a brief hesitation, Lady Ji remembered her duties and none of her fears were realized. When the physician arrived, he found the women smiling over a small bundle.

"The Emperor has a son." Lady Ji smiled.

***

"So now what are we going to do?" Lady Ji asked the physician. "How are we going to get back to the women's palace without the Noble Consort's spies finding out?"

"The First Eunuch has promised us he will work most diligently to come up with a plan. Please be patient. I have started saying that both of you are recovering slowly and that there is hope of a full recovery."

The next week passed. Both women were enthralled with the young prince who had no name. That honor must be given to the Emperor, so they called him little Wu Ming, meaning nameless. Never did a baby receive more hugs and kisses than little Wu Ming, for he was the sole focus of all their time.

One day a messenger came from the physician. He brought restorative teas for the two women. He assured the women the plans were set for their return and the First Eunuch would be there in two days to bring them home. They were to pack their things to be ready.

The two women celebrated that evening and drank the last of their wine. The next morning both awoke with throbbing heads. Lady Ji felt deathly ill as she was not prone to the use of spirits. Lady Jang Yu laughed as she made the tea.

"I shall have to take care of you before I can take care of poor Wu Ming. You are such a baby."

She brought the tea and the two sipped together, but poor Lady Ji vomited immediately and fell back down.

"I'm so sorry, sister. I cannot. I…"

"That is alright. Perhaps later I shall make you a good broth. Rest now." Lady Jang Yu finished her tea. "I shall go and see to my prince. He should be waking soon. I…" the words died in her throat as Lady Jang Yu gasped and clutched her stomach.

"What is it?" Lady Ji said struggling to rise.

"Please…I…" Lady Jang Yu collapsed writhing in pain, froth bubbling from her lips.

Lady Ji dropped to her side calling weakly for help. The village housemaid came in, looked at the two struggling women and ran out in fear, abandoning them. With a horrible gasp, the stricken Lady Jang Yu crossed the bridge.

"No... No ..." Lady Ji cried out. "Don't leave, please don't leave. We need you. Wu Ming needs you." Tears poured down her cheeks as she sat by her friend not knowing what to do. She did not know how long she sat next to her friend's body and only became aware when the cries of Wu Ming became loud enough to break through her fog.

They were alone.

Lady Ji now knew they had been discovered. Was the First Eunuch even coming? She could not wait. When the spies found out that she and Wu Ming were alive, others would come to finish the job. She hurried to gather Wu Ming and tried to sooth him. He was hungry and she had no milk. Steeling herself, she placed him at his mother's breast and let him nurse for the last time, sobbing as she did so.

She hurried to the housemaid's room, changed into that woman's clothing, then bundled Wu Ming as best she could, making a sling across her chest and holding him close. She prayed she'd resemble just another humble peasant woman making her way to market. She dirtied her face and hands, tying an old scarf around her now braided hair. She had little money and traveling would be slow and on foot. With a heavy heart, she covered her friend with her favorite blanket.

"I will protect your son. I swear this to you," Lady Ji said bowing deeply.

The sound of stealthy footsteps outside the house frightened her, so she grabbed her pack and rushed out the back.

***

"There is still no sign of them?" The First Eunuch asked.

"No, nothing. It's been two weeks since I found the body of Lady Jang Yu," the physician said wringing his hands.

"And no one else was there?"

"No. We were found out. The death was definitely by poison and we both know Lady Bao knows her poisons. She's asked me twice how they are recovering."

"What have you said?"

"I told her I hadn't gone because I was ill, but I'd go this week. So, I must go."

"I want to know how she discovered their whereabouts," The First Eunuch said, pacing the floor.

"We must find them before her spies do. Lady Ji saw who it was that delivered the poison so they will stop at nothing to kill her." The physician wrung his hands again. All this intrigue was upsetting to him for he was a quiet humble man, but he had reached his limit and now felt he must resist the evil in the court.

"My spies are as good as hers, said the First Eunuch. "I will increase my rewards. The future depends on our success."

***

Lady Ji had traveled miles in darkness, sometimes stealing milk from goats left unattended and running from a few angry goat herdsmen. What little money she had only bought her meager rations of rice and steamed buns along the road. She'd hidden well whenever riders appeared, desperately trying to quiet a fussy baby. She'd slept in leaky abandoned huts or hidden in the barns of inattentive farmers. A few kind souls had taken pity on the bedraggled 'mother' and offered a warm bed and meal in exchange for a few chores.

So, it was an exhausted, hungry and dirty Lady Ji who stumbled into the tavern just off an alley not far from the Forbidden City gates. This tavern was not a popular one, being on the dark and dismal side, but it suited her purpose. The owner here was from her home province and she hoped that he would remember her. He had been a friend of her father in his youth.

She waited most of the day in a dark corner putting off anyone who tried to approach her. Here she found Wu Ming a great co-conspirator as he always seemed to pick the right moment to cry or whine. At sunset, a boisterous heavyset man entered and went behind the bar. Lady Ji recognized him by his size alone.

Smiling, Lady Ji walked forward. "Excuse me kind sir," Lady Ji began.

"Sir?" the man bellowed. "Ha, it's been a long time since someone has called me sir. What is this? You want money? I have no money. I especially have no money for...ladies...ha!"

"Ah, Ting Won Sun, is this how you speak to a daughter? Have you no respect for a friend?"

"What...what? How do you know me? A daughter? I have no daughter."

"Did you not call me your daughter when you bounced me on your knee? Did you not say I was the prettiest girl in the village?" Lady Ji smiled and tilted her head.

Stunned, the large man stood still blinking stupidly for a moment before realization struck.

"Song Lin Ji?"

She nodded her head and laughed. "So, you haven't forgotten me?"

"But I thought you lived in the palace. What are you doing out here? And dressed like this? And ...with a BABY?"

"Come and sit with me. I have a story to tell you. Right now, my life is in your hands."

***

The First Eunuch had the physician announce at court that both Ladies had succumbed to their illness and that their remains were to be transported back for proper burial.

"We must honor the memory of our lost Lady of Talent. I shall miss my songbird," the Emperor announced at court. "Lady Jang Yu's will be missed also. She could bring a smile always. We shall have a feast in their honor."

A day of mourning was announced. Behind the scenes, the First Eunuch increased his reward to his spies for any news of the missing Lady Ji and a missing baby. Just when he thought all hope was gone, one of his spies came forward with a strange tale from a tavern owner.

***

The caskets were arrayed in splendor on a dais of glorious multicolored blankets of blossoms. Silk drapes encased the area allowing friends to come forward to pay their respects. Food was brought to be burnt for offerings, and small clay figures had been placed in the coffins to be their attendants in the afterlife and some of their material possessions had been added as well. The First Eunuch had announced that both bodies had been washed and dressed at the village because of the distance and time involved in transporting the bodies. He himself took on the duty of placing all items in the casket to prevent any undue distress to the other Ladies.

Lady Bao sat upon the podium with a self-satisfied smile upon her face. Her spies had done their job well. *They thought they could fool me, those two foolish women.* She worried that her man hadn't found the baby, yet. *The housemaid must have taken the child. How long could a dull-witted village woman hide?*

The Emperor stood and toasted his lost Ladies while looking around the room. Lady Bao gracefully bowed her head and forced a tear from her eye, smiling a sad smile.

When the Emperor sat down, the First Eunuch came forward and said, "Your Imperial Majesty, I wish to make an announcement. May I speak freely?"

"Of course."

"I bring you both sad news and wondrous news. Which would you prefer first?""

"What is this? Are we playing a game?"

"I wish it were so, your Imperial Majesty. But this is most deadly."

"Then perhaps, the sad is best first."

"Lady Jang Yu did not die of illness. She was poisoned. So says our court physician."

"What? What say you? Murdered? Lady Jang Yu? What of Lady Ji? Are you saying Lady Ji was poisoned also?"

"No, your Imperial Majesty, Lady Ji is alive..."

"Wait...Lady Ji poisoned Lady Jang Yu," the Emperor interrupted.

"Please, your Imperial Majesty, allow me to tell the tale." The First Eunuch took a breath and signaled the guard to stop Lady Bao from exiting the room.

"Lady Jang Yu became pregnant with your child, but feared for herself and that child after what happened with Lady Sing Lui. She believed Lady Sing Lui was poisoned. Believing this, she asked Lady Ji for help. And here, I must ask for your forgiveness, because I also was fearful for their safety. We spirited them up to the mountains where your child was born. Shortly after the child was born, a man came from the palace and attempted to poison all three. He failed. That man serves the Lady Bao."

The Emperor paled and turned towards the Lady Bao who stood between two guards. His face turned to granite. "Take her." Lady Bao's face paled, her knees buckling. The guards grasped her arms and pulled her up, but she pulled away angrily. Back stiff, she marched away between the guards— never to be seen again.

The Emperor turned back to the First Eunuch. "I-I have a child?"

"Yes, your Imperial Majesty." The First Eunuch signaled and the doors opened. Lady Ji walked in dressed as a servant and carrying a wailing bundle in her arms. She walked up to the Emperor and bowed low.

"Your Imperial Majesty, may I present to you your son. I do believe he is hungry."

Chapter 10

Frankie walked down a dark alley and into the red door without knocking. An old woman sat on the floor behind the table and frowned. "Who said you could enter without an appointment?"

"Are you the shaman, Madam Zin?"

"I am. And you are?"

"I am Frankie Liu. I've heard that you're the real deal. I need a good shaman."

"The real deal?"

"Yeah. I need an evil spirit exorcised."

"Evil spirits surround you. Is there one in particular?" The old woman cackled.

Frankie caught himself looking around half frantic before he stopped himself. He glared at the woman, but stopped himself before he uttered any threats. He needed her help so he better pay her the respect her age and power demanded. He took a deep breath and knelt. "I'm sorry, Auntie." Frankie crawled around the table and began to rub the old woman's shoulders. "How does that feel, Auntie? Good, Huh. I give the best back rubs, yes? This must be thirsty work. How about I send one of my men down for some of your favorite tea?" Frankie signaled one of his men by the door.

"I am partial to Red Blossom's Dragonwell Supreme tea," Madam Zin said with a sweet old Auntie smile.

Frankie knew it must be an expensive choice, but he smiled and waved his man to go and get it.

"You are so sweet to this old Auntie," Madam Zin crooned as she glanced back at his expensive suit and figured he'd be good for a rich commission. She motioned him to sit back down, folded her hands across her abdomen and put on her best wise old sage expression.

Frankie launched into his story of meeting a frightening large evil spirit...minus the whole golden urn part...and asked if she could exorcise the demon.

"Of course. Isn't that why you came. However, I must first evaluate this spirit and see whose spirit it is and why it's haunting you. From what you've said, the spirit has done no harm. Why do you say it is evil?"

"Uh...well...it...threatened me. Yeah, it threatened me." Frankie nodded his head.

"What did it threaten?"

"It said something about facing it's wrath."

"Nothing more specific than that? He didn't threaten to chop you up or cut off your head or eat your liver?" Madam Zin almost smiled as Frankie Liu's face turned green.

"Evil spirits actually do that?"

"Some of them do."

"But you can stop them. Right?" Frankie pointed his finger at her.

"Usually. But that's why I have to assess the spirit and get a reading on what powers I'm dealing with." Madam Zin stood up. Even though she stood no higher than a large fairy, she radiated a vital energy. "Tonight, you are to take me to where the spirit resides. You are dismissed."

Frankie bristled at her tone, but her look shriveled his insides. He didn't want to admit that he found her presence a bit daunting. Besides, she knew how to curse or cure him and right now, he needed her services. She better make good on her promises or he'd make her pay. "Very well, Auntie. I'll send my car to pick you up this evening."

***

At his MSS office, General Shen read over the file again as he waited for Kang to arrive. He removed the information he felt his agent didn't need to know. If anyone could track down these traitors, Kang could. The man was already a legend. His reputation frightened many. Some called him soulless. He was definitely friendless. But he was committed to following orders. A knock on the door interrupted Shen's musing. "Enter."

A black-eyed, mid-sized, well-built man entered and stood before Shen's desk. He nodded to Shen. "Reporting as ordered."

Shen could believe the man's piercing black eyes would miss nothing and he gave off energy like a coiled viper. On a personal level, Shen found the man unpleasant, but as an officer, he was certain that this man was the right man for the job. "Sit."

When Kang had taken his seat, General Shen handed him the altered file and smiled a tight smile at the surprised look on Kang's face.

"This is a very old case. As you can see, we received a transmission from a top-secret satellite launched back in 1982. One we weren't even sure was still functioning. We were attempting to track certain artifacts that were stolen during the revolution. We now have our first clue as to their location. Your mission is to locate them, eliminate the thieves, and bring the items home by any means possible.

"Our local embassy will provide assistance, but you are to tell them nothing of these details. Is that understood?"

"Yes, sir."

"You may finish reading the file here in my office, but it cannot leave this room." With that, Shen stood. "I'm going for a cup of coffee. Take what time you need. Tell the guards if you need anything, or if you have any questions." Shen left.

Kang spent the next twenty minutes reading and memorizing the file. He looked over the photos which were few and of very poor quality. Physical descriptions were conflicting. From the sounds of the battle when the guards invaded the residence, the fighting had been intense and there were many casualties on both sides. Witness statements from surviving soldiers sparked his admiration. These would have been worthy adversaries. The Chang family were indeed formidable. Too bad they had been betrayed by one of their own.

Kang believed in loyalty, first and foremost. In his eyes, there was nothing worse than a traitor. Kang could respect a man who fought for the other side because of his beliefs. Sure he would have to die, but at least the man would die with honor.

After he'd finished the file, he signaled the guard to call the General back to the office. Then he collected his contact papers and vouchers for expenses. He always traveled light, but he had a few weapons he preferred and they'd be shipped ahead and waiting for him at the embassy. Shen handed him his tickets for San Francisco.

***

Bella woke up late Sunday morning, her head pounding. The party last night was dull and boring and she drank too much. She didn't want to admit it, but she wished Jonny was there. Sure, he wasn't the richest or the coolest or the most of anything really, he just made things more fun.

She got up to wash her face and brush her teeth to get rid of cotton mouth. Looking at herself in the mirror she tried to assess what she was feeling. "I don't love the guy, do I? No. Not really. I can do better than him. I know I can." She brushed her hair the required strokes to make it shine, then started her facial regimen.

"Besides, he's a goof-ball." Wash, wash.

"But he makes me laugh." Rinse, moisturize.

"We'd always have to work for a living." Dab under the eyes.

"He's awful cute though." Put on the sealer.

"No. Forget about him. Maybe I'll call Teddy. He's got money and he's always sniffing around me." After saying that, Bella picked up the phone and dialed. It rang and rang, so she had to leave a message. "It's me. Call me back right away."

And she waited. Then, she called again.

And waited.

After two hours she decided to go visiting, but when she got to the store the doors were already locked. When she knocked, no one answered, so she called again and got the same "leave a message". "Damn you, Jonny."

Bella stood outside the shop doors and fumed. *How dare he ditch me. Who does he think he is anyway? Well, Jonny Chen, you messed with the wrong woman. I'll get even with you.*

***

Jonny watched as the blue mist swirled and one of the most beautiful women he'd ever seen emerged from within the fog. She walked, no scratch that, she flowed over to the Admiral and gave him a kiss on the cheek.

"Is the game ready to start? You're going to lose you know." She smiled and turned, noticing Jonny for the first time. "Who are you?"

"Lady Ji," the Admiral said smiling, "May I present Jianyu Chen, our host for the big game."

"Oh, Han and Lei's youngest." The Lady gave a graceful bow towards Jonny and continue to smile. "I am pleased to finally meet you. Tell me, what team do you favor?"

"It's Jonny," Jonny said mechanically. "I'd bet on the Chiefs."

"A most intelligent man." The Lady walked to the fridge and took out a Pepsi then joined the Admiral. The two started to chat like old friends, but Jonny couldn't take his eyes off the woman. She seemed unreal. Her movements were fluid, and when she laughed, all he could think of was music. His brain sizzled.

The Admiral laughed as he watched Jonny's reaction. He leaned forward and whispered. "Now you can imagine how hard it was for me."

"Huh?" Jonny frowned.

"I was a eunuch surrounded by such beauties all the time. Beauty I couldn't touch."

"Aren't you going to let the brothers out? Lady Ji pointed to the urns. Jin will be upset if he misses the game now that we have someone to let us out. I know he wasn't happy that we were going to miss it."

"Sure." Jonny walked over to the urns and grabbed two of them, but when he reached for the one with the arrowhead, the Admiral stopped him.

"I think we should wait before you open that one," the Admiral said placing his hand over Jonny's.

"Why?"

"One thing at a time."

Chapter 11

Chengli and Jin, Yuan Dynasty c. 1279-1368

"Piggy, piggy, piggy," the boys chanted as they followed the chubby nine-year-old down the alley they'd chased him into. They threw dung at his back soiling his best tunic. Chengli gasped as he tried to push his legs faster to reach the street where he knew he would be safe. *Where was Jin when he needed him?*

"You boys," a deep voice bellowed from behind a large bushel. A beggar stood, bedraggled and smelling of the alleyway filth. Chengli stopped, sure he would now be robbed and bludgeoned to death, left in an alley for his father to find and his mother to grieve.

The three boys stopped, unsure what to expect. After looking the man over, they decided he was friend not foe. "This piggy is for sport," the leader spoke for the group. "He thinks he's better than us. We think we should show him he's not."

"But he is better than you," the man said. "Your acts prove that he is. You are all older and larger than he. Your jealousy shows. Now go away."

"You're just an old beggar," the leader yelled, but jumped back when the beggar stepped out and came towards him. When the man reached out, the three boys squealed and ran away.

The man turned towards Chengli. "Are you uninjured?"

"Yes, sir," Chengli bowed. "I thank you for your assistance."

The beggar smiled impressed at the young boy's manners and pleased that the boy had shown him respect despite his appearance. "You are most welcome. Now you must return to your parents for they will be worried."

"May I ask you, sir, if I may bring you some food as a gift for the service you rendered this day?"

"If you wish, it would be appreciated." The beggar smiled at the boy's formal speech.

Chengli ran home, and when his parents saw his clothing, they chastised him until he told them his story. At first, they were grateful for the man's intervention, but when Chengli told them the man was a beggar and that he wanted to return to take the man some food, his father forbade him.

"We cannot feed the beggars on the streets, son. Besides, I don't want you going back down there at night," his father said.

"You could go with me, Father," Chengli replied and looked to his younger brother, Jin, for support.

"No. Now eat your food. We will discuss this no further."

Chengli sulked in silence for his father had the look on his face that said no more words would change his mind. After eating, his father went to the tea-house to meet with his business partners and his mother went into her rooms. Chengli took rice, vegetables, and meat from the store room. Jin offered to go with him, but Chengli declined. "If Father catches me, I don't want him to punish you, too."

When he got back to the alley, he walked up and down looking for the beggar, but didn't find him. Finally, he sat on a bushel to wait. After about thirty minutes, when the beggar walked down the alley, he found the tired young boy asleep on top of the bushel. Looking down at the sleeping boy, the beggar smiled. Laying his hand on the boy's head he looked to the sky. "You've chosen well. He will be a fine man." A faint light glowed about the boy. When Chengli awakened to find himself alone, he was saddened that he couldn't fulfill his promise.

***

Jin had followed his brother at a safe distance. Though he was a year younger, he seemed to be an old soul and was bent on protecting his older brother. He was a scrapper, and the other boys knew not to pick a fight with him, so softhearted Chengli was safe whenever Jin was around.

Jin watched as Chengli entered the alley, waited, then finally fell asleep on the bale of hay. Just as Jin was about to waken his brother to tell him to come home, the beggar appeared. He watched as the man approached and stood over his brother. Worrying for a moment, Jin tensed as the man lay his hand on Chengli's head. *What is he going to do?*

The man looked up and spoke, but Jin was too far away to hear what the beggar said. When the light appeared, Jin's eyes widened in surprise and he began to shake. What was happening? He ran forward, but the beggar turned towards him, and his smile stopped the boy. "Take good care of your brother, Jin."

"How do you know my name?" Jin demanded stepping forward again, undaunted.

"You are a fearless one, aren't you?" the beggar smiled.

"You didn't hurt him, did you?"

"No, I would never do that."

"What did you do?"

"I gave him a blessing, but it's not for you to know. I think it is time for you to go home. Your brother will be safe tonight. I promise you." The beggar waved his hand and Jin found himself feeling sleepy and confused. The beggar reached forward and touched the boy's head. "There, now. Since you two share everything."

"Yes," Jin murmured, "I must go home." He turned and stumbled back towards their house.

The beggar laughed. *These two brothers are quite a pair and will do great things for China.*

In the morning when Chengli returned home, his father was furious. He received twenty lashes as Jin sat by his side. Afterwards, their mother tended to his wounds, sobbing in her quiet, soft manner. While stroking his hair to comfort him, she paused.

"Where did this mark come from?"

"What mark?" Chengli asked.

"There is a small mark on your temple. It almost looks like a crescent moon. Did you get a tattoo? When did this happen?"

"Mother, I did no such thing."

Jin leaned forward to look at the mark. "Huh, brother. There is a reddish mark on your right temple I've never seen before. How could you do this without me?" Jin's laugh was cut short when his mother grabbed his face and turned it to look at his temple.

"You, devil! It was your idea. I knew it!"

Chengli did indeed grow up to be a fine man. Though still wider of girth than he would have liked, his kindness and humor made him popular with others. His father kept an iron grip on the reins of the flourishing family business, but Chengli showed a keen understanding of numbers and his father placed him in charge of the bookkeeping. Now that he was a man of sixteen summers, the time had come for him to have a wife.

He knew his father loved him, but he also knew his father would put business interests and the promotion of family honor before all else. He prayed to the ancestors that his wife would be comely and agreeable. Then, the day arrived.

"Son," his father said as they sat at dinner, "the mayor's daughter has come of age, and I believe she would be a suitable match for you. I plan to approach him tomorrow to begin negotiations. What say you?"

Surprised that his father gave him this consideration, Chengli could only nod at first. Then, he thought about the mayor's wife. "Perhaps there are a few associates that have daughters you could consider, Father? I do not like his wife."

"What does that have to do with it?"

"They would be family."

"They would be useful to our business and increase our status greatly."

Chengli sighed. "But the Mayor is a greedy prideful man. He will demand much for the wedding gifts."

His father sat thoughtful. "You are right there. If he gets too greedy, I will reconsider this path, but I excel at negotiation, so I don't even feel it necessary to pay a matchmaker."

Chengli's younger brother, Jin, looked up from his dinner. "The mayor's wife is a mean ugly old cow. She probably gave birth to a mean ugly little cow." Jin chuckled and stuffed his mouth with rice accepting Chengli's look of gratitude. Only Jin was fearless enough to say what he thought to their father.

"Jin! You disrespect your elders," their father spoke with frustration. Though Jin was a man of fifteen years, he showed no sign of wanting to join the family business. His love was the gambling dens and despite his father's admonitions, Jin's winnings made the warnings sound foolish.

After working all the day to please his father, Jin rushed out most nights to pay his respects to Gong De Tian, the Goddess of Luck. Chengli believed Jin must be her favorite for she seemed to be listening.

Much to Chengli's chagrin, the bridal negotiation went well as the three letters traveled back and forth to begin the process. When Chengli's parents left to go to mayor's house for the actual marriage proposal, Jin consoled Chengli. "Perhaps she'll take after her father," Jin said.

They both burst out laughing at the same time.

"Hopefully not as hairy," Jin added.

The two boys sneaked into their father's cabinet and pulled out the baijiu and poured themselves a glass. They laughed and gasped as they choked it down, the fiery liquid burning their throats. The first sip was so good it had to be followed by a second, then a third. By the time their parents arrived home, both sons lay prostrate on the floor.

"Stupid boys." Father kicked Chengli's foot, but he didn't move. The man sighed. "Jin is a bad influence."

"Leave them be," Mother said. "He takes a wife now. He has a right to some nerves." She walked to the chest and pulled out a blanket and covered her boys, brushing back their hair. Her sons were men now. It both saddened her and made her proud. "We will take the birth-dates to the fortune teller tomorrow to see if this will be an auspicious match."

***

While the family waited for the fortune teller's reading, Chengli groaned as his stomach heaved and his head throbbed. "Why do I have to be here?"

"Because you got drunk last night on my best baijiu." Father seemed to be screaming.

Mother patted Chengli's knee. "You'll live. Your father on ce..."

Father stood as the fortune teller entered and spoke. "The signs are very favorable. This union is blessed, and there will be many children."

Father and Mother beamed and bowed giving the fortune teller an extra gift for her services. They rushed Chengli home where they spent two days gathering the betrothal gifts to be given to the girl's family to let them know the marriage would proceed. Then came the gathering of the wedding gifts.

Chengli was wondering if any woman could be worth all this. At night he dreamed of lifting the red veil and seeing a thin-lipped hairy cow-faced woman with buck teeth. He'd awake with a jump and shout.

"Just turn off the lights at night," Jin teased when Chengli told him his dream and the two brothers ended up wrestling on the floor till mother broke them apart.

The wedding gifts were accepted by the mayor and after another consultation with the fortune teller, a wedding date was chosen according to the astrological texts. Chengli's fate was now sealed.

The day of the wedding came and the bride could be heard wailing. Jin poked Chengli's side.

"See how lucky you'll be. They can hear her all the way to the underworld so her ancestors will send you lots of luck." Chengli had to laugh though his knees were shaking. The bride descended from her sedan chair arrayed in brilliant red regalia and heavy veils. He'd have to wait till the wedding chamber to see his fate.

The tea ceremony began followed by the bride and groom joining a lock of their hair. As the couples did their four bows before the bridal chamber, the bride entered, and the teasing became more ribald as was customary.

"My dear sister-in-law, be gentle with my brother," Jin laughed.

Chengli's friends and cousins laughed and poked each other pushing a flushed Chengli forward into the room where his shy bride awaited.

Finally, they were alone within the chamber and Chengli stood before his silent bride. She was a petite woman and he'd been pleased by her graceful movements when he'd first seen her walk towards him. He bowed to her. "May I lift your veil?"

"Yes, my husband," Jun said. Her voice sounded sweet and soft.

When Chengli lifted her veil, his fears fell away and he fell in love.

***

Chengli sat before his desk engrossed in important affairs of state when a messenger ran in, winded and shaking.

"Mayor, Mayor," the messenger gasped, "they're coming. They'll be here in two days."

Chengli bowed his head for a moment. For the past seventeen years he had built his town into a thriving community, one that gained the attention of the Emperor. Now that fact made them a target for attack and this weighed upon his spirit. He had prepared all he could.

The store rooms were full. The wells were protected as best possible with water barrels filled and stored. His available number of warriors was pitiful however compared to the approaching horde and none could be sent from the Emperor as all were deployed elsewhere.

These were troubled times and the Emperor had ordered him to do what he could to delay the Five Barbarians till the Imperial forces could marshal their way farther north. But Chengli was no soldier, he was an administrator, albeit a good one.

Jin came in and upon seeing his brother's face said, "So, what are you going to do, brother?"

Chengli hung his head. "I need an idea. Do you have any?"

"I think I may. I said a prayer to Gong de Tian, and she sent me a dream. Send this message to the khan of the barbarian tribe." He handed Chengli a scroll.

"What is it?" Chengli asked.

"It is a challenge."

"A challenge for what?"

"I have challenged the khan to a game of Tien Gow."

"What? Are you crazy? What is that going to do?" Chengli was stunned. His brother had pulled some crazy stunts before with his betting and only Chengli's position had saved his hide a few times, but their town was at stake now.

"Their Khan is a rabid gambler, worse than I am. In this missive, I have bragged of my prowess and belittled his barbarian abilities. He will not be able to help himself."

"Are you possessed? Do I need to call the shaman?"

"Did you not just ask me for an idea? Have I not saved you on many occasions?"

"That was from bullies and from father. This is our home, our families. How can I risk all to a game of Tien Gow?" Chengli shuddered at the thought.

"Go to the temple, then. Say your prayers. Ask your precious gods to help you if you reject my offer. I will be the one facing the barbarian. I will be the one putting my life at risk to save our town." Angered, Jin stomped out the door.

Chengli felt shamed for berating his brother so he went in search of him. Unable to find Jin, he found himself at the temple where he did pray until he fell into a deep sleep. When a dream did indeed come to him, he was sitting on a bale of hay in an alley and an old dirty beggar came to sit next to him.

"You have grown to be a good man, Chengli, just as I knew you would," the beggar said.

"Thank you, sir. I remember you." Chengli smiled in recognition. "You never came back that night. Why do you come now?"

"I still wish to return the great kindness you once showed to me. So, I say to you, listen to Jin. You both have been working towards this moment."

With those words, he faded away and Chengli awoke. He rushed back to his office to find Jin waiting and the message was sent to the khan's camp. The brothers waited anxious for an entire day until the rider returned with the khan's answer. Seems the khan was indeed a rabid gambler and indeed was challenged to prove himself superior to any Chinese townsman. The game was set. The next morning, Jin set out with only two soldiers to act as his escort and the khan's flag of truce to guarantee his safe passage.

***

Jin entered the barbarian camp with more bravado than he felt. Warriors sat before the felt-made gers that were spread out as far as Jin's eyes could see. As the Chinese gambler rode by, the warriors sharpened their sabers and bared their teeth making Jin feel like a fat hog on his way to the butcher. He heard the muttered prayers of his two escorts as they rode beside him, their hands on the hilts of their jians.

The smell of the camp overwhelmed him. He wondered if these barbarians ever washed. The odors of dung, animal and human, mixed with numerous unwashed bodies, carcasses of animals being carved for food, and corpses of enemies left for display. Jin was sure the later was for his benefit alone. These people were truly barbarian. His town would be helpless before this horde. He placed a perfumed cloth beneath his nose and inhaled its scent, but it was of little help.

They stopped before a large round ger in the middle to the encampment where the guard motioned for him to dismount. Two barbarian soldiers grunted at him. They were short stocky men with harsh scowling faces he could not envision ever smiling. They pulled back the openings and pushed him inside. He staggered in and almost fell before regaining his balance. When he looked up, there sat the Khan, calmly appraising him as he chewed on his dinner. The silence was oppressive as the two men stared at each other. Jin gathered his thoughts and bowed.

"Mighty Khan, I am Yang An Jin, and I am your challenger." Jin took a breath and waited for the Khan to reply.

A man stepped forward and in a halting mixture of archaic Chinese and Cantonese spoke to Jin. "The great and all-powerful Khan welcomes you to his ger and offers you hospitality. Please be seated." With that a woman came forward to offer Jin a bowl of milk tea and a plate of bread and cheese that Jin was careful to take with his right hand being forewarned this was the custom. Jin left some on the plate and in his cup to let them know he needed no more. Through the interpreter, a thin-lipped bowed little man, the Khan informed Jin that they would begin the challenge after a good night's rest.

Jin was escorted to a small ger behind the Khan's and two guards were positioned outside the doorway. With a sigh, Jin lay back and looked at the ceiling wondering how he would sleep knowing what the next day would bring and how his town was depending on him. A rustle startled him out of his thoughts

The drapery at the doorway was pulled back and a woman entered carrying a small silver bowl. She knelt beside his bed and offered him the bowl motioning him to drink. He sat up, brought it to his nose and smelled the warm milk-like smell...koumiss, he surmised. He took a sip and smiled his thanks. She smiled in return and reached forward to slide her hand down his face. Jin's shocked expression made her laugh. She leaned forward and placed a kiss upon his lips causing him to jerk back. Her quizzical expression showed that she was trying to decide what would please him.

With a graceful movement, she stood and slipped her robe from her shoulders. Jin found himself mesmerized looking at the lovely young woman and the word barbarian slipped away. He spent a night he would never forget with a barbarian he would dream of for decades to come.

***

Three days had passed since Jin had left. Chengli paced his office restless and worried as the long days dragged by. At night, he tried to play with his children as Jun worried for her beloved brother-in-law. Only once did his temple mark burn and that was the night Chengli assumed they had arrived at the khan's camp so he feared that Jin had already fallen. He pictured his brother tortured in a boiling barbarian pot or crushed under a pile of stone. Late at night he'd go to the temple to pray.

"Gong de Tian," Chengli prayed, "look out for my brother. Surely after all these years he must be your favorite. I know he is brash. I know his wit is sometimes irreverent, but he has always been good to me and my family. We cannot be without him."

On the third night, Chengli bowed low touching his head to the floor and stayed there till the first rays of the sun began to peek through the window. He must have dozed a moment for he felt hazy when the morning noises of the town brought him awake. He felt a burning sensation at the mark on his temple as the shouting outside grew louder and louder. Then he heard his name.

"Chengli," he heard Jin's voice yell. "Come out of there!"

Chengli ran to the door to see Jin sitting atop his horse bedraggled but smiling with his two escorts smiling beside him.

"Jin!" Chengli stumbled down the stairs as he ran. "You're alive?"

Jin slid off his horse and the two brothers embraced laughing. "Looks that way."

"Did you win?"

"Of course, I won. Do you see any barbarians?"

"The Khan is honoring his wager?"

"The Khan may be a barbarian, but his honor is sacred to him." Jin broke out of Chengli's hold. "Now, what is my fee is the next question."

"What?"

"Well, I did risk life and limb." Jin held up his fingers listing his sacrifices. "I ruined my best tunic in that dirty disgusting camp. I had to eat things I don't want to discuss. So, I'm thinking I should at least get some prime property I've been looking at. And, I do believe I'm ready to settle down. So, maybe I'd like to have you negotiate a good wife for me."

"I think I need to call the shaman for surely my brother has been possessed." Chengli laughed.

"No, brother. But I do believe I've come to finally understand that my life is passing me by and I need to grow up. I'd like a good woman like you have." Jin thought briefly of his barbarian, but after a sweet goodbye, she'd left with the horde and never once looked back. He sighed. He was ready to see the benefit of having someone steady by his side.

"Come, let us go home and celebrate," Chengli said. "We have lots to tell the village and I must send a message to the Emperor. My wife is most anxious for her brother-in-law. We must reassure her. I believe her help will be very useful in obtaining you a suitable wife."

"Please, no ugly, hairy, cow-face woman."

The brothers laughed.

***

Jin's plan not only saved his home from immediate attack and had allowed time for some imperial forces to arrive, but he had wrested an oath to spare his town for the khan's lifetime. If the khan hadn't died in battle five years later, they would have remained safe, but fate is never that kind.

Because of Chengli's guidance, the town continued to thrive. However, he and Jin knew they'd need to worry over future attacks. China suffered sporadic upheavals from rebellions within and barbarians without, so Chengli decided he needed to increase his cities' defenses. He wanted to build a wall around the city and increase the number of their guards. This would require a serious influx of cash into his city budget.

"Taxes," Chengli said shaking his head. "I see no way around it. I will have to increase taxes."

"Don't you say that dirty word," Jin replied sipping his wine. He watched his youngest son play outside chasing some imaginary bug and laughing hysterically. *Who knew I'd turn into this? Huh, a family man.* He turned back to his brother. "We can raise money by letting the people have some fun."

"You've got another one of your ideas?" Chengli sat back and folded his hands over his enlarging belly.

"I say we have a contest for something valuable like a... a jade statue."

"A jade statue!" Chengli interrupted, "I need to raise money, not give it away."

"Have another drink and listen. You offer the statue to the winner. In order to win, you must buy a ticket. Make the ticket a reasonable amount...say a copper or two...and people will gladly spend their money for the opportunity to win jade. Make a big production out of picking the winner and everybody will be happy. You're your coffers will be full, your defenses will be built, and your citizens won't complain about their taxes."

Chengli sipped his wine as he thought over his brother's idea and a smile crept over his face. *Ah, my brother once again comes to my rescue.* He laughed and lifted his glass as the brothers toasted each other.

The Jade Contests became a great success. Chengli ran them four times a year and funded his city's defenses entirely on the ticket sales. His reports back to the court of the Ming Emperor once again gained the notice of court administrators and his decreased demands on the Emperor's coffers earned their respect.

***

Two decades passed and the town continued its growth as did the brother's families. Both Chengli and Jin became widowers but their many children and grandchildren gave them great joy. Strangely, all their sons and grandsons were born with a small reddish crescent moon birthmark on their right temple. The brothers were honored by their town and considered wise, even if Jin still liked a good game now and then.

When a plague struck the area, both brothers became ill. Though the entire town prayed, it was to no avail. They died the way they lived–together.

The family grieved, but as they prepared the bodies for burial, there was a knock on the door. The eldest son answered to find an old shaman standing there with a small chest. "May I help you?" he asked.

The shaman bowed. "I have a great gift for the Yang brothers, Chengli and Jin."

"I'm sorry," the son said, "they have crossed the bridge."

"We know this. That is why I have come. Please accept this. Open the chest and all will be clear." With that the shaman left.

The son took the chest into the house and when the family opened it, they saw two beautiful golden urns and simple instructions explaining that after the forty-ninth day of mourning, a shaman would return to collect the urns. At first, the family argued over what to do.

"They're taking father and grandfather away!" they shouted. There were tears and fears, but no one could argue with the emperor's seal or the shaman who had delivered the urns. The pure gold of the urns made it obvious to the family that this was meant to be a great honor.

So, the family of Yang Ho Chengli and Yang An Jin followed those instructions and the two brothers became residents of the Golden Urns.

Chapter 12

JONNY SAT IN THE chair watching as the four spirits argued over the game. The two brothers chose different teams so argued incessantly. When they weren't arguing, Jin flirted shamelessly with Lady Ji. Jonny's head pivoted back and forth trying to make sense of what was happening and what he was feeling.

"Jonny," Lady Ji said, smiling. "Would you please make us some popcorn?"

Jonny shook his head. "You're dead. Sorry, but you are spirits...how can you eat?"

"Special privileges! And we never get fat." Lady Ji laughed.

"Nothing could dim your beauty," Jin said smiling.

"I'm fat already," the Admiral quipped.

"A veritable mountain of a man." Chengli laughed.

"My brother, the politician ever," Jin sighed.

In a daze, Jonny did as was requested. The game finally ended and the winners gloated over the losers. Lady Ji planted a kiss on Jin's head and he pretended to faint.

"I may be the gambler, but I almost never beat the Lady. This goes in my book." Jin placed a hand over his heart. The three others laughed as he picked up the remote and changed the channel to Jeopardy. Within minutes, the four were shouting out answers before the contestants could hit the buzzer.

Jonny couldn't stand it any longer. "I don't get this. What's with you guys? How can you know this stuff? You're dead!"

The Admiral had been watching the boy during the game and found himself liking him despite his first impression. Jonny's struggle to hold on to his sanity was impressive. Most would have run screaming from the room when presented with such crazy circumstances. Granted they had played it up big, but it had been great fun. And fun was often missing in this existence they'd been sentenced to.

"How can we advise if we don't know?" the Admiral said. "The Guardians see to it that we learn. We read, we watch, we listen."

"What the hell is a guardian?"

"Well, since you already know about us, I guess we better let you know the truth. Your family are the Guardians...have been for...oh, about a thousand years or so."

"Huh?" Jonny stood there, eyes blinking and frowning.

"Your ancestral family was selected and took the blood oath to serve and protect the urns and us."

"A b-blood oath? What's that?"

"It's an oath given to the gods where you pledge with your blood for yourself and your progeny to fulfill the task given." The Admiral watched the wheels in Jonny's brain spin as he took in the information and tried to understand it.

"What happens if you don't do it?"

"Typically, you die. The spirits and Guardians aren't very forgiving to oath breakers."

"But I never took any oath!"

"They don't see it that way. Your family has the obligation. The entire family are Guardians."

The Admiral now realized he had overstepped his bounds and created a problem for Han. *What to do?*

Lady Ji stepped forward and laid a hand on Jonny's arm. "Please don't worry about this. Han and Lei will explain when they return. Someone had to stay to watch the store. They gave you a great responsibility because they trust you. All will be revealed in time. You weren't supposed to find out about us this way."

"Trust," Jonny laughed. *Right.* He wanted to believe her, but deep inside he just couldn't. He'd have to think about what he could believe.

***

After the game was over, Ting-a-Ling made some of his special braised short ribs with soy and orange sauce and decided to take some to Jonny to cheer him up. Though he knocked, Jonny didn't respond, so Ting took out his key and entered the shop deciding to leave the dish in the fridge with a note.

Just as Ting was locking the shop's front door to leave, he heard a noise behind him. When he turned, there stood Frankie, two bodyguards and an elderly woman.

"Hey, old man, Jonny in there?" Frankie said.

"No, sir. I was just leaving him something in the fridge. I don't know where he is," Ting said.

"Now you wouldn't be covering for him, would you?" Frankie said.

"No, sir."

"Then why don't you let us have a little look around to be sure." Not waiting for an answer, Frankie took the key from Ting's hand and opened the door. One guard shoved Ting inside, causing him to fall against the counter and slide down to the floor. With a sigh, the old man got up and brushed off his pants.

"Jonny, hey Jonny," Frankie called out. "Come on out here. We need to talk."

When there wasn't any answer, Frankie sent his men upstairs to look around and when they returned shaking their heads, Frankie pulled out his cell. He called Jonny, no answer. After a silent curse, he called again and let it ring. Finally, Ting-a-Ling heard Jonny's voice.

"Hello?"

"Hey, kid, where are you," Frankie asked.

"Why do you want to know?" Jonny answered.

"I got someone here who would like to speak with you." Frankie put the cell against Ting-a-Ling's mouth and motioned for him to speak.

"Jonny, I left some ribs for you in the fridge."

Frankie pulled the phone away. "Isn't that sweet. He sure is a sweet old man. I sure hope my boys weren't too rough, but we need to talk to you. I think you better get over here and talk to us."

"What do you want to talk about? You made it pretty clear you never wanted to see me again." Jonny's brain was racing. Frankie was downstairs! What could he possibly want now? He didn't have any cash to pay off his debt. Besides, it had been wiped and if Jonny put out the word that Frankie went back on his word, that wouldn't look good for Frankie...unless Jonny wasn't able to talk. *Crap. Am I a dead man?* Jonny began to sweat.

"What's the matter, Jonny," the Admiral said.

Jonny covered the mouthpiece. "Um, I think the casino boss is after me again."

"Is that the guy I met?"

"Yeah."

"You sure didn't get any of my luck, did you," Jin laughed.

"You better bring down that urn," Frankie said. "I changed my mind. I'm gonna take it after all."

"What about the evil spirits?" Jonny asked.

"Don't you worry about that. I brought a shaman with me."

"Does that mean the deals back on then? I'm not bringing the urn unless I get my deal." Jonny wiped the sweat from his brow. *What am I going to do?* Now that he knew what the urns were, he couldn't give one to Frankie. He looked at the four spirits to see them looking back at him with smiles on their faces. He covered the phone again. "Can a shaman hurt you?"

Lady Ji walked over to him and placed a hand on his cheek. "Aren't you sweet for asking. Yes, if they are powerful enough. But there are four of us. Unfortunately, we have squandered our power by being out for so long to watch the game. We're not at full strength. However, we can give a good showing for ourselves, if necessary."

"Listen," Frankie growled, "if you don't want the old man to get hurt, you'll get over here and stop negotiating. I want the urn."

"Who cares?" Jonny hung his head. *Sorry, Ting.* "He's just an old man who works for my father. I want my money."

Frankie shook his head, then laughed. "That's my boy. All right. You bring the urn and the deal is back on, but only if the shaman can get rid of the spirit."

Jin motioned Jonny not to speak. "Listen, don't take that deal. Tell him that's not acceptable. You need a better deal. It's not your fault if the shaman fails or if Frankie can't handle a spirit. You need the debt canceled and the ban lifted. That's a show of good faith on his part. After all, you're being a good sport here."

"Don't you think I could get killed asking for that?" Jonny said.

"Listen to my brother," Chengli spoke up for the first time. "If there's one thing he knows, it's gamblers."

"Make the gambler gamble," Jin laughed.

Jonny rubbed his forehead. Sometime during all this his, head started to ache. "Okay."

"Hey," Frankie yelled over the phone, "what's your answer?"

"I'll make you a deal, Frankie. I'm being a good sport here. I made you a good deal, then, you threw it back at me. Not only that, but you banned me and ruined my reputation. Now you come into my store, threaten me and an old man whose done you no harm, and you expect the same deal? Well, now you're going to have to have some skin in the game, as they say. So, even if you throw the urn back at me, the deal stands. My debt is canceled and the ban is lifted. It isn't my fault if your shaman fails or you get scared. Deal?"

"Why you..."

"Deal or no deal?"

Frankie simmered for a few minutes and looked at Madam Zin. She sat placid and smiling. "You can do this, right?" His finger jabbed at her.

"I've never failed," she said.

Where did this kid get the balls to work a deal like this? I'm going to have to watch him. "Alright. You've got yourself a deal. How long 'til you get here?"

"I got here while we were talking. I'll be down in a few minutes. Don't come up or I'll consider it a break-in and shoot."

Frankie fumed. Jonny was going to pay for the added insult.

The four spirits huddled in the center of the room murmuring to each other and making Jonny very nervous.

"What are you guys going to do?" Jonny asked.

"You are going to present the Admiral to this Frankie person and insist that they do the reading here so that you can see this "so-called" evil spirit. When everything starts to happen, it's important that you pretend to see and hear nothing. Frankie must believe that he is the crazy and possessed one. Can you do that?"

"Sure. I can act with the best of them. But what about Ting-a-Ling?"

"I'll take care of him along with the guards," Lady Ji said. "Unfortunately, it won't work on the shaman, but it's her show. It's Frankie we have to worry about. If we play this right, he won't believe the shaman anyway."

"See, Jonny, it's the women you have to watch. They're the devious ones," Jin said laughing.

"And none more so than a concubine," the Admiral added and dodged Lady Ji's slap.

The Admiral re-entered his urn and the others faded away as Jonny took a deep breath. He left the room and started down the stairs. When he entered the back office, he saw Ting-a-Ling seated back against the wall with a guard on each side. Jonny almost laughed. What did they expect the old man to do? Frankie was seated at the desk and an older, distinctive woman walked about the office looking at the pictures on the walls.

"Did you bring it?" Frankie said first thing.

"Of course." Jonny put the urn on the desk.

The shaman had turned when Jonny entered and stood staring at him as he'd placed the urn before Frankie. Her eyes widened just a bit, then narrowed. Jonny wasn't sure what was happening, but his skin felt funny, almost like an itch he couldn't scratch. He took a step toward Ting and noticed that he and the guards looked heavy-eyed and seemed to be leaning back against the wall.

Maybe it was his imagination but there was the faintest haze next to them. *Do I hear laughter in my head?* Jonny almost laughed until he saw the bruise forming on Ting's cheek. *Frankie, you'll be sorry.*

"Well?" Frankie said.

"Be patient," the shaman said. She picked up the urn, closing her eyes and making a strange sound almost like humming. After a moment, she handed the urn to Frankie and said simply, "Make the spirit appear."

Frankie just looked at her. "Oh. Okay...um...appear, spirit. I command you!"

Nothing happened.

The shaman shook her head. "There must be a ritual to open the urn. Follow the ritual."

"Ritual," Frankie blustered, "I-I don't know anything about any stupid ritual. Jonny, you do the ritual."

"I didn't open the urn. I think you're crazy. I don't know anything about any evil spirits." Jonny shook his head. "If you opened it before, open it again."

"What did you do before?" the shaman said.

Frankie paused in thought for a moment. "Wait a minute. The spirit said something about a question."

"Well, then ask a question," the shaman said with exaggerated patience.

"I don't know what question I should ask."

"Ask him the meaning of life," Jonny said with a smirk. "I always wanted to know that."

The shaman gave Jonny a glance and signaled Frankie to just get on with it. "What did you say the first time?"

"I asked "What are you for I wonder"?" No sooner had the words left his mouth than the urn began to grow warm and Frankie dropped it. The lid flew off with the flash of light and there stood the Admiral in all his glory. He began to swell in size and his glow turned an angry red. A deep angry roar began. Frankie jumped up blinking and screaming.

"There he is...there he is. Cast him out...cast him out!" He looked around the room stunned to see his bodyguards and the old man looking as if they were napping. Jonny looked around the room with a frown on his face.

"Frankie, are you okay?" Jonny asked. "There who is?"

The shaman had covered her eyes instinctively, but now they opened wide as if she recognized the apparition. She'd heard legends, rumors, but never believed, never thought in her life she'd see such a thing. She felt others in the room although she couldn't see them. Their power felt tremendous. She could feel it surround her and she wanted to bathe in it. She looked at Frankie.

That man must never possess it...must never know of it. She saw the truth of what was happening in Jonny's eyes. Ting was in a trance as were the guards who had hurt him.

"Frankie," the shaman began, "there is great evil in this urn that will bring death to you. You must never touch it. You must never tell anyone about it or the spirit will hunt you down. There is a powerful demon at work here. Even I dare not interfere. Beg for forgiveness. Hurry!"

Frankie dropped to the floor and cowered, shaking as the Admiral growled. "I warned you." The smell of sulfur grew. "Shall I take you for the demons to feed upon?" The Admiral waved the sulfurous fumes to surround the shuddering man.

"Please s-spare m-me," sobbed Frankie, choking and gasping.

"Lucky for you I have eaten my fill already. GO. If I ever see you again, your liver is mine!" With a blaze of fire, the Admiral disappeared back into the urn and the lid flew up to snap shut.

"We must leave this place and never return," the shaman said.

Jonny walked over to Frankie. "Hey man, are you okay? Did you fall?"

"You saw it, right? Right?" Frankie screamed up at Jonny, hopeful.

Jonny almost felt bad until he thought of Ting's face. "See what?"

The guards snapped out of it and rushed over. "Hey, boss, what'sa matter?"

Frankie stumbled to his feet with the help of a guard, still shaking and pale. He took a deep breath and then noticed everyone was looking down. His pants were wet.

Chapter 13

At The Retreat

Han finished the histories of the urn residents as Lei brought in their lunch. The family ate in silence as the boys digested the stories until Min looked over at his father.

"Hey, wait a minute, that's only five residents. Didn't you say there were six urns?"

"Yes, Min, there are. I'll tell you that story a little later. After we eat, I want to go over some of the duties and responsibilities you'll have." Han wiped his hands and smiled his thanks at Lei.

The brothers finished up and settled back again to listen.

"Do we need to take notes?" Min said with a smile.

"Just listen," Lei said.

"First of all, think of the urn as their home, their charging station. While they are inside, they are asleep. They can leave for hours at a time, but the more energy they use, the sooner they need to return to recharge. The older they are, the more powerful they are. So, my dear friend here, Physician Ho, may look like a nice old man, but he's the strongest. The Admiral is next, then the brothers, then Lady Ji."

"What about the sixth urn?" Bolin asked.

"Like I said, we'll talk about that later." Han replied. "To open the urn all you need do is ask a question, any question will do, but you must be touching the urn. You can touch as many urns at one time as you wish. Sometimes, however, you may wish to ask a private question.”

“What kind of questions?” Min asked.

Han considered his answer. “Think of the urns as an—early computer. They contain accumulated knowledge and wisdom to help the Emperor make decisions. Anyone can ask a question, even another spirit who is already outside of their urn.

“Remember to watch the time they are out also so they don't get depleted. Jin can still get too...enthused...and loose lose track of time.”

“Loose lose track of time?” Bolin said. “You sound like he's out and about.”

“He can be. They all like going out. Sometimes they stay as spirits and don't use that much energy, but sometimes, they go corporeal and get involved in the real world. You have to keep an eye on them when they do that. Only take one or two at a time or you might get in trouble. Also, they can change appearances if they so desire.”

“How so?” Min asked.

“By age. Physician Ho doesn't, but the Admiral will, as will the brothers.”

“How about the Lady?” Min said.

“Since she died young, she has no need to make herself look young. I did see her make herself look old once to talk to a young child who was crying for his grandmother. She has a weakness for young children since she never had any of her own.

“Everything is kept in a secret room behind the storage room. There's an old clay Buddha figurine on the top shelf that opens a panel into the room. I'll show it to you when we get home.

I've tried to make it as comfortable for them as I can since they spend a lot of time there. There's a shield above in the attic to block any radiation or frequency detectors. They've told me that when they first exit the urn the burst of energy can be detected. So, they must never exit the urns anywhere other than the attic room. Our home is somewhat protected, but downstairs, other eyes might see."

"Is Mom a Guardian?" Bolin asked.

"No, son," Lei answered, "I've never taken the oath. Only blood relations of the family may do so. That is why you must choose your wives very carefully."

"Why?" Min said smiling, "Did we have any Romeos and Juliets?"

Lei looked at Han. "You might as well tell them now."

"I wanted to wait. It was bad enough that we had one of the family betray us to the revolution, but to misuse an urn was unforgivable." Han paused and took a breath. "One of our ancestors betrayed his oath to save his lover. He used an urn for her."

Chapter 14

SUNDAY NIGHT

Frankie and his men left taking the shaman with them. The shaman looked back at Jonny and Ting with a strange smile and nodded. When the front door closed, Jonny locked it and put up the closed sign. He returned to Ting.

"Are you okay?" he said scratching the back of his head and looking everywhere but at Ting.

No answer.

"You know I didn't mean it. I was just negotiating. You have to know how Frankie thinks. I'd never let him hurt you."

"Yes, Jonny, I know."

"Can I get you some noodles?"

"No, thanks." Ting sat silent and stared at the floor. Jonny had never seen Ting act like this. He'd always forgiven him before.

"Ah, c'mon, man," Jonny moped, "you gotta forgive me."

Ting stood up and patted Jonny on the shoulder. "Everything's fine." Then he walked out of the office, opened the front door of the store leaving Jonny dumbfounded.

***

Wang Ting exited the store to find Wu Zhang, the shaman, waiting for him outside.

"Are you okay?" Wu Zhang repeated the question.

"Yes. You needn't worry." When the shaman made no move to leave, Ting couldn't help but ask. "So, Madam Zin, you're working for the likes of Frankie Liu now?"

Wu Zhang shrugged. "He said he was threatened by an evil spirit. Even a bad guy needs to be protected against evil spirits. Have you forgotten everything?"

"I've forgotten nothing."

Wu Zhang sighed. "Can we perhaps go and have a cup of tea together?"

"For old times' sake?" Ting said with a hint of a smile.

"Yes, that would please me very much." The smile Wu Zhang returned still made Ting's heart skip a beat.

The two walked the two blocks to the nearest tea house, sat at a table, ordered their favorite blend and gathered their thoughts. Wu Zhang spoke first.

"I hear Jonny calls you Ting-a-Ling. I thought I was the only one you let call you that."

"You were."

"You must be fond of the boy." She nodded her thanks as the tea was served and took a small sip.

"I am." Ting tried not to stare at her face, but it had been at least twenty years since he'd seen her up close. She was still lovely. Her vitality called to him. His aches and pains disappeared in her presence and he felt young again. Ah, if he could do it all over again, would he make the same decision?

"Did you ever marry?" Ting couldn't stop himself from asking.

"No. Seems like every man agreed with you. No man wanted a shaman for a wife and I couldn't give up my calling. So, there you have it. Did you marry?" She asked, but she already knew the answer.

"No."

"Why not?"

"You know the reason why not." Ting looked Zhang in the eye. "Are you enjoying yourself?"

"Yes, maybe."

Ting laughed and shook his head. "So, it looks like we grew old together after all."

Zhang decided it was time to change the subject. Memory lane was getting downright painful. "What about the Chen family? Are they good to you?"

Ting blinked at the change in topic, but went along with it. "They treat me like family."

"I sure get a lot of strange vibes in that place." Zhang took a sip and tried to look nonchalant.

"There are no evil spirits in the Chen's store or in their home, Zhang. Go look somewhere else for business."

"Don't get angry, Ting, but I definitely felt something from that urn. I just don't want anything to happen to someone you care about." Zhang leaned forward and touched Ting's arm. She didn't mean to be calculating, but she could feel the residual energy from a spirit. So, there had been more than one spirit in that room. *I knew it! I have to talk to that Jonny and see if I can get a read off of him.* "Can I talk to Jonny?"

"That's up to him. I don't speak for him."

"Please, give me his number?" She frowned when Ting called Jonny on his phone.

"Jonny, Madam Zin would like to speak with you. You okay with that?" Ting listened, then handed the phone to Wu Zhang. She walked a short distance away so Ting could not hear what she said.

"Mr. Chen, I wanted to apologize for my association with Mr. Liu. He only told me he was threatened by an evil spirit," Madam Zin paused.

"I understand."

"I was wondering if I could speak with you in private?"

"About what?"

"About the urn, Mr. Chen."

"I have nothing to say to you about the urn, Madam Zin. Frankie is nuts."

"I know you do not want to talk about it, but I recognized the spirit. I know who the spirit was, and if you do not wish me to reveal the information, it would be best if we spoke in private." Madam Zin could hear Jonny's intake of breath. She didn't want to threaten him, but she had to meet the spirit.

"What do you intend to do?" Jonny said.

"I intend no harm, Mr. Chen. Meeting someone like him would be a dream come true. You cannot know what it would mean to me. You know who I am and what I believe. His is the most powerful spirit I've ever seen or felt. Not seeing or meeting him would be like flying to Mars but not stepping foot on the planet. Can you understand?"

"Wait. I'll call you back."

Wu Zhang heard a click. Her pulse raced.

***

Damn. What am I going to do? Jonny went up the stairs to the room and touched the urn.

"What are we going to do?"

"That was quick," the Admiral said taking spirit form. "Listen, I need to rest. What has happened?"

"The shaman wants to talk to me. She said she meant no harm, but then she said that she knows who you are and threatened to reveal that information. I don't trust her. She was working for Frankie."

"Do we have another choice?"

"Can you guys do some more of your hoodoo stuff?" Jonny said.

"We're all low on energy right now. We were out a long time in corporeal form, plus the others used a lot of energy keeping Ting-a-Ling and the two guards subdued. They are all asleep and recharging. I'd rather not awaken them. The shaman just knows about me, so why don't we let her see me and find out what she has in mind. Your father will handle the rest when he returns."

"So, do you want to meet her tonight?" Jonny asked.

"She's still here?"

"She's with Ting-a-Ling."

"Send him home and have her come to the downstairs office." With that the Admiral returned to the urn.

Jonny called Ting-a-Ling's cell and asked for Madam Zin. Jonny gave her the instructions then headed down the stairs to unlock the front door.

After sending Ting home with a brief and abrupt "thank you", Madam Zin walked back to the store. Jonny let her in and she followed him to the office.

"How do you know who the spirit is?" Jonny asked.

"Don't you know anything about Chinese history?" Madam Zin said.

"Not much. I'm an American."

"Your ancestry is Chinese. You should know something about where you came from. We have the longest continuously recorded history in the world."

"Like I said, I'm an American."

Madam Zin sighed. "The ignorance of youth. Please...I wish to meet the spirit of the urn."

"First, what assurance do I have that you will keep silent about what you see today," Jonny said. "Do I have to threaten to have him eat your liver?"

Madam Zin laughed. "No, but I will give you my word that I will never reveal to Frankie what I see today."

"If you do," Jonny said, "I'll tell Frankie you were in on it."

Madam Zin's eyes widened in surprise. "You're a bold young man to threaten me. Aren't you afraid I'll cast a spell on you?"

"Maybe. But just remember, I have a spirit that can eat your liver."

The two looked at each other for a few minutes then both started laughing. A truce had been declared.

Jonny pulled out the urn and placed it on top of the desk.

Madam Zin looked at the golden urn in awe and touched it with reverence. "Are you who I think you are?" She closed her eyes. When she opened them, there he stood. Tears filled her eyes and she dropped to the floor and performed a kowtow three times.

"My Lord, Admiral Zheng He!"

Chapter 15

ADMIRAL ZHENG HE, 1371-1433, Ming Dynasty c. 1368-1644

Ma He woke up to a beautiful morning. Allah spoke to him and said his fate would change today. No more boring chores. He bounced out of bed, dressed and ran out the door, ignoring the calls of his mother.

"Ma He, you will be the death of me!" she wailed.

The ten-year-old headed down the road where he'd heard the noises from many horses and soldiers clanging. General Fu Yonde chased the Mongol pretender and that made Ma He laugh. He watched as the general approached in all his finery. The general spied the solitary young boy and paused.

"You there," the General commanded, "Have you seen the pretender?"

"He jumped into the lake," Ma He replied, smirking.

Displeased, the General spurred his horse forward leaving the disrespectful boy behind.

Later that day, while Ma He was finally finishing his chores, soldiers came to his home and without any warning, grabbed him. Despite his mother's tears and his father's pleas, they took him away to the General's camp where he was put into a cage along with a few unsavory characters. His flippant words came back to haunt him. The general strode by with a satisfied smile.

On the third day, four soldiers came and pulled Ma He and two teenage boys from the cage and dragged them to where a large man stood with a knife. With a flick of his hand, the man motioned for the oldest boy to be brought forward. The boys seemed to understand what was happening and began to scream and struggle.

Ma He was confused and shrank back. Surely, they hadn't come this far only to be slaughtered now. The boy was held fast by the soldiers and before Ma He's astonished eyes, the knife flashed and the boy's genitals hit the ground accompanied by his anguished screams.

The man shoved a wooden peg into the remaining hole to allow urine to pass and the boy collapsed. The man motioned the second boy forward whose struggles intensified past hysteria so the soldier hit him with the hilt of his jian and the boy fell, senseless. The procedure was carried out.

The man turned to Ma He. "I was told to save you for last. You must have angered the general greatly. Come boy. I will be as quick as I can."

Ma He shook and trembled as his knees gave way. The soldiers dragged him forward by his arms. The boy found he could not look away from the knife, and as it raised upward, he fainted.

The pain brought him around. He lay in the cart on the dirty straw with the odor of unwashed men surrounding him. He could hear the sobs of his fellow victims and the curses of the other prisoners for the boys to cease their wailing.

The night was dark, but Ma He could see a few stars so he concentrated on trying to count them one by one by one. Only then could he divert himself from the fear and pain.

"What will become of us?" one boy sobbed the question aloud that the three victims were all thinking.

"I heard the soldiers say you were all going to Beiping as a gift for the Prince there," one prisoner muttered. "You're to be servants there. Now cease your moans for we must sleep."

The trip lasted many days and during that time, Ma He prayed, truly prayed, perhaps for the first time in his life. He'd always felt he was destined for great things, now he was to be nothing but a lowly eunuch servant. How could this be? Was this what Allah really wanted for him?

He spent the next few days pondering his fate and what he was to do. His father had impressed upon him that whatever you are to be in life, be the best you could be so you could hold up your head and be proud. So, Ma He decided.

He would be the best at...whatever Allah had chosen for him.

The general had all of them dumped at the back entrance of Prince Zhu Di's palace in Beiping. By this time, he and his cage mates were scrawny malodorous lumps of human flesh.

"What have we here?" A large hefty eunuch stood before them in his fine silk robes with arms crossed and a look of disgust.

"They didn't let us out to attend to any personal hygiene, sir," Ma He stood and said with a bow.

"No?" The First Eunuch spoke with arched brows.

"No. I made the others pee over the side, but without a shit stick or paper, we did the best we could."

"And you organized this?"

"Yes, sir."

"Pushy little brat." One man staggered to his feet. His rotten breath and missing teeth gave away his history of neglecting personal hygiene.

"Up, all of you." The First Eunuch commanded.

After they stumbled to their feet, the First Eunuch walked around the group evaluating them. He pointed to the two other teenage boys and Ma He and they were directed to follow the house eunuchs to a side room. The others were taken away to the street markets to be sold.

Inside there was a large tub. They were ordered to strip, but before the other two could obey, Ma He climbed the ladder, and with a loud whoop, jumped into the water. The two others looked at each other, then followed suit.

The First Eunuch watched as Ma He scrubbed vigorously, so he knew the boy was used to being clean. He saw the way the others followed him even though they were older, so he knew the boy was a leader. This boy would please the Prince if he was as smart as the First Eunuch believed him to be.

They were each given a long-belted robe to wear and taken to the dorm where they were to sleep until their training was complete. They devoured the simple dinner that was provided. After days of eating nothing but scrapings from the bottom of the soldiers' bowls, the rice and vegetables tasted wonderful.

The doctor was called to attend to the boy's cuts as it was obvious no care had been given and one of the boy's wounds was already festering. Ma He's was inflamed, but he'd done a fair job of caring for it confirming the First Eunuch's impression that the boy had rudimentary knowledge of wound care. Tomorrow would be a big day when they could evaluate the three boys more completely.

"Tomorrow your new lives begin. Forget all that came before. Sleep now." The First Eunuch turned and left.

And so, Ma He's training began. The First Eunuch found himself pleased with the boy's progress. Obviously, the boy had had some schooling before being taken, but he absorbed knowledge like a sponge. His writing skills were exceptional and that would please Zhu Di, who would soon need a new scribe. Of the three boys, Ma He excelled the most in all areas. The only thing the First Eunuch found irritating was the boy's constant requests to write to his family.

"Your old life is gone. What makes you think you are worthy enough to justify the expense of a messenger to Yunnan? Get back to work."

Despite the rebuffs, Ma He continued to ask, until one day in a fit of pique, the First Eunuch snapped and yelled, "If you think you are so important, ask the Prince. If he says yes, so be it."

Ma He bowed and ran off. For a moment, the First Eunuch stood stunned, then trembled in fear. The boy wouldn't really approach the Prince, would he? He rushed after the boy, but arrived too late. Ma He was prostrated at Zhu Di's feet.

"My Prince," he heard Ma He say.

"Yes," Zhu Di answered and waved away his guards who'd already drawn their swords.

"I wish to make a request."

"I see." Zhu Di smirked. "I live to serve. What is your wish?"

"I wish to write my family."

"Oh? And what would you say."

Ma He paused for a moment and glanced sideways at the First Eunuch who stood anxious and sweating on the sidelines. He realized for the first time that he just might be in terrible trouble. "Well, my Prince, I'd want to tell them that I serve the Prince of Yan, greatest of all the princes, and that I'm treated very well. I would say someday I hope to serve the Prince in a great battle and win him a great victory."

"You would say all that would you?" The Prince smiled to himself. He was silent for a moment then said, "You may send one letter." Then, he looked at his guard. "Ten lashes only." And walked away.

The guard grabbed Ma He by the arms and took him to the front court where they administered his punishment. No sound escaped Ma He's lips as the bamboo stick struck his bare back ten times. He remained on the block for one hour, then a guard came and took him to the dorm where the First Eunuch waited with the doctor.

"You, stupid boy," the guilty First Eunuch shouted as he wiped away the blood from Ma He's mouth. "You cannot just run up to the Prince and ask for a favor."

"But you said..."

"I know, I know. I am to blame and equally stupid. I was angry." The First Eunuch sat by Ma He's bed. "One should never speak in anger."

Good to his word, Ma He got to write his letter to let his family know that he was fine and doing well, thereby alleviating their worry. He did not know that his father was already dead and buried by his eldest son and Ma He's brother.

Four months later, the First Eunuch approached his Prince, bowing low.

"My Prince, I believe I have found a good candidate to replace your scribe."

"You do, do you?"

"Yes."

"Who is this man?"

The First Eunuch cleared his voice. "My Prince, he has just turned eleven years old. He is a young Muslim boy from the Yunnan province captured by General Fu Yonde. The general took him prisoner and had him castrated, then brought to you as a gift."

"A gift? Really? And you think this boy would want to serve me? A young Muslim boy who we have castrated. Why would he?"

"He has ambition."

"Ah, a most deadly sin." The Prince thought for a moment. "What great crime did this boy do to gain the ire of my general?"

When the First Eunuch explained, the Prince laughed long and hard. "I must meet this brazen but brave young man."

"You have already met him, my Prince."

"I have?"

"He was the young boy who requested permission to write his family."

Intrigued, the Prince said, "Take me to him."

When they arrived at the classroom, the students were discussing history and a fierce debate was going on between two boys. The First Eunuch pointed to the younger boy. He was the taller of the two with thick dark hair, bright flashing intelligent eyes that stayed focused on his opponent. The assignment was to defend the position of two generals from a famous past battle. Both boys were passionate. Zhu Di found himself drawn to Ma He's thought processes and logic. Ma He laid out his position well and the Prince thought, with training, this boy could be more than a scribe, he could be a fine soldier, maybe even a captain.

He turned away and signaled the eunuch to follow him. "I disagree with you," the Prince said. "I want him trained with my guard. I will follow his progress there. Maybe he will get his wish after all. We will choose someone else to replace my scribe."

***

Over the next fifteen years, Ma He trained hard and well gaining the trust of Zhu Di. Although there was an eleven-year difference in age, a friendship formed between the two as they found they shared similar interests and a similar sardonic sense of humor. This sense of humor disappeared quickly however, whenever either man felt threatened.

Both excelled at swordplay and practiced with their jians daily. Warrior training encouraged the men's competitive natures, so there were often crossbow or archery contests either standing or from their chariots. Ma He was the only soldier who would not just allow his Prince to win, further earning Zhu Di's respect. Ma He became a trusted adviser.

Prior to Ma He's capture, imperial politics had become a quagmire. Despite Zhu Di's superior abilities, the aging emperor followed tradition and chose his eldest son to become the next emperor. Zhu Di was named Prince of the Yan province like his other brothers and uncles who each had their own province. Then, when the empire suffered the death of the eldest son from an illness, once again, following tradition, the aging emperor named the teenage son of the deceased as emperor instead of Zhu Di.

The teenage grandson, fearful of a rebellion, began to strip his uncles of their power including forcing one uncle to commit suicide. Hoping to delay the emperor's attack of his province while he plotted his rebellion, Zhu Di feigned mental illness. In 1399, however, the emperor sent 500,000 warriors to capture Beiping, Zhu Di's capital. While Zhu Di gathered his army away from the city, it was up to the women and Ma He to defend it. The women fought throwing pottery, furniture and anything they could find. Meanwhile, Ma He defended the reservoir, the city's main water source. Creating these delays made it possible for Zhu Di to return and defeat the emperor's army earning Ma He more honors.

The war against the young emperor ended in 1402. The Emperor's palace burnt to the ground and three unidentifiable bodies were found in the rubble. Zhu Di was ruthless, killing all who had opposed him along with their families, their friends, and even their neighbors.

In the new administration of Zhu Di, called the Yongle Emperor, Ma He was given the title of Zheng He for his meritorious actions both in Beiping and in the taking of Nanjing. He was named as Grand Director of Palace Servants and later as Chief Envoy. But his real passion was yet to come. This passion took place over the next three decades. Together with Emperor Zhu Di, the now Admiral Zheng He built a treasure fleet of 317 ships capable of holding thousands of men. The treasure voyages were about to begin.

***

Emperor Zhu Di and Admiral Zheng He stood aboard Zheng He's ship admiring the finished vessel. Zheng He felt his chest expand with pride. Well, Father, look at me now. I have done my best.

A laugh escaped.

"Proud of yourself?" his friend asked.

"Yes, my Emperor, at this moment, I am."

"So, you have all that you wish?"

The question caught Zheng He off guard and he hesitated. "Of... of course. What more could I possibly want?'

The Emperor nodded thoughtfully, then smiled. "Good, good. Let's return to the palace. You will need a good night's sleep before you leave on your grand adventure in the morning. And remember," Zhu Di's eyes turned cold and hard, "I want you to keep your eyes open for my nephew. I don't believe those bodies were he and his family. I know he's out there somewhere and I'll have his head."

"I will. If I find him, he will not escape me."

Zhu Di's eyes relaxed again revealing Zheng He's friend. "Excellent. I know I can trust you. Besides, I want to show you my new idea. I'm going to build a new palace. It will be called "The Forbidden City"."

"That sounds impressive." Zheng He laughed.

"I thought so. It will make someone think twice before attacking me."

After the two parted for the night, Zheng He returned to his quarters, disrobing and donning a black silk hanfu. He ate a light supper for he felt a strange restlessness and had no appetite.

How could he sleep tonight? A knock disturbed his thoughts. He opened his door and stood stunned.

"We are a gift from His Imperial Majesty," a beautiful courtesan said in a lilting voice. "May we come in?"

He stepped aside and two beautiful females and one strong male courtesan entered.

A gift indeed.

The next morning, Zheng He arrived at the dock with a bounce in his step and a twinkle in his eye that his men hadn't seen before. When the Emperor arrived soon after, the two were heard actually laughing, and the men wondered at this. The friendship between the two was well known, but they were usually more circumspect.

The Emperor read aloud his commission for the voyage, a Buddhist monk said a blessing and so on the morning of July 11, 1405, the first treasure voyage left Nanjing harbor.

A few weeks later, the sailors became restless and uneasy. None of them had been this far from home or on vessels this large. From nine masted battle ships capable of carrying patrol boats to five masted ships carrying men and horses, no fleet like this had ever sailed from China. So, when a great storm appeared on the horizon, Zheng He felt the tension mount and feared he'd have a mutiny on his hands. The portents were not favorable.

As the storm clouds gathered, lightening coursed through the clouds and static electricity charged the air making Zheng He's body tingle. He found himself shouting a prayer along with his men.

"Goddess Mazu, protector of seafarer's, protect us."

A light gathered above his ship and coalesced above his sails, all nine glowing as the charge ran down the masts. Zheng

He couldn't help himself. Drawn to the light, he reached out and touched the mast. The charge coursed through his body, the hair on his head rose creating a halo, the static charge made the hair on his arms almost crackle. Mazu sang to him of his future. He saw visions and laughed with joy.

His men fell to their knees. From that moment on, they would give their lives for the man who Mazu had chosen.

Chapter 16

Monday AM

The plane landed early at San Francisco's International Airport. Grabbing his carry on, Kang went through customs then headed directly to the Chinese consulate on Laguna St. where they expected him. There he collected his weapon's case and received another file to read. The Consul was courteous providing local information needed for this operation. Kang rejected his offer for additional help for the time being. Grabbing a coffee, he sat and read the file, memorizing important facts. Hunger pushed him towards the nearest restaurant as he planned his route around Chinatown.

The satellite signal received was so brief that only the city was pinpointed. That left a large area for Kang to cover. The Consul's file had an alphabetical list of names for residents that were considered recent immigrants meaning they arrived in San Francisco after the revolution. Kang doubted the list was complete, but one had to start somewhere. He looked at the first five names: Bai, Cao, Chang, although he doubted the family kept their original name, Chen, and Dong. Perhaps he could cover those today. Being methodical, he'd just go down the list.

Jonny and Ting-a-Ling stood behind the counter, both glum and silent. Finally, Jonny couldn't take it anymore.

"Ting, are you still mad at me?" Jonny's voice had a definite whine. "I said I was sorry."

"I'm not mad at you, Jonny." Ting looked up and patted the young man on the shoulder. "I told you that last night. Remember?"

"Then what's the matter? You're not acting like yourself. Are you sick? Did those guys hurt you more than you're saying?"

"No, I'm fine. Really."

Jonny looked at the older man and noted the sadness in his eyes. Then he remembered the shaman using Ting-a-Ling's phone. "Why did you let Madam Zin use your phone?"

"Because she asked me to let her talk to you and I didn't want to give her your phone number." Ting turned to walk away, but Jonny grabbed his arm.

"Wait a minute. Where were you?"

"At the tea-house."

"With Madam Zin?"

"Um...yes."

"Alone?"

"Yes."

The tone of voice got through to Jonny. "You know Madam Zin, don't you?"

"Yes."

"How well do you know her?" Jonny's smile started slow and reached his eyes. The image of Ting-a-Ling with a woman was kinda hard for him to imagine. The two of them were...well...old.

"Not that it's any of your business, but when we were young, we were engaged."

Ting's direct answer stopped Jonny's laugh before it could start as did the obvious sadness in the man's eyes. "What happened?"

"I walked away."

"Huh? Why?"

"I couldn't handle all the supernatural stuff. I didn't want to compete with ghosts and spirits and the other world. This world was more than enough. I thought if I walked away, she would come after me." Ting hung his head.

"But, she didn't."

"No, she didn't. I guess she didn't love me enough."

"Maybe she thought you didn't love her enough." Jonny tried to imagine Ting as a passionate young man. He failed. "What did you look like when you were my age?"

Ting-a-Ling laughed. "You mean when I didn't have wrinkles?" Ting opened his wallet and pulled out an old worn photo handing it to Jonny. Jonny felt a bit stunned. Ting stood beside a vibrant woman with long black hair and flashing dark eyes. Ting had always seemed strong for his age, now Jonny understood why. Though of medium height, Ting's physique was defined and spoke of strength. Wu Zhang's face drew Jonny's attention. Though not beautiful, she had a presence even the camera captured. Ting's smile as he gazed at the woman showed his love with an intimacy that came close to being embarrassing to any viewer. Jonny handed the photo back.

"You really did love her, didn't you?" Jonny said.

"Yes, I do...did."

Jonny thought for a moment. "It's not too late, you know. Why don't you give it another try?"

"I should get to work." Ting-a-Ling started to walk away.

"I don't know if I could walk away from someone I loved as much as you love her," Jonny said. "I don't think I'd be brave enough to live alone after that."

The conversation stopped when the front door opened to admit a family of four and Jonny went to work entertaining the kids while Ting-a-Ling helped the parents. The bell rang again and a tall Chinese man entered and signaled he just wanted to browse. After the couple rang up their purchase and were leaving, the door opened again and in walked an agitated Bella.

"Jonny! I have a bone to pick with you," Bella pranced to the counter. Ting walked back towards the Chinese gentleman to try and guide him away from what was looking like trouble.

"Good morning, Bella," Jonny said with caution. "What can I help you with this morning?"

"Help me with? Is that all you have to say to me? After not answering my calls yesterday?" Bella's voice dripped ice.

"I'm sorry, Bella, but I was busy." Jonny knew that was the wrong answer the moment he said it. "Um..."

"EXCUSE ME!" Bella's voice went up three octaves. "YOU WERE BUSY?"

"Ah, c'mon Bella. Give me a break. I didn't have time to..."

"JONNY CHEN, you are so HISTORY. UNDER-STAND?" Bella heaved a giant sigh. She looked straight up to the heavens. "I can't believe I ever hung out with such a giant LOSER."

She stressed the word loser while glaring at Jonny. "GOODBYE, FOREVER."

With that last pronouncement, Bella left the store leaving the three men staring after her.

Ting-a-Ling was the first to recover. "I apologize for this unfortunate scene." He bowed. "Is there something our poor establishment may assist you with?"

Kang looked at the old man first then returned his bow with a slight bow in return. He glanced over at the young man pouting behind the counter and smiled. Jianyu Chen. Youngest son of Han Chen. Owner and proprietor of Golden Dragon Antiques and Collectibles. Kang ran off the family's data from the consul's file. The family lived a quiet life. Solid. Safe. Boring. That felt suspicious all by itself. But Kang believed a Guardian would have training and confidence enough to handle one spoiled belligerent female. This confused angry young man was no Guardian.

"No, thanks. Enjoyed the show." With that, Kang left.

Ting-a-Ling joined Jonny at the counter. "You upset?"

"Not really." Jonny shrugged, frowning. "I should be," he murmured, then asked, "Can you handle the store? I think I need a break."

"Sure."

Jonny went up to the apartment and made some lunch. While he sat down to eat, he went online to read up on Admiral Zheng He. After an hour, his food was cold and his brain sizzled. *This can't be real. No wonder Madam Zin reacted the way she did. Star Trek even named a star-ship after him! I can't believe this.*

Jonny tried to look up the other residents but couldn't find their names online. He'd have to ask his father and he couldn't ask his father. Curiosity burned in his brain. He wanted to know their stories, but after his father's return, he'd be cut out of the picture.

"Jonny, I need you down here," Ting-a-Ling called up on the intercom.

"Be right there."

***

Jonny locked the shop's front door and headed up to the apartment. He reheated lunch and ate then went upstairs to the hidden room to stare at the urn cabinet. The Admiral had told him to give them at least a day to recharge when they'd said goodbye.

"I probably won't get to see you again," Jonny had said.

"You can't know that," the Admiral replied.

But Jonny did know that. After the Shaman had met the Admiral, Jonny had ordered him back to the urn despite her pleas for a chance to really speak with him.

"You just asked to meet him. I let you meet him. That was the deal." Jonny felt bad, but the Admiral was weak and had signaled the need to go back to the urn.

Madam Zin had stomped her foot in frustration. "You have to give me another chance to speak with him. Please!"

"I will consider it. It's late. I gotta go."

Now Jonny knew her frustration. He wanted to be around the spirits and have the chance to talk to them. He wanted to know their stories. *Me, the guy who hated history.*

Jonny relived every moment with the group and knew he wanted to be with them. Not knowing what he felt, he got angry, jealous. His brothers would get to work with them, be with them, help them. *He'd be excluded!*

He walked to the cabinet and opened the door. The last urn beckoned him. This one didn't need to rest. He grabbed it and closed the door. A funny sensation started almost immediately. The urn grew warm and his arm tingled.

"What the..."

Instinct had him reach for the lid even though he knew it was sealed. His mind was blank. To his surprise, the lid came off. He stared at it with a stupid expression until he realized there was no flash of blinding light. Instead, a steady stream of what he could only call glittering stars flowed out—just like Disney or Vegas. Within seconds a form took shape and went from ethereal to corporeal. A woman stepped forward and looked straight at him.

"Jianyu," the woman said. She ran to him, threw her arms around him and kissed him.

Jonny's arms encircled her of their own accord and he found himself kissing her right back. Passion rose up inside him like he'd never felt. His heart pounded. He became lightheaded, staggering back, he broke the embrace. His hand went to his head as his vision blurred. He heard the woman's voice as if from a distance, then everything went black.

Chapter 17

WEI ZAN, THE HULI JING

Oh, my, he is beautiful, Wei Zan peered down from her perch on the cliff. Her nine white tails swished of their own accord. She crouched low to stay hidden and observed the man as he made camp. After watching his efficient movements while pitching his shelter and building his fire, she was then treated to the sight of him stripping off his shirt and stepping into the pond to wash away the dirt of the road.

Her hunger called to her, and since she could read the vitality of this man, tonight she knew she would be well fed. Sitting up, she was just preparing to go down when she heard horses approaching. She looked down at the man and saw that he also heard. Exiting the pool and grabbing his shirt, he went to the fire and armed himself.

Four riders entered the clearing. The man stood by the fire, relaxed, his sword hanging loose by his side.

"Sir," the leader said, "What brings you to our territory?"

"Just passing through," the man replied.

"I see. What is your business?" the man demanded.

"My business is my own."

"My Lord may not agree."

"That is not my concern."

"I'm afraid it is." The leader signaled his men and they surrounded the man who still had not moved. The leader drew his sword. "You will need to come with me and explain your business to my lord."

"I'm afraid I must decline for I cannot be delayed."

"That is not my concern," the leader threw the man's words back at him.

Wei Zan did not like the idea of her plan being interfered with. This man would lose his vitality or indeed maybe his life if they fought. *Hmm. What should I do? I don't like to interfere with humans if I can avoid it, and there's four of them. However, I'm very hungry! Let me think...ah...yes.*

With a swish of her tails, Wei Zan went into action. By the time she ran down the small cliff, her transformation was complete. Gasping, she ran into the camp.

"Help me, please, help me," she gasped and collapsed at the hooves of the leader's horse.

The horse shied back and the leader took a moment to get his mount under control. "What?" the leader looked down and saw the most beautiful woman he'd ever seen looking up at him with pleading frightened eyes. They shimmered with tears as one escaped and traced a trail down her porcelain cheek. He could not look away. He dismounted. "Are you alright?" he asked, the strange intruder forgotten.

"Please," Wei Zan said, "I need to be taken to see your lord. Can you take me there?" She exuded her glamour and the men became obedient with smiles on their faces. They may not have been as handsome, in fact, a couple caused her to shudder, so she would just settle for their breath. But the leader was passable and virile.

The men turned as one and followed their leader away from the man who stood there smiling. Wei Zan frowned almost suspecting that the man knew what was happening, then shook her head. *Nonsense!* He was only a human.

After they'd ridden for a half hour and she was sure her man was safe, Wei Zan feigned fatigue and asked her escorts if they could rest. They stopped in a clearing and the men laid down to rest and under her influence, soon closed their eyes. Wei Zan smiled and laughed softly taking the leader's hand. "Seems like your men have left you undefended." She raised his hand to her lips. He was mesmerized as he followed her into the forest, and they lay down on a soft bed of autumn leaves.

Later, a white fox came out of the woods and approached the sleeping soldiers. She walked over to the first sleeping soldier and leaned over. With each exhale, a soft glow of energy left the soldier's mouth to enter the white fox's mouth. After a few moments, she left the weakened man, best not to take too much energy, and walked to the next soldier. Afterwards, her yang energy full, Wei Zan left her victims to the whims of her forest.

In the morning, the three soldiers woke confused, tired and confounded as to where they were and how they got there. They found their leader naked in the woods, and with much difficulty, roused him. He also seemed very confused and couldn't explain his state of undress. Embarrassed, they all decided it was best not to discuss this event with anyone lest their fellow soldiers think them fools or worse yet, mad.

After taking her nourishment, Wei Zan had returned to the campsite only to find the man gone. "May you live in interesting times!" Wei Zan cursed up to the moon. Then putting her abilities to work, sniffed the site and set off tracking her prey. She couldn't have explained why she had fixed herself on this man because her essence had been replenished. But the man's face was before her so she followed, her tails swishing as she ran in pursuit.

Chang Jianyu set up his camp believing the soldiers would be unable to follow. If his suspicion was correct, he had been saved. But why? He couldn't quite understand. He was fulfilling his duty and could not be late. Exhausted now, he climbed into his shelter and fell into a deep sleep.

***

Wei Zan found the camp before the man loaded up to leave the next morning. She stayed hidden, deciding to watch over him during the day. Her forest was known for trouble, so she set herself to a parallel course.

The day grew warm for autumn, but the man's stride never faltered. He tied a cloth about his forehead to keep the sweat from his eyes and poured some water over his thick black hair to cool his head. He ate a late meal, barely stopping by a river where once again she was treated to the sight of his bare-chested glory. My, my. Tonight, she'd visit his shelter.

However, a small town came into view and there were dogs everywhere. Big ones, little ones. Wei Zan cringed as their yapping pierced her skull. She dared not enter the town. Her nine tails swished angrily as she retreated back deeper into the woods. She jumped up into the trees where she could keep vigil over the town and see when her man left in the morning. Please be to the gods, let him leave in the morning. Don't let this be his destination.

***

Her man went to an inn where he treated himself to a meal of boiled beef, rice balls, steamed vegetables, and folded eggs. Taking clean clothes, Chang Jianyu walked next door to a small bath house. After so many days on the road, this was heaven. The slave from the inn took the sweaty clothes and promised they'd be ready in the morning.

He spent an hour walking about the small marketplace before heading back to the inn for a good night's rest in a comfortable bed.

The next day he would be back on the road heading up north for the Emperor. He looked at the pouch that never left his side. Sometimes he wondered if his family's decision not to hire guards was a wise choice, but usually, it had worked. Who attacked poor travelers? And, his blade was sharp, as was his skill.

The next morning, he left at dawn. For some reason, he felt an itch between his shoulders that let him know he was being watched, but no matter how often he looked, he could see no one.

The day continued much like the others until late afternoon when a small group of men appeared before him blocking the road.

"Good evening," a large man with rotting teeth said displaying them with pride.

"Good evening," Jianyu said with a polite bow.

"Oh, see this, men? We have someone with proper manners." The man smiled broader, if possible. "Were you raised in a noble house?"

"No, but I appreciate a man whose size and importance are greater than my own."

"A diplomat! I like you. And because I like you, I will only take half of what you have in your bag."

"A truly generous offer. Such a great heart resides in such a great breast. It saddens me to say I cannot do as you ask." Jianyu shook his head.

The man's face darkened. "Do you mock me?"

"No, sir. I would not dare. These possessions have been cursed by a shaman. I have been sent on a journey to save myself. If I fail, a demon will kill me."

Fear flitted across the men's faces. "You've been cursed?"

"Yes. I angered the powerful shaman by refusing to marry her daughter. In this bag is a sacrifice to a demon and if I do not deliver it to his hidden temple, he will come for it and kill all in his path." Jianyu trembled. "I cannot pass this burden to anyone else."

One man behind the smiler pushed at him. "Let's get outta here. We don't want no part of no curse." The men started to back away.

The smiler looked at Jianyu, then backed away, too. "Be on your way." He waved his hand.

Jianyu bowed again and hurried past. After a short distance, his smile broke out. The curse story worked well whenever it came to the lower-class thugs. Superstition was a powerful tool. After walking for another hour, the sun dipped below the trees and he decided it was time to set up camp.

He left the road and walked into the forest thinking he'd be safe from other travelers. There was a small stream with fresh water that provided a small trout for dinner. As he was finishing his meal, two men approached and they didn't look like they'd be easily fooled.

***

Wei Zan rolled about laughing as the man spun his tale of curses and demons to the fools on the road. *This man is clever. This man is funny.* She had never seen anyone quite like him. When the four soldiers had come into his camp several days before, she'd watched as he pulled his sword. His relaxed, easy stance bespoke his skill and confidence, yet he didn't feel the need to display it before these fools. When called for, he'd use words instead of swords.

She followed the man until he started to set up his shelter. She couldn't wait! Her tails swished in anticipation. Just as she was getting ready to transform, she smelled two men approach. She sprung up into a tree and looked down recognizing the villains.

These men were not fools. They made their living by robbing and most often leaving no witnesses. Wei Zan felt a growl rise up in her throat.

The man stood and pulled his sword as the two entered the camp. He felt the threat as the two men separated to either side.

"If you hand over your pack," one man said, "no one will be hurt."

"If you leave now, I can say the same."

Wei Zan was furious. Another delay. Her man could get hurt or killed. *Not this time!*

A scream echoed from the treetops. Startled, the men looked up as a large form surrounded by blue mist swirled overhead and landed between them and their prey. Wei Zan swelled in size and her white fur glowed an angry red as she growled deep in her throat. Terrified, the would-be bandits scrambled away screaming as they ran. Wei Zan let her glamour fade and turned to face the man in her true fox form.

Wei Zan stood still allowing the man time to adjust to her appearance and strangely, he didn't look frightened.

"You've been following me, haven't you?" the man said.

Wei Zan nodded her head. As a fox, she was unable to speak.

"You also helped me the other night with the soldiers, didn't you?"

Another nod.

"Why?"

With a tilt of her head, Wei Zan walked over to the fire and sat down in an obvious invitation. After a moment's hesitation, the man sat down next to her. Wei Zan curled up and placed her head on his lap. Looking up at him, she blinked another invitation. The man laughed.

"You are a brazen one, aren't you?" He laughed again, but he started to scratch her head, then behind her ears.

Wei Zan sighed with happiness. She looked up again, and somehow, he knew what she was asking.

"My name is Chang Jianyu and you, my dear little fox, are my guardian. Thank you." The two sat like this for a long time just being together with Wei Zan resting her head on Chang Jianyu's lap and he just scratching her ears. A bond was forming...unexpected and unknowable.

***

Wei Zan didn't go to Chang Jianyu's shelter that night or the night after that. She traveled with him in her true form disappearing into the brush whenever other humans approached. At night, she kept watch over him to protect him from any threat.

When he arrived at his destination, he told Wei Zan to stay outside of the city.

"Little fox, I have to go into the city. It is a large city with many people and many dogs. It is too dangerous for you to follow me. You must stay here."

Wei Zan shook her head. She didn't know Chang Jianyu's task, but he always seemed to get into trouble. He needed her! She could transform and go in as a woman. But it seemed like Chang Jianyu knew what she was thinking.

"And even if you're in the form of a woman, what if you come across their dogs? What will you do? Can you stay safe? Will your fear not cause you to reveal yourself? You'd still be vulnerable. You could be killed." Jianyu sighed in frustration. "Please stay here. I am not a child. I am a grown man and have been taking care of myself for many years."

Wei Zan growled. Humph! She decided not to argue with him so she plopped herself down by the fire curling up to sulk.

"Thank you."

Chang Jianyu gathered up his pack and headed into the city to make his delivery to the temple. When he arrived, he unlocked his case, took out two objects and closed the lid. The abbot took the objects telling Jianyu to return in forty-nine days to collect them. Rather than stay in the city, Jianyu decided to go back to his camp in the woods and pass the time with his little fox.

Disobeying Jianyu, Wei Zan cast a glamour of a black dog and followed him into the city going over the rooftops. She cowered a few times at the barking of the village dogs, but those canines would be unable to reach her. Wondering what his business was, Wei Zan crept down inside the temple to watch as he spoke to an abbot. She was too far away to hear, even with her fox's ears, but she saw the flash of gold. *So, my Jianyu is not as simple a man as I believed.* Her fascination grew.

Chang Jianyu turned to leave, so Wei Zan hurried to return to camp before he could discover her missing. Her energy began to weaken having expended too much since meeting Jianyu. She'd almost reached the outskirts of city when one leap landed her on a group of roof tiles that crumbled causing her to crash down to the ground with a loud thump. The tiles fell on top of her, cutting her head and shoulder. Howling in pain, she heard voices yell from across the street. The neighborhood dogs began to bark.

As her fear mounted, she was unable to hold her glamour. She struggled to her feet. In her present weakened state, the dogs would kill her. The barking came closer along with the sound of thumping feet. She couldn't hide because the dogs could smell her. She took a couple steps to try to leap to the next rooftop when a cloak covered her and strong arms wrapped her up tight. Frantic, she struggled.

"Ssh! Little fox, I've got you," Jianyu said.

Wei Zan felt herself slung over his back as he set off at a fast-paced walk and soon the frightening sounds of the city were left behind.

When they arrived back at the camp, Jianyu took her out of the cloak and tended to her wounds by firelight. He was silent, but she felt his anger, so she just curled up. She desperately needed to replenish her energy deciding that when Jianyu fell asleep, she'd leave and either find a nearby cavern where she could restore her energy, or another camp.

"Did you really think I didn't know you were following me?" Jianyu burst out through gritted teeth. "Do you think me a fool? Don't you know what would happen to you if you were caught?" The sting of his words was lessened when he began stroking her head. "Your kind are meant for the forests, not the cities." His voice was almost a whisper.

The two sat together for a while, then Jianyu spoke again, "I'm going into my shelter now. Get some rest. If you need me, I am here."

When he woke in the morning, she was gone.

***

Wei Zan found a cavern where nature's energy was pure and strong. She slept, exhausted, allowing her body to heal and absorb the energy offered by the earth to one of its special creations.

Three days passed before she woke feeling refreshed and energized. She shook her head and considered what to do next. Her heart wanted to return to see Jianyu, then she took note of the fact she no longer thought of him as Chang Jianyu, but Jianyu. This was not good.

I should stay away! He's a human. No good can come of getting close to a human.

But her paws took her back to the camp where she found Jianyu roasting a fish by the fire. She watched him from the trees again trying to decide what she should do.

"I feel your eyes," Jianyu said looking about. "I've been waiting for you. Are you well?"

Wei Zan pulled back in indecision and leapt up into the trees where she watched him all morning. What to do? *I should just leave. Why do I feel like this?* Jianyu read a book, fished for his lunch, then laid out by the fire and took a nap. She became angry that he seemed so relaxed when she felt so unsettled. *Silly, he thinks of me as just a fox! I should leave it that way.*

But the truth was Wei Zan didn't want to leave it that way. When the sun set and Jianyu had built his campfire, Wei Zan slipped down out of her tree. Spinning her magic, she transformed into her other self. Holding her head high, she walked into Jianyu's camp.

"You've finally returned," Jianyu spoke without looking up. "Why did you stay away so long? I was worried."

"What are you talking about?" Wei Zan said feigning ignorance. "I'm lost. I just saw your campfire. Can you help me?"

"Do we really need to play that game?" Jianyu looked up.

Wei Zan flushed and took a step back as if to run.

"Please don't run away. I know you're my little fox. Please come and sit by the fire." Jianyu patted the ground next to him. "Are you hungry?"

Wei Zan hesitated, then nodded her head and stepped forward to sit beside him. He handed her a cup of rice with flakes of cooked fish leftover from his dinner. "I saved it for you." He looked into her eyes and Wei Zan felt her heart flutter.

"Thank you." She took the bowl and ate with her fingers.

"I waited for you that night. Why didn't you come into the shelter?" Jianyu asked. "I know you needed to replenish your energy."

"I couldn't."

"Why not? I offered."

"I just couldn't."

"Are you recovered now?"

"I am well." Wei Zan shifted uncomfortably. Jianyu kept staring at her the same as all the other men had stared. She wasn't sure what she expected, but she didn't want him to just be enamored.

"You are very beautiful. I guess I knew that from when I saw you before. May I ask you your name?" Jianyu said tilting his head, curious if she'd tell him.

"It's Wei Zan."

"Which is your true form...the fox or the woman?"

"Does it matter?" She tilted her head. "They are both me."

Jianyu laughed. "As was the dog?"

"Yes, that was a glamour."

"So, that was why you were injured when you fell."

"Yes. With a glamour, I am real, with an illusion, I just control what people see."

"So, what I'm seeing right now, is you." With that Jianyu reached forward and touched Wei Zan's face.

The stroke of his fingers down her face sent traces of shivers through her body. She couldn't help but think of him stroking her fur, and she could not look away. *I am the seductress, so why do I feel like I am the one being seduced?* His eyes grew closer until hers grew heavy. She felt his hand slip behind her head and deep within her hair as their lips touched.

When he pulled his lips away, she almost cried out. Jianyu stood and scooped her up carrying her into the shelter. *Indeed, I am seduced.*

***

Wei Zan woke in the morning startled to see Jianyu staring down at her. She had always left the men before and always slept alone. The sensation of waking up with someone felt odd but somehow comforting. Jianyu's warm smile made her smile in return. *What is this feeling? I feel so funny inside. Like sunlight.*

"Hungry?" Jianyu said.

"Yes, but not for food."

Laughing and wrestling turned into earnest lovemaking leaving both spent. "Now, I'm hungry," Wei Zan said laughing.

The two left the shelter for the morning meal and then went down to the stream to clean up. They spent the day exploring the surrounding woods, talking, laughing, and touching. Wei Zan loved hearing the sound of Jianyu's voice as he told stories of his family and his youth growing up. *Family...what was that like? This* became the pattern for the next passing weeks as they waited for the time Jianyu needed to return to the city to continue his duty.

"What is it that you do?" Wei Zan once asked him.

"I can't say," Jianyu replied. "But I want you to return with me when I'm done."

"We will see."

***

"I'm heading back to the city to pick up my items. Please promise me you will not follow me this time," Jianyu said as they lay side by side.

"I promise. Can I wait for you at the outskirts of the city? I will stay human."

"No, please. Your beauty will only lure men and cause a different kind of problem. This campsite is off the road and secluded. You're safer here. Promise me." Jianyu looked into her eyes, brushing back her hair from her face.

"Yes." Wei Zan sighed with contentment. "How long will you be gone."

"Two maybe three days. I can't be sure how it will go. Promise me you will wait."

"I promise, but I may visit my grotto and return in three days."

After a lingering goodbye, Jianyu picked up his pack and headed out leaving Wei Zan idling about the camp doing one chore and then another just to feel his warmth and smell his scent. *This is foolish. I best be going.* After transforming back to her fox form, she trotted off towards the grotto. A few days of sleeping and replenishing her energy would help her heart not miss Jianyu the way it missed him right now.

***

Jianyu's trip into the city was uneventful. When he arrived at the temple, the abbot received him in his private quarters where he presented the two urns.

"The families of the two brothers were distraught, but have come to understand the honor that is being bestowed upon their loved ones," the abbot said. "Blessings to you and your family."

Jianyu took the urns and headed to an altar outside the city where a shaman waited for him. This shaman was familiar with the rituals that needed to be done. "Their spirits will be quite weak at first and need time to cultivate their strength. Your family has lots of work to do since you have never done two at the same time before. Are you prepared for this?"

"My family is ready. Tomorrow at sunrise we must do the first cleansing ritual at dawn and I shall greet the brothers on behalf of my family." Jianyu bowed his head.

The shaman opened a back wall in his private altar. The two golden urns were placed on that altar where they would spend the night being blessed. Incense burned and prayer sticks were placed before them in the sand pots.

"Do you have somewhere to stay?" the shaman asked.

"Yes. I will return tomorrow at dawn." With another bow, Jianyu left and went back into the city. He spent the afternoon walking about the marketplace, picking up a few treats he thought Wei Zan would like and buying a few books for his brothers to read. He saw a bracelet that would look beautiful on Wei Zan's graceful wrist, a ribbon that would shine against her ebony hair, and fine silk that would make her face glow. Engrossed as he was in his private thoughts, he didn't notice a man following behind.

At dawn, Jianyu rose, returning to meet the shaman at the altar where they entered his private shrine. After taking down the two urns, the shaman said a prayer and handed the urns to Jianyu.

"Their spirits have been within for the required forty-nine days of mourning. I can feel that they have sufficient energy to manifest themselves. However, do not let them expend too much energy this first time, just enough to explain to them what is happening so they can come to an understanding. Start gently. It will take time for them to understand and accept their new place in the world. They will have to be trained the same as any shaman or scholar. Their abilities will grow over time as they gain strength and knowledge."

"Should I open the two urns together?" Jianyu asked.

"I am unsure. Let's try one first and if he does well, then we will open the brother's urn."

Jianyu picked up an urn, spoke under his breath, gave a twist and the lid came off with a smooth movement. With a brief flash of light, a soft blue mist exited followed by a glow that formed into a slender elderly man who stood calm and composed before them. He looked around the room, confused for a moment, then smiled.

"This must be a dream. If so, it's a strange one. I was sure I had died. If I did, I sure expected the afterlife to look better than this."

Jianyu burst out laughing. He liked this man. "Who are you, sir?"

The spirit sighed. "Guess it's not a dream then, or you wouldn't be asking. Same thing with the afterlife. You'd know my name. Now, I have a mystery." The man's head cocked to one side as he bowed. "I, sir, am Yang An Jin. Who, may I ask, are you?"

Jianyu, impressed with the man's demeanor, decided to be frank and upfront with the facts. "You, sir, are indeed dead. However, the Emperor wants to honor you and your brother for the service you gave to China. Your ashes have been placed in these blessed golden urns. They allow your spirits to continue to live in the mortal realm where he wishes you to continue to serve by acting as advisers. You will be able to continue to grow in knowledge and spiritual power."

"Here I thought I had retired."

Jianyu found himself laughing again until he caught the look from the shaman.

"You do not wish to serve?" the shaman asked stiff-necked.

"And if I don't?" Yang An Jin said still smiling.

"Your ashes will be removed from the urn and returned to your family. Your spirit will no longer be able to manifest in the mortal world. You will be just as gone as all the other people before you. The Emperor will be told you refused his gracious offer."

"What did my brother say?" Yang An Jin said. The smile was gone. The shaman's voice made Jin wonder if some retaliation would fall on the Yang family.

Jianyu picked up the other urn. "Shall I open it and we can ask him?"

"Please."

Jianyu spoke the words again and opened the urn and within moments an elderly corpulent man stood before them, dazed until he saw his brother.

"Jin, what's happening?"

"Chengli, do not worry. We find ourselves in a new adventure it seems." Jin approached his brother.

"But, didn't we die?" Chengli shook his head. "I remember hearing weeping."

"Yes, brother, we are indeed dead, but seems like we aren't going to stay that way."

Jin explained the Emperor's plan to his brother, and Chengli, ever the patriot, said they must serve their country.

Jin sighed. "My brother has spoken, and where he goes, I must follow."

Jianyu smiled at the brothers. "I will be taking you to my home where I, my family, and our descendants will care for you. There we will help you learn and grow. We will teach you everything that you need to know about what abilities you can master now and in the future. For instance...you can appear to be any age that pleases you."

Jin laughed. "Are there any beautiful women in this spirit world I need to impress?"

Jianyu could sense the shaman's displeasure with Jin's frivolous talk, so he changed the subject. "I will come again this afternoon to collect your urns and return to my camp. You need to return to the urns now because staying outside of the urns consumes energy and you are not that powerful yet. In the future, you will be able to stay out longer."

"What happens if we stay out too long?" Chengli said.

"If too long, you could lose form and fade away. We'd lose you forever. But we won't let that happen. So, back to your urn."

"How do we do that?" Chengli asked.

"Just think 'home'."

With that, both spirits floated back into the urns and the lids snapped tight.

Jianyu rushed back towards the camp, anxious to see Wei Zan, perhaps these feelings caused a carelessness that made him neglect his usual caution. A shadow approached, certain of his ability to surprise the oblivious young man. Just when the shadow prepared to attack, Jianyu spun and drew his sword. The shadow fell to the ground and rolled, shouting "I surrender, little brother."

Laughing, Jianyu sheathed his blade and offered his hand. The two brothers embraced. "Why are you here, Fo He?"

"Nothing good, I'm afraid. The Emperor's brother attacked the palace. The Emperor is safe, but we had to move the urns to another location. The traitor wants the urns. I'm here to guide you. I've got two urns and First brother has two. Father and the others are acting as decoys till they can be sure they are either free of being followed or have killed those who dare. We will meet them later. Are you ready to head out?"

"No, I must return to my camp first."

"Why?"

"Um...I left something there."

"Very well. Let's go."

The brothers talked as they went with Fo He filling Jianyu in on the events of the attack. The family tried to avoid palace intrigues. Their public task was to be stewards of the antiquities that the Ming Emperor prized. They were in charge of all his treasure; however, the urns were secrets of the Chang family alone. No other servant was aware of the hidden cabinet within their quarters.

When they arrived back at the camp, Jianyu packed up the last of his gear while looking around and pacing.

"What's the problem? We best get going." Fo He said.

Just as Jianyu was about to tell his brother about Wei Zan, four men rushed into the clearing, swords drawn. They surrounded the two brothers.

The brothers dropped their packs, drew their swords and stood back-to-back in defensive position.

One man stepped forward and addressed Fo He. "Thank you for leading us here. I thought we'd only get you. Now, we get two of you. Give us the packs and we will let you live. Our Lord only wants what's inside."

"I'm afraid we can't do that."

With a shrug, the men attacked.

***

Wei Zan trotted through the brush back towards the camp until she heard the sounds of battle. With a leap, she was up into the trees and soared over the tops until she had an aerial view of the fight.

Jianyu and another man stood back-to-back fighting four other man. The blades flashed faster than she could follow. All were expert swordsmen, but she felt a thrill of appreciation to note that Jianyu was still the best. One man cried out and fell, dead. Jianyu struck at another, who fell back, but a cry from a third man caused Jianyu to leap backwards to stand over him. Wei Zan could see the resemblance between them. Brothers! Jianyu had spoken of his brothers. Now Wei Zan saw the determination on Jianyu's face. He'd die to defend his brother. Then her sensitive fox ears heard a rustle. When she looked towards the sound, she saw a man come out of the woods at the side of the clearing behind Jianyu. He pulled out an arrow and prepared to fire.

Without thought, Wei Zan leapt forward intercepting the arrow and felt it pierce her lung driving all breath from her body. She knew then that she would never leave her forest. All she could do now was try to protect Jianyu and his brother from the forest's retribution. She struggled to hold on. With the last of her strength, she sent out her energy to mark Jianyu and his brother lest the forest take them also.

Stunned by the sight of the white fox, the attackers stood for a moment until Jianyu's wail rang out. "NO, WEI ZAN, NO!" He crumbled to the ground grasping her body in his arms. Fo He looked on, shocked and confused at the sight of his brother holding and crying over a white fox. He tried to struggle to his feet, but fell back to the ground. He saw the attackers press forward once again and cried out a warning to Jianyu as he held up his sword to defend his brother.

A wailing sound rose up all around them, as if the forest itself was crying out. Wind swirled, blowing dirt into the men's faces and blinding them. Vines sprang up everywhere, entwining legs and bodies and growing about the would-be assassins until they strangled on their own cries. Fo He shrank in terror. Two men were pulled up against large trees where the tree bark grew around them until only the tree remained. Ivy vines grabbed one man's ankles and he disappeared up into the treetops. Other vines went down the throat of the archer and exploded out of his body. His muffled screams gurgled away until silence returned to the deep woods.

"Oh, gods! Jianyu..." Fo He trembled where he lay.

Oblivious to what happened behind him, Jianyu rocked back and forth, sobbing, repeating the name, "Wei Zan."

Her last bit of strength gone, Wei Zan looked up, smiled and let out her last breath.

"Jianyu, please! What's happening? Who is this?" Fo He reached out to Jianyu.

The fox's body began to glow in Jianyu's arms. He looked around in panic. With a strange glint in his eye, Jianyu jumped up and ran to grab Fo He's pack. Pulling out a case, he put in the code and opened the box. He removed an urn and spoke the ritual.

"What are you doing?" Fo He shouted. "You can't do that. Stop it!" He struggled once again to rise, but was unable. You don't know what they'll do to you!" He crawled forward and grabbed at Jianyu's leg.

"I don't care!" Jianyu kicked his brother away. He approached Wei Zan's body now glowing bright, flickering like a loose gathering of stars. He feared it would break apart at any moment and scatter. So, unsure if his desperate idea could possibly work, Jianyu put the opened urn within the cluster of stars. "Please," he begged, "please stay with me, Wei Zan."

As if in a dream, Wei Zan's spirit heard. And stayed.

Chapter 18

Han lay in bed, Lei snuggled up against him as always. He'd had a good life, with good sons, but there was such a feeling of unfinished business when it came to Jonny. He'd thought there would be time enough to understand, but now it seemed there wouldn't be. Part of him blamed the fortune teller. They should never have gone to her. Some family traditions should have died in the old country.

But his family had always consulted fortune tellers on the naming of their children, so Han and Lei did the same. Bolin was named after the great hero of the family for he inherited his traits. The teller foresaw that Bolin would grow to be a wise Guardian. Likewise, Min would be quick and clever—the negotiator of the family. He grew to be exactly as she predicted, forever a peacemaker between his brothers.

Then came Jonny. The fortune teller hesitated and didn't want to speak at first. Then she said his name was to be Jianyu and looked at Han and Lei saying, "You understand what I am telling you?"

They understood all too well. Jianyu had been reborn. Just as there had been many sons named Bolin in the family, there had never been another Jianyu. But what that would mean to their family, they hadn't understood.

From the very beginning, Jonny rebelled against all things Chinese. He hated tradition, he hated rules. "I'm an American," was his mantra. He wanted hamburger and French fries not stir fry or chow mein. He resented the martial arts training and dropped out to take boxing. Han did manage to convince him to try fencing as long as the swords were western.

How could Han ever trust him to be a Guardian? Jianyu had betrayed them before. Would he betray them again? What would happen if the Huli Jing were set free? And, Jonny would want to set her free. Somehow Han knew that was true. How would the modern world react to one? Could the Guardians even control her?

Han hated to lay these responsibilities onto his sons but he had no choice.

"Stop worrying," Lei's soft voice murmured.

"Did I wake you?"

"I can hear the roar of your thoughts." Lei laughed. "The boys will be fine, just as you were. After all, they have all the wisdom of the spirits to help guide them. Have faith."

"I know. I know." Han's laugh rumbled deep in his chest. "Isn't it usually the woman who's the worrier and the man who's the comforter?"

Lei hugged him tight and rose up to kiss his cheek. "I need to get up and feed you. You need to eat a little more today if you could, please."

"I will try."

The family gathered around the breakfast table and Han tried not to be irritated as everyone watched every morsel he ate. He forced himself to eat and Lei's relieved sigh was his reward. After cleanup, they walked over to the temple and Physician Ho joined them.

"This is our last morning here before we pack up and head back tomorrow morning," Han said looking at his sons. "Any questions?"

"I have a question," Min said raising his hand.

"Yes."

"What happened to our ancestor who used the urn for his lover?"

Han bowed his head. *Min always had to ask.* "The family took a vote and he was ostracized, shunned. The penalty was supposed to be death, but the vote was one shy of the total needed for that. His brother spared him and the urn was forever sealed so the creature could not be released."

"Creature?" Bolin said, surprise in his voice.

Physician Ho took up the story. "The last urn contains a supernatural being called a Huli Jing. Some believed your ancestor may have been under the undue influence of this creature and not totally responsible for his actions."

"Nonsense," Han argued, "the Guardians were aware of those beings and trained for such encounters."

"You mean there are such creatures?" Min said astounded.

"Why do you sound so surprised when you're sitting across from me?" Physician Ho said smiling.

"Every continent has its own supernatural realm," Han said. "I've never heard of a Huli Jing in the Americas, but they're spirits that still live in the forests of China. Back then, the forest took the lives of the men who killed their Huli Jing, but somehow spared our Guardian ancestors. We could never quite understand how that came to be."

"What powers do they have?" Bolin asked.

"That can be a research topic when we return if you're interested. These are creatures of China you will not see here in America. You have other duties to concentrate on first."

The rest of the morning Han made the brothers recite their roles as Guardians and taught them the ritual for sending a spirit back into an urn.

"I myself have never had to do this. It is only for emergencies and we do our best to avoid those in the first place. The last time it was invoked was when the house was invaded by the revolutionary army. The spirits would have fought. Indeed, the Admiral's first response was to fight, but his energy would have been used up and depleted too quickly by the sheer number of invaders. The Guardian overrode him and sent him back to his urn."

"Could the Admiral really fight and kill?" Min said.

"In corporeal form, his sword is deadly."

"I guess we better not piss him off," Min said after a moment of silence.

"Min," Lei said, but smiled.

"Sorry, Mom."

"Father," Min said, "I have another question."

"Yes, son."

"When we get back, how are you going to handle Jonny? He has the right to know you're sick. He also has the right to know about the family legacy. Bolin and I talked last night and we don't understand why he's been left out."

Han looked at Bolin. "You agree with Min?"

"Well, I agree that you have to tell him you're sick right away." Bolin flinched as Min punched him in the arm. "I'm not as certain as Min is about the legacy. Jonny is so stubborn about all things China, but Min thinks this might be the thing to bring him around. I'm just not as sure as Min is."

"There are facts I can't speak of yet that make me hesitate. I will give this long careful thought I promise you. For now, keep the secret."

"Yes, Father," Bolin said.

"Crap," Min said.

"Min," Lei said.

Chapter 19

Monday Night

"Jianyu, Jianyu." Wei Zan knelt by Jianyu's side patting his cheek. "Are you okay?" For the first time she looked around the room and froze. *Where am I?*

Calling on her powers, she placed her hand on Jianyu's chest and read his energy. It was strong. Reassured, she stood and took another look around. Walking to each object she didn't recognize, she touched them and tried to get a reading. Nothing—until she reached a tall box that felt cool to the touch. *Curious.* Since there was a handle, she pulled it. *Food!* All kinds of food. *What miracle was this?* She reached in and pulled out an apple. *Wondrous.* She pulled out a container and opened it. Looking inside she frowned at what appeared to be noodles covered in red sauce. She smelled it. *Interesting.* She pulled out drawers and opened containers, recognizing some things and shaking her head at others.

Closing the door, she went to an open bag on the counter and reached into it pulling out a thin, crisp roundish pieces of...something. She couldn't read what was written on the bag. *Strange. What language is this?* She took a small bite. Salty. She smiled.

Putting the bag down, she walked back and sat next to Jianyu. *What to do?* She sighed. Maybe, if I give him a little jolt of energy he'll wake up. Maybe...just a gentle slap or two. She considered both, then gave Jianyu a quick slap. Nothing. Another, a little harder. This time, he began to stir.

"Jianyu!"

***

Jonny wandered in a foggy place seeing snatches of pictures he didn't want to see, feeling emotions he didn't want to feel. Confused, he saw himself doing things he'd never done, saying things he'd never said, being with people he didn't know. And, he saw the woman. He saw himself with her. He saw her death. The intensity of his loss made it difficult to breathe. He had to wake up. HE HAD TO WAKE UP!

He forced his eyes open and looked up into the woman's eyes. They seemed to sparkle as she smiled down at him.

"Jianyu, you're finally awake," she said. "I was so worried."

Her accent was strange, but he understood everything she said. *How was that possible?* He felt intense longing just looking at her, his heart pounding, his breath rapid. What was happening to him?

"Who are you?" Jonny managed to ask. "What are you doing to me?"

Wei Zan blinked, startled. Placing her hand on his chest again, she read his energy once more, this time going deeper. When she withdrew her hand, she collapsed, her head dropping to her chest.

"You're not MY Jianyu."

"What do you mean by that? Your Jianyu?

"Tell me, where am I?" Wei Zan wailed looking at Jonny with a pleading look he couldn't resist.

"You're at my home."

"Is this the palace?"

"Palace? No-o. We're not that fancy. We live above our store on Grant Ave."

"Grant? Is that in Beiping?"

"Again, no. It's in San Francisco."

Wei Zan put her hand to her head as it spun. She had to close her eyes for a moment to gather her thoughts. "What year is it?"

"It's 2023."

Wei Zan began to tremble. First her hands, then her entire body began to shake. "What happened to my Jianyu? He would never have left me alone like this. What did they do to him?"

Jonny shook his head. "I don't know. I don't know anything about the history of these urns. I only found out about them a couple days ago."

Wei Zan's obvious distress pulled at Jonny until he couldn't stand to see it without offering comfort. He reached forward and his hand covered hers. The reaction was immediate. Wei Zan's breathing slowed and her body stopped trembling. She looked up at him, her brow furrowed. She grabbed both of his hands and held on.

"I feel him in you. You are him. He's come back for me."

Stunned, Jonny pulled away. "That's crazy." Jonny stood up and backed away. He looked around the room as if looking for an escape. He didn't know what to do or what to think. He needed the Admiral, but when he started towards the urns, Wei Zan stopped him.

"Jianyu," Wei Zan said frightened by the look on his face, "do you honestly not remember me?" With those words, she wrapped her arms around Jonny and kissed him.

Jonny found he couldn't move. Her body molded itself into his. One hand threaded up through his hair as the other nestled between his shoulders pressing him close. Desire overwhelmed him and left him feeling dizzy. He clutched her to him backing towards the couch where they fell into a heap. He moaned deep in his throat.

"Wait," Wei Zan gasped, breaking the kiss. "Wait." She pushed against Jonny's chest and rolled. He fell to the floor as she struggled to stand up.

"W-what?" Jonny shook his head, dazed.

"I'm sorry. I'm so sorry, Jianyu. I swore I'd never do that to you." Wei Zan hung her head in shame.

"Do...do what?"

"You really don't know anything, do you?"

"I told you I didn't." Frustrated Jonny tried to stand, but fell back down.

"Maybe I don't deserve to be set free. Maybe I deserve to be locked up. Forgive me!" With that cry she broke apart into glittering bits.

"No, wait," Jonny yelled reaching out toward the lights.

But it was too late. The lid snapped back in place. The urn was sealed.

"I don't understand," Jonny yelled to the room. "What just happened?"

Chapter 20

Tuesday

Jonny woke up feeling groggy and dull headed. After two cups of coffee, he didn't feel much better. Everyone would be home today and he'd never see the spirits again. He'd never know all the stories. And Wei Zan. *What about her?* He dreamed of her all night. His heart still pounded. Jonny shook his head and turned on the shower. Maybe he'd make it a cold one.

After a breakfast of cereal, Jonny walked downstairs to open the front shop door. Ting-a-Ling came in a few minutes later and the day began.

"What time are your parents going to be home?" Ting asked.

"Around lunchtime, I guess."

"You going to tell them about Frankie?"

"Hell, no."

"Did you put the item back?"

"Yes."

"What item did you use? Where did you get it?" Ting-a-Ling looked at Jonny with an odd expression.

"Just around, you know, private stuff. Let's get to back to work."

"Nobody's here."

"Well, then, let's clean up the place." With that Jonny grabbed the duster and began to furiously dust the shelves.

Ting frowned and bit his lip. His boy was up to something and Wu Zhang knew what it was.

***

Han and Lei got the boys all packed into the Enclave and they headed back down the mountains towards home. The ride was quiet as each digested what had been said and what would be expected over the coming weeks and months.

"When are you going to tell Jonny," Min asked breaking the silence."

"We'll tell him tonight," Han promised.

Min got out his phone and played some games, while Bolin read a book. Lei kept a watchful eye on Han to make sure he didn't do too much, but he seemed excited to be going home and did fine. When they pulled up to the back of the shop, Han jumped out of the SUV and ran up the stairs shouting to the boys to unload.

Lei laughed. "I think your father is glad to be home."

"I think he's just glad to see the store still standing," Bolin said and got a punch in the arm from his brother.

Han went down to the shop to see how everything was going and was pleased to see Jonny charming a family with small children doing his sleight-of-hand. The kids were laughing and the parents were smiling. Ting then escorted the mother around while

178

the father stayed with the kids. Han watched their teamwork and nodded at the amount of the sale it generated.

When the family had left, he walked over, "Good work, you two."

Startled, they both turned. "Father!" Jonny said. "Welcome home. Did you have a nice trip?"

"Very nice. Did all go well here?" Han was surprised to see guilt on his son's face for a moment before it disappeared behind a smile. Han looked back and forth between his son and Ting.

"Yeah, great. Didn't it, Ting-a-Ling?"

"Yes, Mr. Chen. All went well. You can see our daily receipts. I left them in the register. If it's okay, I'd like to take a little extra time for lunch today?"

"Sure, sure. I'll send one of the boys down to cover for you. Take the afternoon if you'd like. You worked all weekend." Han turned and reached for the intercom. "Bolin, come down and cover for Ting Wang this afternoon."

"Yes, Father," came the reply.

"Thank you." With that, Ting-a-Ling bowed his farewell and left. Jonny wondered what Ting's plan was. He bet it had to do with Madam Zin. *Good for you.*

Han was over at the register checking the receipts and nodding. "It looks like you did pretty well this weekend. I'm pleased. No real problems then?"

"What, you didn't believe me?" Jonny's hackles started to rise.

"No, no," Han said backpedaling. "I'm very happy. Listen, we want to have a family dinner tonight so please don't make any plans for this evening. We haven't seen you for days. Okay?"

Surprised, Jonny only nodded, then shrugged. "Sure."

When Bolin came down, the brothers looked at each other with their usual 'huh, you' expression and went to their separate corners. Bolin's sales style was the opposite of Jonny's. No one could match his knowledge of the history and value of each piece. He was a collector's best friend.

That evening, Lei outdid herself with dinner. She picked one thing that was a favorite of every member of her family. There was salt and pepper shrimp, dumplings, pumpkin mochi with red bean paste, beef chow mein and char sui. Not to mention, her famous fried rice. No one could complain that she favored any one person over the other. She called her family to the dinner table saying a prayer. *Please let this dinner go well.* After dinner would be another matter.

As they gathered around the table, she could feel the tension in the air so her first mission was to set the stage to put everyone at ease. She began with telling stories. Stories were always good, especially silly stories of childhood. She talked about her first crush on a boy who she heard grew up to be a triad assassin. He died in a shootout. Han talked about never having a first love except Lei. Lei talked about her first kiss. He was a young boy who wrote her a poem in seventh grade that promised he'd love her forever. Han talked about the fact he'd never kissed anyone but Lei.

Pretty soon the boys were laughing and calling their father hopeless as Lei continued her litany. This boy had asked her to marry him; that boy had asked her to marry him; of course, she said no. Han never asked anyone but Lei, and of course, she said yes.

"It doesn't matter how many came before me," Han smiled. "It only matters that I was the last."

The dinner was a success and with full stomachs they went to the living room. "I need to talk to you boys."

If Jonny noticed how silent everyone became, he didn't say anything. He took his seat and watched as everyone did the same. Silence fell.

"What's up?" he said. "I feel like I'm the only one here that doesn't know what's going on. Am I right?" He looked from brother to brother. They looked away. "Right. What is it?"

Han decided to say it outright. "I'm sick."

Jonny sat up straight, shocked. He didn't know what he was expecting, but this wasn't it. "What do you mean, sick? How sick?"

"I have cancer."

Again, Jonny looked at his brothers, but neither looked him in the eye. Shit. This is bad if they're not looking at me. "How bad?"

"It looks like it's terminal. I have enough time left to be sure everything will be okay with your mother and you boys."

"When did you go for treatment?" Thoughts were racing through Jonny's head. His father was a rock. He couldn't be DYING.

"It's too far advanced for treatment so we decided not to waste my remaining time feeling sick and being away from the people I love. I'm going to live until I die. Please understand. This is the decision your mother and I have made."

"Without asking us?" Jonny looked at his brothers. "You're okay with this?"

"We weren't at first, but we've accepted it now, I guess," Min said.

"At first? How long have you known?"

"Dad told us this weekend," Bolin said. "I was angry at first, too. I wanted him to fight, but physician...but he convinced me that his way was what was best for him."

"What physician?" Jonny demanded.

"Just one of my doctors," Han said.

"You got to speak to one of his doctors?" Jonny asked Bolin.

"Not really. I misspoke. I meant to say that what Dad's physician said to him helped me to understand why Dad made this decision."

Then Jonny remembered that his father had taken an urn up into the mountains. The Admiral said the first urn was a physician. So, two plus two gets you four. That physician was going to let his father die. Without even trying!

"Bull!" Jonny yelled.

"Jonny!" Lei said.

"Sorry, Mom, but, Dad, you have to try. You can't just give up."

Han sagged back against the chair and Lei rushed to his side. "That's enough, Jonny." Her tone was one he'd never heard before. She took her husband's hand then turned to Jonny. "Every man must make his own choice when it comes to how he wants to live his life and that includes how he wants to face the end. Do you think this was easy for us? Do you think we were ready for this?" Tears gathered in her eyes. "Allow us our dignity. We need your support, not your anger."

Jonny looked around the room and again felt excluded. He was the last to know, the odd man out. What he thought, what he felt, was discounted.

"Do what you want then." Jonny got up and left. Tears blurred his vision as he stumbled out of the house and walked down the street.

***

The family sat in silence until Han spoke. "He'll be back. We'll talk with him again then. For now, let me take you up and show you the room." They all stood and followed him up the attic stairs in silence to the large storage area and to the back wall where Han turned the Buddha on the top shelf and the wall panel slid open.

"What the..." Min said. "I never knew this was up here."

"Me neither." Bolin walked in first and looked around the room. "This is some set up, Father. Where are the other urns?"

Han laughed. Bolin was all business. "Here." Han walked to the cabinet and opened the door showing the five other urns. He reached for one and his hand froze. Wait a minute, they weren't in the usual position. Did he move them? Did Lei? She must have cleaned. He shook his head and focused on the job at hand.

"Each urn has slightly different markings so you can tell whose urn is whose. You'll learn them fast enough. The one with the red cord and arrowhead, we don't open. That's the Huli Jing."

"Can we meet them tonight?" Min asked.

"Yes. Briefly."

Over the next hour, Bolin and Min were introduced to the other four urn residents. Both were intimidated by the Admiral, and both fell half in love with Lady Ji. Chengli and Jin put the brothers at ease and after a few of Jin's jokes, Bolin and Min were laughing like they were old friends. The brothers had to keep reminding themselves that these were spirits. They just seemed like...people.

"It's late," Lei said seeing Han droop with fatigue. "Time for bed. We'll be setting up a schedule for the boys to carry out their duties. Teach them well." Lei gave the spirits a bow. "Good night."

With a return bow, the spirits disappeared back into their urns and the lids snapped shut. The family returned downstairs and headed to their rooms. Han fell asleep almost immediately, but Lei lay awake until after midnight when she finally heard Jonny come up the back steps. She got up and met him as he entered the kitchen.

"Are you alright?" Lei said.

Jonny looked at her for a moment, put his head down, then said, "I'm sorry, Mom. I'll do better." With that, he gave her a quick hug and walked back to his bedroom leaving a bewildered mother standing in the kitchen.

***

Jonny had wandered the streets not really paying attention to where he was going. So much was happening in his life he couldn't fathom which way was up and which was down. The world had changed. He wanted to run away. Then he remembered his mother's face—his mother's face. She was the one person in this world who was always on his side, who always had a smile for him and who he knew loved him whether he was being a jerk or not.

Jonny brushed the tears from his eyes. His father couldn't be dying! He was so confident, so strong, so stubborn. A crack appeared in Jonny's reality. He found himself in front of Madam

Zin's red door. He stood there for countless minutes feeling stupid and unsure.

The door opened. "Are you coming in or what?" Madam Zin asked.

Startled, Jonny said, "You really are psychic, aren't you?"

Madam Zin laughed and pointed up at the security camera. "I only take credit where credit is due. Follow me."

Jonny stumbled in after her and took a seat on the floor before her table. She sat on her cushion and looked at his distressed face. "Tell me, boy, what's happened?"

"Don't you know? Aren't you a shaman?" For a moment Jonny's usual disdain of all things Chinese raised its head, but it crumbled under the old woman's gaze.

"Very well," Madam Zin said, "you came for a reading, I'll give you one." She took out her bag and slipped a few dried herbs onto her tongue, closed her eyes, then began a soft cadence on her drum.

"What are you doing?" Jonny asked.

"I'm calling my spirit guide. Please be silent." She continued the drumming and began a soft low chant.

"This is stupid." Feeling foolish, Jonny started to get up.

"Death threatens your house," Madam Zin intoned.

Jonny collapsed back down. His hands clenched. "Who told you that?"

"Who do you think? You have your spirits, I have mine," said the shaman as she peeked out of her eyes for a moment. "The Admiral has friends. I want to meet them."

"Wait a minute. Stop." Jonny's chest tightened in a moment of panic. "I don't know what you're talking about."

Madam Zin opened her eyes. "Don't be afraid. I see danger, but it's unclear. Be strong. Your family needs you."

Jonny stood up, shaken. "I don't believe this. I'm outta here."

"Aren't you forgetting my bill?" Madam Zin looked up at Jonny with raised brows.

"How much do I owe you?" Jonny sneered with false bravado.

"I want to meet the spirits. That's what you owe me."

Chapter 21

THE NEXT MORNING THE family sat at the breakfast table staring at their food with quiet intensity. No one seemed to have the courage to be the one to speak first. Min couldn't take it anymore, so he finally broke the silence.

"We need to come up with a work schedule so Father can take it easy." Min looked around the table for agreement.

"Sure," Bolin said.

Jonny nodded. "Does Ting know?"

"We'll tell him today," Han said. "After work."

Silence fell. Everyone finished eating and headed to their respective tasks for the day. Han stayed in the kitchen to help Lei clean up. The two went about the job with the rhythm of a long-standing ballet. When they were done, they turned to each other and Lei walked into Han's arms. They stood together for a few moments just enjoying each other. Lei tried not to think about the future, tried not to wonder about how much longer she would have Han here and be able to hold him like this. She sighed. A few small tears escaped.

With a sudden cry, Han doubled over. Lei struggled to support him as she guided him to a kitchen chair while he fought the spasm of pain.

"Shall I call the doctor?" Lei asked, her voice shaking.

"No, just give me a minute. It's already passing." Han took a couple of deep breaths and tried to relax as the spasm left. He had pain medication in his room, but resisted using it for it dulled his senses and he wanted to delay that feeling as long as possible. "See, my dear, it's gone. I'm fine now."

***

Bolin came down to the store and called Jonny and Ting-a-Ling over. "Min is going to go over the bookkeeping for taxes so he'll be busy all day. Father is tired from all the driving so he's taking the day off. I'm going up to start an inventory, so we'd like you two to handle the store for today. Any questions?" Bolin looked at Jonny. He needed Jonny to stay in the store so he could go up to the urn room.

Jonny started to object, then decided to go along with the plan. After all, he had nothing else to do. He slept very little last night and when he did, his dreams were bizarre. His head hurt. His eyes were blurry. If he could, he'd go get drunk. "Sure."

With a nod, Bolin left. Ting-a-Ling turned and looked at Jonny with a concerned expression. "You don't look so good. Bad night?"

"You could say that."

"Do you want to talk about it?"

Jonny opened his mouth to say he couldn't just yet, but the front door opened and a family entered. Jonny pasted on a smile and walked over. "Good morning," he said. Then he looked at the little girl. She was about six years old, bright-eyed, red-haired, and all smiles. "I bet you like flowers."

"How did you know?" the little girl asked.

"Because you have them growing out of your ears," Jonny said as he pulled a rose from one ear, a daisy from the other and handed them to the little girl.

"Oh, Mommy, look!" she squealed jumping up and down.

Her brother, who appeared to be about eight, leaned over to look into his sister's ears. "I never saw any flowers in her ears."

Jonny knew a doubting Thomas when he saw one. Kids need to believe in magic. "I have a trained eye to see special things others can't see," Jonny explained.

The little boy tilted his head back and frowned. "Really? Like what?"

"Like I bet you are a hard worker who likes money."

"How do you know that?" the boy said.

With a wave of Jonny's hand, he pulled a dollar bill out of each of the boy's ears. "See, the ears don't lie."

The boy's eyes lit up. Jonny could see the battle rage inside the boy between what he saw and what he believed. He wondered which would win. At eight, Jonny hoped it would be magic. "Come over here and I'll show you a few games you two can play while your parents' shop."

Ting-a-Ling began escorting the smiling parents around the store. Once again, their teamwork paid off with a large sale and happy customers. The two gave each other a high five and at lunch time, Jonny treated Ting-a-Ling.

When closing time came, Madam Zin walked into the store creating an odd dynamic. Ting believed she'd come to see him, Jonny believed she'd come for him. Madam played it cool by walking about the store waiting as they closed up. Then Han walked down.

"Ting," Han said, "I need to talk to you for a moment, please."

With a sideways glance at Madam Zin, Ting-a-Ling nodded and followed Han to the break room leaving Jonny alone with the shaman.

"What are you doing here?" Jonny asked.

"I want to talk to the spirits."

"That's not possible right now."

"Why not?"

"I can't get into that with you. Please don't talk about this in front of my dad."

Madam Zin paused to consider for a moment. The light dawned. "He doesn't know that you know, does he?"

Damn. "Please don't say anything. I'll tell him when the time is right. You'll just make trouble if you tell him, then I'll never let you talk to any of them. Get it?" *When in doubt, bluff.*

The kid is good, but who does he think he is if he thinks he can bluff me? "You owe me two-fold now and I collect on my debts. Don't make me wait too long."

The two adversaries stared at each other for a moment, then they nodded in silent agreement. A noise behind them made them turn and they saw Ting-a-Ling come out of the break-room. The tears in his eyes let Jonny know he'd been told of Han's illness, but before he could move to go to his friend, he was surprised that Madam Zin rushed forward.

"What is it?" she asked touching Ting's arm.

Ting shook his head. Madam Zin looked over his shoulder at Han walking out of the break-room. "Did they fire you?" Her voice rose, but as she went to step forward, Ting grabbed her hand.

"Stop," Ting said. "Come with me." Pulling her by her hand, Ting led her from the shop. They walked down the street until they came to the nearest tea shop. There Ting told her what Han had said to him and she felt foolish for not guessing the truth immediately. But she hadn't seen Han's death! *Was she slipping?*

The two decided to get dinner so they walked to their favorite restaurant and talked for a couple hours. The years fell away just as it always did when they were together. They didn't even notice that their hands were touching, but an observer did.

***

Bella watched as Ting and Madam Zin left the tea house. *That's strange. Isn't that Jonny's store clerk? What's he doing with the old shaman? Isn't she the one Jackie Ling said he got for Frankie?*

Bella followed the two to the restaurant and went inside. She took a table across the room from them and behind a pillar. She ordered a bowl of noodles as she continued to watch the two old lovers. *Isn't this interesting?*

***

Everyone's asleep. Jonny turned the Buddha and the door slid open. He went to the cabinet and pulled out the urn with the red cord. *I have to see her again. I can't stop thinking about her.*

"What are we?" Jonny asked.

Wei Zan stood before him. The two stared at each other for a moment before she spoke. "You called me again? You've forgiven me?"

Jonny looked into the woman's eyes and saw love looking back at him. It confused him. His heart raced and he felt an almost overwhelming desire to hold her. *Where was this coming from?*

"What are we to each other?" he repeated.

"We're lovers."

Jonny took a step back. "How can that be?"

"All I can think of is that you're fighting the memories. If you let them come, you will understand. I'm confused also. When I died, Jianyu asked me to go into the urn, so I did. Now I see his image in front of me, but my Jianyu has been gone for hundreds of years."

"This is so unbelievable. A week ago, I would have thought I was either stoned or crazy."

Wei Zan laughed. "May I ask a favor of you?"

"Um, I guess."

"I have been asleep for a very long time. I would like to see this new world I find myself in. All I have seen is this small room. Please, may I see the sky?"

"Oh, of course. We can sneak out. Everyone's asleep. We have to be quiet though until we get out of the house." Jonny motioned Wei Zan forward. "We'll need to get you some different clothes though. Yours kinda stick out."

"How about this?" In a blink, Wei Zan's clothing changed to match Jonny's. She wore jeans and a white tee shirt that did little to hide her endowments.

"Um, maybe you should wear a different shirt. I'll get you one of mine on the way out." They exited the attic room. Downstairs, Jonny grabbed a shirt for her, a couple of jackets, and a cap his mom had made for him. They tiptoed out of the house down the back stairs.

When Wei Zan stepped down onto the pavement, she stopped and frowned. Looking around and then up, her eyes filled with tears. "There are no trees, no grass. Where am I to draw my power?"

"What do you mean?"

"I'm a Huli Jing. I prefer to replenish my energy from the earth."

"I can take you to the park. There's lots of trees and grass there. Will that do?"

"Yes, please."

The two started to walk out of the alley when a cab drove by and Wei Zan made a strange barking sound and jumped behind Jonny. Jonny laughed and took her hand. "It's only a cab. It's okay."

"What's a—cab?"

"It's a method of transportation, a way to get around town."

"You mean like horses or carts?"

"Yes, just faster. They use mechanical engines, not horses."

"Amazing." Wei Zan looked up at the city lights and the tall buildings of the city. "Everything looks so big and bright. Can I ride in one of those—cabs?"

Jonny laughed. "Sure." He waved down a cab and the two got in. I know where to take you so you can see lots of trees and grass." He looked at the driver. "Golden Gate Park, please."

During the ride to the park, Wei Zan stayed glued to the window looking at buildings, lights, people, cars, trucks, and exclaiming like a child at Disneyland. Jonny could see the cabdriver glancing in the rearview mirror with a look that said "what kind of weirdo is this?" But when Wei Zan leaned forward and touched his shoulder to say a sweet "thank you", the man melted. The goofy smile he gave back to her told Jonny she'd made a conquest.

"I can wait for you?" the cab driver offered with another hopeful smile.

"No, thanks. We're good," Jonny said.

They walked into the park and Wei Zan breathed in the air and was able to relax. "This is better," she said. "The air where you live is not good. At least at the park I can breathe." With a laugh, she took off at a run and surprised, Jonny took off after her. He wasn't sure how long they ran, but he was gasping by the time she stopped.

Wei Zan collapsed onto the ground in a field and lay down on the grass throwing her arms out. She called on the earth to fill her up and could feel the vibrations of life roll up and into her. A breeze began and the leaves rustled. Searching for beings of her kind nearby, she was saddened to realize she was all alone. Indeed, she felt no other super naturals within this park.

"Have the humans here killed off all the forest spirits? Am I in danger?"

"I never heard of there being anything like that here. Is a Huli Jing a… forest spirit?"

"I can get strength from nature." Wei Zan looked away.

"Then what did you mean when you asked if I'd forgiven you?"

Wei Zan started to get up, but Jonny stopped her. "I can look it up if you don't tell me. It'll be better if you just tell me yourself."

Wei Zan's voice was a whisper. "Huli Jing can take energy from humans."

"How?"

"When I kissed you, I started to take some of your energy. I was afraid you'd send me back to the urn. I can bedazzle and control humans this way. But then I realized what I was doing. I was so ashamed, I went back on my own." Wei Zan stared down at her hands.

Part of Jonny was horrified, part of him was fascinated. He remembered the intense feelings. Were they real or not?

"So, were we lovers, or weren't we?"

"I think I need to tell you about MY Jianyu." So, Wei Zan began to speak, slowly at first, then with a tenderness that Jonny found humbling. He realized that this incredible woman actually sacrificed herself to save him, or the past him...other him...whatever. *What do you say to someone like that?*

"Don't worry about what you did. I forgive you."

Wei Zan turned to him with a smile like the sun. "Truly?" She threw her arms around him and kissed his cheek. A memory flashed of Wei Zan splashing in a pool of water, smiling, then leaping forward to wrap her arms and legs around him. Jonny's breath caught in his throat. When she drew back, he leaned forward to kiss her, but the barking of a few dogs stopped him.

Wei Zan paled with fear. "We must leave." She stood up.

"What's the matter?" Jonny rose beside her.

"Dogs. I hear dogs. They're coming."

"I'm here. There's nothing to be afraid of. I won't let them hurt you."

The barking grew closer.

"No. You don't understand. I must run." Wei Zan broke into a run as two large dogs came out of the trees. Jonny felt it strange, but they must have scented her fear for they ran right at Wei Zan. Jonny ran after them shouting for the dogs to stop. Before he could reach them, he was blinded by a brief flash. The howling of the dogs changed and when Jonny looked, Wei Zan was gone and, in her place, ran a beautiful white fox with...Jonny blinked a second time...*how many tails?*

The dogs closed in fast, so when the fox reached the trees, she took a leap up into the treetops.

Chapter 22

WEI ZAN TREMBLED IN the treetops and tried to leap from one to another, but the dogs followed, baying and growling. Have I lived all these hundreds of years to be torn to shreds now?

Jonny arrived at the base of the tree and shouting at the dogs, tried to drive them away, nearly getting bitten himself. He ran over to the nearby brush and picked up a large fallen branch then went back to confront the dogs. After a few good swats from the branch, the dogs gave up the hunt and ran yelping away.

"Wei Zan," Jonny shouted up the tree, "you can come down now. They're gone." He looked up and found her huddled form near the top of the tree. "Please, you're safe now." After a few moments, the white fox began to descend.

Jonny stood still, afraid if he moved, she would panic again. How could such a powerful creature be so afraid of dogs? He would definitely have to look this up when he got home. Now he regretted not paying attention to his Chinese history. Although this wasn't really history, was it? This was mythology. But, when she landed at his feet, he couldn't say she was a myth, could he? Just like he couldn't say spirits weren't real. Life has become very strange.

Wei Zan collapsed at his feet and curled up in a ball, so Jonny sat down beside her. Before he knew what he was doing, he began to stroke her fur, paying special attention to her ears. When she sighed and looked up at him, he laughed. "You're so brazen," he said and shook his head. Where did that come from?

Curious, he counted her tails...nine. I wonder what that means?

"Can you talk," Jonny asked.

Wei Zan shook her head. No.

"Can you change back?"

Wei Zan found that her panic had subsided enough for her to regain control. She changed and once again took on her human form, sitting beside Jonny. "Thank you for saving me," she said kissing his cheek.

"You're welcome." Jonny couldn't wait to look it up at home. "Why are you so afraid of dogs?"

"They've been used for millennia to hunt us because they are our natural enemies and can kill us."

"But you are a spirit now. How can they kill you?"

Wei Zan sat up startled for a moment, then started to giggle. The giggle turned into a laugh, then grew until she could barely breathe. Jonny could only laugh along with her.

When the laughter died, Jonny stood and offered his hand. "Let's take a little walk before heading back."

The two walked through the park just talking about their lives, Wei Zan told Jonny about her life as a Huli Jing, about her bond with her forest and the creatures that lived there. While they walked, Jonny began to see what she was saying. A small gray fox followed them for a while until Wei Zan sat down and gave him her attention. She looked up at Jonny. "He's a cousin."

To Jonny's surprise, up waddled a young skunk. He started to back away when Wei Zan laughed.

"You are safe." She scratched the black and while white head until the animal rolled over presenting an itchy belly.

A rabbit was next, and when the coyote appeared, she wiggled her finger at him saying only "behave". Her sweet laughter made Jonny smile, but the coyote obeyed. She stood up and told them all to go home.

Jonny told her about his dreams which they both decided must be actual memories from his past life as Jianyu. He remembered bloody sword battles and what it felt like to pierce another human with a blade. He shuddered. "It's weird. In my dream, I don't think a thing about it. But when I wake up, I look at my hands, expect to see blood and it grosses me out."

"So, you're saying in this time, men don't have to defend themselves?" Wei Zan said. "What a wonder that would be."

"Well, sometimes we do, but no one uses swords anymore."

"What do they use?"

"Guns, mostly. And knives."

"Isn't a knife just a short sword? We used knives back then, also. What is a gun?"

"It's a weapon that shoots a small projectile of metal into its target." Jonny pulled out his phone and showed her a picture of a gun.

She looked at it and frowned. "It is just a smaller arrow." She grabbed the phone. "What is this thing?" As she spoke, she stumbled and her form seemed to flicker. The phone fell to the ground.

"What's wrong?" Jonny said grabbing to steady her.

"I am very tired all of a sudden," Wei Zan said.

"We better get you back." Jonny picked up his phone and called for a cab to meet them at the nearest exit.

Wei Zan struggled to keep up feeling herself fade as they ran. By the time they arrived at the street, she was incorporeal. Jonny flagged down the cab and gave him the address. Even though he could see Wei Zan, Jonny realized the cab driver couldn't. Why could he see her and the driver couldn't? Another mystery.

When they got to the house, they rushed up the stairs. Wei Zan's faint form caused Jonny's gut to twist. "Hurry, get back inside the urn."

"How?" Wei Zan voice was barely a whisper. "I'm too weak."

"I don't know." Frantic now, Jonny grabbed the Admiral's urn and asked, "How does Wei Zan get back into the urn?"

The Admiral appeared. He took one look at Wei Zan's condition and Jonny's frantic expression and knew what had happened.

"Say the command 'fachu hui jia'," he ordered Jonny.

When Jonny said the words, she obeyed and disappeared back into the urn. Once the lid had snapped closed, the Admiral turned to Jonny.

"You've been very foolish and taken a great risk. What happened?" he demanded.

"Will she be alright?" Jonny asked.

"Yes. But she'll need a long time to recharge. She's never been out before. Now answer my question."

So, Jonny told the Admiral about opening Wei Zan's urn and having his past life memories being returned.

"She's a Huli Jing, Jonny," the Admiral said, "how do you know you are not under her influence. They are seductresses. They'll do whatever they wish to gain whatever they want. Your past life was ruined by her. You dishonored your vow. She did not deserve an urn."

Angry, Jonny lashed out. "Then why didn't they open the urn and let her spirit die?"

"A Huli Jing is a very powerful being. The more tails they have, the older and stronger they are and she has nine tails. Once she had entered the urn, they were afraid if they let her out, she would be malevolent and do great harm. It was safer to keep her a prisoner."

Jonny collapsed onto the chair. "You don't understand anything. She's not like that at all. She died protecting me. I love her."

"No, Jonny, YOU don't love her. Jianyu loved her. Don't get confused." The Admiral sat beside him. He could feel the boys' confusion and he felt sorry for it, but there was danger here. A Huli Jing had great power and if she regained it, he doubted they'd be able to control it. "It's very late, best you get some sleep."

"Please don't tell the others about this," Jonny pleaded.

"I can't promise that, but for now, I'll stay silent."

***

He'd been on a few wild LSD trips before, but for Andrew Bigham, this one beat anything he'd ever experienced. And, he was mostly sober. At first, he'd thought his dogs had taken off after some rabbit. He'd freaked when he saw that poor girl running. If they attacked a girl, they'd be put down for sure. Before he could even try to call them off, there was a flash of light. There in her place ran a white fox. *A white fox! With how many tails?* Holy Mary, Mother of God! He shook his head. *Am I having a flashback? This can't be real!*

He heard, then saw the man running after them and followed, watched the man pick up a branch and chase the dogs away. He got pissed when his dogs got hit. *Hey, first things first.* He watched when the fox came down from the tree and turned back into a woman...a beautiful Chinese woman. *Oh, yeah. Hey, stupid, get your phone!* He scrambled through his pockets, pulled out his phone and started a video.

This is wild. This is good. I can make some money with this. A story like this could get me on the news. Maybe get me enough for some of the good stuff. Yeah. Good. Right. He couldn't wait to get back to the homeless camp. Who should he tell first?

Chapter 23

KANG'S PATIENCE WAS BEING tested. He'd wasted days of checking out names and he'd found nothing...just spoiled descendants of traitors who seemed to place money over honor. Luxury homes and offices, big cars and fancy clothes, and forgetting where they came from seemed to be very prevalent. Capitalists all. Disgusted, Kang decided to get a drink and headed for a small bar close to his hotel.

He took a seat in the corner so he could watch the goings on and ordered a Liberty Ale. At least San Francisco had some good beer. After a couple of drinks, he was bored and getting ready to leave when a reporter came on the TV with a smile and announced that a few days ago a local homeless man by the name of Andrew Bigham had video of a "ghost" in Golden Gate Park. She then played a cellphone recording of a man and a woman walking through the park from a distance where the faces weren't clearly visible. The poor-quality video did show, however, at one point that the woman's figure began to fade in and out, then faded away completely. The man began to rush, then ran to a cab stand. There, the recording ended.

"There you have it, ladies and gentlemen. Golden Gate Park has it's its own lady ghost. Shall we name her? KRON4 has decided to have a contest to name our lovely GGP lady. Send your ideas to..."

Adrenalin pumped through his blood erasing boredom and bringing on a natural high. *This has to be something.* He smiled. *Andrew Bigham. Golden Gate Park.* He threw a tip on the table, another rude capitalistic custom, but he didn't want to stand out or be remembered and stiffing the wait staff would make him memorable.

He took a cab toward Golden Gate Park asking to be dropped off by the homeless encampment. "Listen, buddy, I have no idea where that is and I don't want to know," the cabbie said."

"Then get me into the park as far as you can."

"I'll take you in the Haight Street entrance. I can't park. You'll have to ask around if you want to know where the homeless camp is."

Kang nodded. He had no intention of asking anyone anything. He erred in even mentioning that to the taxi driver. *Foolish. I must be tired.* He looked at his watch. It wasn't even 10 PM.

After being dropped off, Kang grabbed a map of the park and set off looking for the encampment. By process of elimination, he marked out areas he thought were most likely areas for the homeless to infest. The first area was a bust, but he lucked out on the second.

He came across two drunks snoring, oblivious. He kicked them, but they didn't rouse. *Useless.* He walked to the next group huddled by a small fire talking and caught the last part of their conversation.

"...can you believe his shit?" one dirty middle-aged man said. He scratched his lice-infested head, sneezed and wiped his nose with his sleeve. "If half of what he says is true, why don't he got video of that, too? Huh? He musta doctored up that phone. I'm tellin' ya."

"Do ya really think he's got the know how?" a smaller version replied. "He ain't no rocket scientist, ya know."

"He's been braggin' about getting good money, too. Says another TV station called and wants to do an interview. Can you believe it? There'll be no livin' with him." The third man looked cleaner than the others, but had a mean look in his eye. "I think he should share a little of his luck with his friends, don't you?"

"Where did he camp tonight?" the first man asked.

"The usual spot. His dogs will be a problem, though," the small man said.

"I can handle them," the leader said pulling out a knife. "Never did like those damn mutts anyways."

"Shall we make a visit?" the first man said, laughing as he stood up.

Kang hung back and followed as the three led him to where Andrew Bigham slept. *The small man was right.* The dogs went on alert and growled the moment the three showed up as if they knew the men's intentions.

The knife wielder lunged at one dog and sliced him across the shoulder. With a yelp, the dog retreated, but the second dog bit down on the man's arm and held on. The man's scream finally roused Andrew from his drugged slumber, but it was too late to defend himself. The first man jumped on top of him as the smaller man began to rifle through Andrew's pack looking for any cash or drugs.

Kang decided it was time to act. He stepped in, pulled the man off Andrew and threw him across the clearing. The small man looked up in astonishment.

"Do you want to follow your friend?" Kang asked in English.

"Uh, uh...no, sir," the man stammered looking up at the menacing figure.

"Then leave now."

Which the man did.

Meanwhile, the dog still had a hold on the knife wielder's arm. Kang walked over and commanded. "Good dog, down."

Amazingly, the dog let go and sat. The man stumbled back, panting, and looked up at Kang. "Who the hell are you?" he demanded grabbing hold of his bleeding arm.

"I'm a good Samaritan."

"You shouldn't butt into other folks' business." The man looked like he wanted to act so Kang decided a preemptive warning was indicated.

"If you try to do what you are thinking of doing, I will use that knife of yours to carve out my initials...in several languages."

A frightened look replaced the belligerent one and the man began to back away. After he left, Kang turned back to Andrew and found the man nursing his injured dog. He walked over followed by the second dog who took up vigil by his fallen comrade.

"Is the animal alright?" Kang asked.

"He's hurt pretty bad, but I'm good with animals, so I think he'll be okay. Thanks, mister." Andrew looked up at the Chinese man dressed all in black. To tell the truth, the man had a scary looking intensity about him. *I wouldn't want to get on that man's bad side.* But that man had saved him and his dog.

"I don't know how I can thank you. You can see I don't have much. But, if you hadn't come along, I'd have had a lot less. Please, can you give me a hand a minute? I keep some first aid supplies in my pack."

Kang knelt down and held pressure on the wound where Andrew indicated while Andrew rummaged through his pack. The dog whined in pain and Kang found himself rubbing the dog's head with his other hand and speaking to the animal to reassure it. Andrew returned and put some antibiotic ointment on the cut and wrapped gauze around the worst area. When Kang stopped applying pressure, he was surprised that the dog licked his hand. Clearing his throat, he stood up.

"Good dog," Kang repeated.

"I raised both these guys from pups. They were dumped off as strays. I may not have much, but I got them."

Kang watched the trio and, for once, changed his mind on how he was going to interrogate his subject. "Why did those men come after you?"

"I guess because I got a little money recently and they thought I had it on me."

"You don't?"

"Hell, no. That's like asking to be robbed. I hid it real good. Believe it or not, I use to have a pretty good life until I got into the drugs. I ruined it all." Andrew threw his arms around to encompass the park. "Now this is my world." He laughed.

"How did you get the money?"

"Do you watch the news?"

"Sometimes."

"You will probably see me on the news here again real soon. I gave a video to the TV station. I saw something in the park the other night. Supernatural. You'd never believe me if I told you the whole story, but I got part of it on my cell, so they have to listen to part of it. I'll get my fifteen minutes of fame out of it and enough money to keep me going for a bit."

Kang sat down on the grass. "Tell me the whole story. I'll believe you."

Chapter 24

Han snored in bed as Lei fretted on how to approach Jonny. She'd seen the late-night news report and recognized the cap she'd made for him. Luckily, Bolin was on duty upstairs. She wasn't sure where Min was, but she thought he might actually be on a date. The way he had avoided answering her when she asked where he was going was a dead giveaway. She heard the back door slam as Jonny came in and she went to meet him. "Where have you been?"

"I went for a walk." Jonny said.

"You were gone for a long time."

"I had a lot to think about." Jonny tried to walk past her, but Lei took his arm.

"I saw a strange video on the news," Lei said.

"Oh?"

"Yes," Lei said. "Seems like they're saying that Golden Gate Park has a ghost. Isn't that funny? They want to have a contest to name it. Want to help me come up with a name?"

Jonny paled. "Um, that's...dumb. Who believes in ghosts these days?"

"Well, seems like a lot of folks do. I bet we can come up with something good with your imagination." Lei pulled him into the living room and pushed him down into a chair. She sat across from him. "It's funny, though," she mused. "I thought I recognized the man's cap. It looked a lot like the one I made for you last Christmas. You know, the red one." Lei stared at Jonny and waited for his reply.

Jonny flushed a bright red and looked away.

"Oh, Jonny, what have you done?" Lei wailed softly.

"Please," Jonny begged, "Don't tell Dad. He won't let me see her again if you tell him."

"What did she do to you?" Lei said as tears threatened. "Don't you know how dangerous she can be?"

"I wish everyone would stop saying that!" Jonny said with his hands clenched. "She didn't DO anything to me...other than save my life and pay for it by being locked up for centuries." Jonny took a deep breath. "No one even gave her a chance."

"But, Jonny, you don't understand the power Huli Jing have over men. You never cared to learn. How could you possibly know if you're being manipulated?"

"I know because Jianyu knows," Jonny almost yelled.

"W-What did you say?" Lei gasped with her hand on her chest.

***

Bella sat drinking alone at the bar, her sour mood making her snap at everyone. When she saw Jackie Ling rushing by, she grabbed his arm. "I've got some news I think Frankie might be interested in," Bella said with a slight slur.

"Yeah, what's that?"

"Remember that shaman you told me about? That Mada
m...what's-her-name...Zin?"

"Yeah?"

"I saw her all cozy like having dinner with the old man that
works for the Chen family."

Jackie Ling straightened up. "You sure about that?"

"I followed them to the restaurant and watched them have
dinner. I'm sure. They seemed like old friends, holding hands and
everything. How can Frankie be sure they didn't play him for a
fool?" Bella smiled. "Wouldn't Frankie at least want to know?"

Jackie looked at Bella long and hard. "What did Jonny do to
you?"

Bella stared back, silent.

"You sure must hate the man." With that, he got up and
left.

***

Frankie sat in his office, angry, pondering what his next step
should be. His men had started murmuring behind his back and
he caught a few sideways glances that he didn't like. Just when he
thought he couldn't take another slam, Jackie Ling, his second in
command, entered.

"What is it?" Frankie growled.

"Gregor Prinkin raided one of our warehouse games. Two
dead."

"How much did they take?"

"Estimate is close to $150 G."

Frankie knew then that his rep was broken. He'd have to hit hard and fast to restore it or they'd pick his bones bare—and he'd have to do this personal.

"Get the boys." He looked up when Jackie didn't move. "What?" he growled.

"There's something else you gotta know."

Chapter 25

Physician Ho stood behind Bolin at the doorway to the living room. He'd come downstairs to check on his friend in time to hear Jonny's confession. He could feel the surprised tension in Bolin, but when the man moved to go forward, Physician Ho placed a hand on his shoulder to stop him. Pulling him back, he placed his fingers to his lips. "Let them speak."

"Does this mean Jonny knows about all of you?" Bolin asked.

"Apparently. I am not surprised. Everyone has been acting a bit strangely since we've returned. I sensed something, but I did not realize that Wei Zan had been allowed out. This is most interesting."

"You aren't frightened of her?" Bolin said.

"No, I do not believe I am. I never agreed with the decision in the beginning, but I was not asked. The Emperor was furious that a precious urn was used thus, and the Guardians felt betrayed. We spirits discussed it, of course. The Admiral agreed with the decision, as did the brothers. Lady Ji and I, however, believed Jianyu. We, perhaps, are more tenderhearted and believed in love."

"So, Jonny knows that he is the reincarnation of... man, this is so crazy," Bolin paused to take a breath, "of Chang Jianyu?"

"It seems so. It has taken many centuries for him to return. Perhaps he's returned to free the woman he loves. Perhaps, he just wishes to be with her. I can understand this desire of his soul. Don't we all wish for a great love such as this? His was taken away too soon. This, too, I understand."

"What should we do now?" Bolin asked.

"You should go to bed and rest. I will check on your father. We will let your mother and brother talk. Things must unravel in their own good time."

"Can I tell Min?"

"Could I stop you?" Physician Ho smiled.

Bolin laughed. "Probably not."

"So be it."

"What are you going to tell the others?"

Physician Ho looked thoughtful for a moment, then said, "I think it's time for a long talk."

***

Frankie stood over the bodies of Gregor Prinkin and four of his lieutenants. They hadn't expected his rapid response or the attack on their headquarters. They'd beefed up security on their own illegal gaming dens, but that had worked in Frankie's favor.

Frankie nursed a knife wound on his arm and wrapped one of his silk handkerchiefs around it. Shallow though it was, it hurt like hell. It had been a while since he'd been on a strike like this, but his men now looked at him with respect again. Putting a bullet in an enemy worked wonders in this business.

Jackie Ling walked up with a black bag and dropped it at Frankie's feet with a smile.

"How much?" Frankie asked.

"Over $400 G. Got some jewels, too. Don't know their worth. Some art, also. You know how Gregor liked to put on airs. I'll have the guys take the stuff to the warehouse and have it priced."

"Sure. Now about the other matter."

"I sent a couple guys to pick up the merchandise and bring it to the location you said."

"Good." Feeling rejuvenated, Frankie knew this time there would be no problems with any damn spirits. If there were, heads would roll.

***

Physician Ho examined Han's pulses while the exhausted man slept. He placed his hand over Han's chest to check the man's energy levels, one of the benefits of being a spirit, and felt disheartened. Within a few weeks, his friend would no longer be able to hide the depths of his disease from any observer.

Sitting on the bedside, the old physician said a prayer for his friend's soul. A deep sadness filled his heart. He'd said so many goodbyes—too many—and with no end in sight. Strong young men had died violent deaths for them, and he'd watched old men die in his service. Foolish really. He sighed.

His thoughts were interrupted when Lei entered the room. She stopped, startled. "I didn't know you were here," she said.

"I told Bolin I was coming down to check on Han. I'll be going upstairs now."

"How is he?"

"He's fine for now." Physician Ho saw no reason to worry Lei further. She had other things on her mind tonight. "Did you wish to speak of anything?"

"Um..." Lei hesitated. She seemed hesitant to speak.

"Do not worry about your youngest. He has greater strength than he knows."

"Do you really think so?" Lei's hopeful expression made the physician's heart ache.

"Yes. I've seen it many times. The rebellious ones are often the ones who will fight the hardest when the time comes to fight. They just have to believe. Never doubt that he loves you." The physician reached out and patted Lei's hand, a rare gesture. "Now, I must return."

"Thank you," Lei said with moist eyes and a smile.

Physician Ho became ethereal, bowed and exited the room making his way back towards the stairs to the third floor. He heard a cell phone ring in Jonny's room and paused. I shouldn't be listening, but who would be calling at this late hour? Only trouble comes after midnight.

"What the hell!" Physician Ho heard Jonny say. "They had nothing to do with any of that!" Then silence as Jonny listened before he burst out, "If you harm one hair on Ting's head... Yes, that's a threat. Where do I bring the urn?"

Physician Ho withdrew as he heard Jonny come towards the door. Jonny peeked out into the hallway and then went up the stairs to the third floor. The physician waited until Jonny reappeared with Wei Zan's urn under his arm and disappeared back into his room. He listened at the door while the enterprising young man and the devious Huli Jing concocted a wild plan of their own. Smiling, he entered Bolin's room and woke the young guardian up.

"Physician Ho, what is it? Is it Father?" Bolin sat up.

"No, your brother needs you."

"Min? Is there trouble with the urns? What's wrong?" Bolin shook his head to clear it.

"No, Jonny is in trouble." The physician then relayed the plan he overheard and added, "I think the Guardians need to help."

"I'll get Min."

"I'll get the Admiral. He'd never forgive me if I let him miss all the action." The physician smiled.

"Do you have enough power to call him out?" Bolin asked.

"Yes, if I have already been called out, but I will need to go back in right after. This has been a busy night."

So, while the brothers prepared for battle, Physician Ho went up to their room and took out the Admiral's urn. Becoming corporeal once again, he spoke the command to "come out" that only he could speak as the primary and oldest spirit, "Chulai."

When the Admiral appeared, he knew there were big happenings because the physician had only twice before used his power to command a spirit from out of their urn, both events had been devastating to either the family or their country.

"What is it?" the Admiral asked, his warrior's face solemn. Gone was his elder form, in its place was the young Captain who fought beside his Emperor.

As the physician briefed the Admiral, Bolin and Min entered the room. Because Physician Ho had been unable to hear the location where Jonny was to take the urn, the Admiral would only be able to follow the energy of the urn once it was opened. Min got on the computer and searched public records for listings of all of Frankie's properties to find possible locations. One warehouse stuck out as a likely possibility being listed as vacant at present. The three decided on their course of action and taking the risk, headed in that general direction.

***

Jonny took a deep breath as he walked up to 'Godzilla and Kong' standing guard outside the warehouse door. "Frankie told me to come, so I came."

With a smirk, Kong opened the door and Jonny entered. Kong followed leaving Godzilla to stand guard. They walked down a corridor and through another door into a huge room with a tall steel beam ceiling. A few large crates were pushed up against the walls, and old rusted barrels were interspersed haphazardly throughout. The cold concrete floor had multiple stains, some Jonny could identify, others he didn't want to give too much thought to.

Ting and Madam Zin sat bound in chairs up against crates on the back wall. Jonny walked towards them until Frankie came out of the shadows and said, "You can stop there."

Jonny saw that Madam Zin, despite being a little mussed up, looked none the worse, but Ting had a black-eye, blood encrusted forehead, and swollen left cheekbone. *He saw red.* "Must make your guys feel really tough to beat up an old man."

"The guy was tougher that he looks." Kong laughed, then grunted when Jonny elbowed him in the gut with enough power to send him to the floor. "Why you little..." he gasped.

"Cut the crap," Frankie ordered. "I want my urn. Madam Zin has assured me that she will dispel the evil spirit this time. No more tricks or you'll all be dead. Understand?"

Jonny looked around at the men bordering the room. *Damn. He hadn't planned on this many.* He took a deep breath and blew it out. He was counting on Wei Zan an awful lot and she'd been out of commission for a long time. Not to mention, she might still be at less than full strength after almost dissipating.

"You'll have to untie me," Madam Zin spoke up. "I can't work like this."

Frankie motioned to one of his men who cut her ropes, then took the knife and held it to Ting's throat. "Get my message?" Frankie asked looking at her.

"Yes." Madam Zin rubbed her wrists to return the circulation. "I know my craft." She looked at Jonny and nodded. She opened her long black case and pulled out a string of beads, a mask, a whip, and an embellished sword. "You can release the spirit whenever you're ready."

"Wait a minute," Frankie interrupted pointing at the items. "What the hell are those for?"

"The beads help me diagnose the type of spirit I'm dealing with, the spiritual whip helps me fight back the evil spirit, and the heavenly sword pierces the spirit's heart sending it back to hell."

"Now I know you were playing with me! You didn't have any of those the last time." Frankie spit out in anger.

"That's because I only asked to see the spirit so I could evaluate what I was dealing with—if you remember," Madam Zin said. "I never tried to fool you. I'm a professional." Madam Zin turned her back to Frankie and gave Jonny a look he couldn't quite comprehend.

Jonny looked at the items and grew nervous. *Was Madam Zin for real? Could she really exorcise Wei Zan?* Somehow, he didn't believe she wanted to do that especially since she thought he was bringing the Admiral and she adored him. Jonny had to believe Madam Zin was up to something.

Madam Zin put on the mask and started a soft chant. "I am ready."

"Why the mask?" Frankie demanded.

"I don't want the demon to recognize me."

"What about us?" Frankie all but yelled.

"You are no threat. You have no power."

"Oh, alright then, let's get on with it. Jonny, open the urn." Frankie took a step back before he realized it then stepped forward again. "Everyone, be ready."

"What day is today?" Jonny asked.

With a rushing sound, the lid popped off the urn. Black smoke poured out, and from within, a deep voice intoned "it's a good day to die". A large red-scaled serpent with glowing red eyes emerged and flew up coiling through the air. The men stood frozen, mouths gaping until the hissing maw opened to display large dripping fangs. The men broke, screaming and scrambling to get away. They fell over each other, shot uselessly at the flying demon and cried for their mothers.

Frankie stood frozen. In wet pants.

Then, a terrible thing happened. The power drain on Wei Zan was too much. Her energy flickered and she collapsed onto the floor. The serpent shape disappeared, and in its place, lay an exhausted nine-tailed white fox. She looked up at Jonny and hung her head with shame.

Everyone else in the room came to a standstill. Jonny ran forward to try and grab Wei Zan, but Frankie's voice rang out, "Take one more step and you're dead."

Jonny froze as Frankie walked over and stood over the fox. "What the hell is this?" he asked.

"I don't know," Jonny said.

Frankie turned and struck Jonny sending him to the floor. "Give me one good reason why I shouldn't kill you right now."

"I really don't know what's going on, Frankie. I brought the urn just like you said. I'm no demon expert. How could I possibly know what goes on inside a demon's head. That's her business, not mine." Jonny hated himself for passing the buck, but for right now he had to stay alive to protect Wei Zan.

Frankie started to say something to Madam Zin when another voice was heard.

"Didn't I say if you interfered with the Guardians that I would eat your liver?" A large glowing warrior walked into view wearing ancient Chinese armor carrying a long sword and growing in size as he came. The gleam in the Admiral's eye set Frankie off. "Fire," he screamed at his men.

Jonny motioned to Madam Zin to hit the floor, then jumped up and ran to Ting to take him to the floor, the knife-wielding guard having long abandoned his duty. Jonny looked up from the floor to see the Admiral laughing, but then was shocked to see his brothers across the room taking out Frankie's men quietly and efficiently while the Admiral held everyone's attention. Not wanting to be left out, he got up and joined in.

He ran towards Min, who was closest and fighting two men, Kong being one of them, and threw himself on Kong's back. With his arm locked around the giant's neck, he held on and squeezed until the man toppled. Trapped beneath the giant's body, he pushed until Min kicked the unconscious man aside and offered him a hand. Then they turned to meet the next assailant. The battle didn't last much longer and left Frankie standing all alone in the middle of the room facing the gloating Admiral.

Bolin joined them as they walked up behind the Admiral and waited to see what the Admiral would do. The feral gleam in the Admiral's eye warned Jonny that the Admiral was done having fun and his mood had turned deadly.

"I only give one warning," the Admiral said in a reasonable voice. "And I always keep my promises." With that, he swung his mighty arm in a large arc only to have his arm grabbed a strong hand.

"Who dares?" he roared turning red-faced with anger. He spun around.

Wei Zan had taken human form now and stood quietly waiting for the Admiral as he struggled to regain his temper. He was struck for a moment by her beauty. His arm dropped to his side.

"What are you doing?" he demanded.

"Admiral Zheng He," Wei Zan said bowing, "this man does not deserve the honor of being slain by your sword. We should let the people of this time deal with him. Jonny has told me that they put people in cages for their entire lives for the crimes they commit. Surely there could be no worse punishment than to never walk freely again."

The Admiral looked at Wei Zan and then the brothers. They waited for his reaction. He sighed. He hadn't blooded his sword for centuries. "I suppose we are to call the police? And exactly what are you going to say? These men have seen too much."

"I can take care of that if you will permit me." Wei Zan bowed again.

With a wave of his hand, the Admiral granted his permission wondering how the Chen brothers would react to watching a Huli Jing at work.

Wei Zan looked at the brothers and said, "I will need to take their energy. These men will not be harmed so please do not interfere." With that she started to walk around the room and stopped by each of the fallen men. She stooped over each and as they all exhaled, she breathed in. Bolin and Min couldn't help but be shocked as they watched the mist-like yang energy transfer. Min shuddered. Bolin was fascinated. Jonny finally began to understand his family's concerns.

When she was done, she returned to the group. "None of those men will be able to remember what happened here. Their memory will be foggy and dreamlike. As for Frankie, I believe we should give him a compulsion."

"A compulsion?" Jonny asked.

"Didn't you say that this man was evil?"

Madam Zin spoke up. "I overheard the men talking about a hit on another gambling house tonight. Will that help?"

Wei Zan looked at Jonny and he explained. "That means they attacked another group of men."

"That will do." Wei Zan walked to a frozen Frankie who stood trembling at her approach.

"What are y-you?" he stammered.

"You poor thing," Wei Zan purred stroking Frankie's cheek. "Don't be afraid. I'd never hurt you."

"You w-wouldn't?" Frankie took a couple of deep breaths. Her beautiful face floated before his eyes. Her soft voice and smooth hands relaxed his jangled nerves. She had saved him from that demon. She was an angel. She kept stroking his cheek, murmuring his name and telling him everything would be fine. He believed her. She said if he would just tell the nice men what had happened, she would stay with him forever and keep him safe. He should call the nice men at 911. She placed her hand on his chest and kissed his cheek. Love burst out of his frozen little heart. He'd die without her!

"Will you do that for me?" Wei Zan asked tilting her lovely face with a soft smile.

"Yes!"

Chapter 26

WEI ZAN WALKED OVER to Ting and placed her hand on his chest. "Are you in pain?"

"I think my ribs may be broken," Ting said as he took short shallow breaths.

"I will help you up," Wei Zan said. She poured some of her new energy into the old man as he struggled to rise. "You will be fine now. I think you are just sore. Rest." She didn't complete the healing of all his bruising because once again her energy was waning. She looked over at Jonny. "I must return to the urn, now."

Jonny ran over to grab the urn and brought it back to her. "Thank you. You saved us all." He went to hug her, but she faded to ethereal, smiled, then returned to the urn at his command. The lid snapped shut.

The Admiral walked over followed by his brothers and stood beside him.

"Go ahead and say it," Jonny said expecting a lecture.

The Admiral nodded. "Pretty good plan for a novice. Next time though, don't leave us out of all the fun." With that, he returned to his urn. Bolin slipped the urn into his backpack and reached over for Wei Zan's. Jonny shook his head, cradling her urn with his arm.

"We better get out of here," Bolin said deciding not to make an issue of Jonny's possessiveness. He pointed to Frankie who was on his cellphone calling 911.

Jonny nodded and walked over to grab his pack slipping the urn inside.

Madam Zin spoke up, "I'll call a cab and take Ting to my place. My neighbor's a doctor and he owes me one." She grabbed her pack and looked over at Min. "You there, make yourself useful and put my things inside."

"I feel fine now, really. As soon as I got up, the pain seemed to go away. I know I look awful, but I don't need a doctor," Ting said.

"Who asked you," Madam Zin said. She took his arm and pulled him along. "You boys go home. I got him."

The brothers choked back a laugh and followed the couple out of the warehouse. As they exited the alley, they could hear sirens in the distance. Jonny breathed a sigh of relief. Will I really be free of Frankie forever? Brother, no more gambling for me. Time to get my act together.

When they walked out to the street, they said goodbye to the couple, then walked to where his brothers had parked the Enclave. Jonny started to laugh. "You brought Dad's pride and joy?"

Bolin shrugged. "If we had to bring back your body, it wouldn't fit in the Cobalt."

After a shocked moment, the tension broke and the three burst out laughing. They laughed until tears ran down their cheeks.

"Did you see Jonny riding Kong's back?" Min choked out. "Talk about having a monkey on your back." And off they went again.

"Well, if you knew how to fight, I wouldn't have had to save you," Jonny gasped.

Bolin was the first to settle. The three sobered and took some calming breaths realizing how lucky they were to be alive. Min spoke first.

"Wei Zan is really something, but she's very scary, too." He looked at Jonny.

"I know."

"Who thought of the serpent," Bolin asked.

"She did," Jonny said. "I told her how scared Frankie was of the Admiral and how superstitious he was. She said a serpent would scare all of them and it was her best illusion. Unfortunately, she couldn't hold it as long as she hoped. You guys really saved us."

"Yeah. Talk about perfect timing." Min puffed out his chest. "My computer skills are supreme."

Bolin punched him in the arm. "Don't take all the credit. We all deduced which warehouse was the most likely site and we lucked out." Bolin turned to Jonny. "The Admiral couldn't trace Wei Zan's energy until she exited the urn. Once he felt it, we were able to get here in time.

"Well, enough talk. We better get home before Mom and Dad realize we're gone."

Jonny climbed in the back seat letting his brothers in the front, a silent reminder of family position.

The ride home was quiet as each brother came to a new understanding of what had happened this night and what it would mean.

"We'll have to tell Father," Bolin said as they pulled up to the back of the house.

"Not me," said Min.

"Not me," said Jonny.

"I know. I'm the eldest." He pretended not to hear the snickers.

The three exited the vehicle and climbed the stairs, entering the back as quiet as possible. When Jonny closed the door, the light turned on. They all froze.

"Where have you been?" Han asked. "And what's in the packs?"

Lei rushed into the kitchen. "Han, what are you doing up this late? Do you need anything? I can..."

"I need to know where my boys have been." Han looked from one son to the next, settling on Bolin. "Tell me."

"Maybe I should..." Jonny started to say.

Han held up his hand to stop him and Jonny's voice faded away. "Bolin?"

"Yes, Father." Bolin began to speak in a calm clear voice and told their father about the events of the evening right down to the tiniest detail of what cab had picked up Ting and Madam Zin.

Damn. Jonny was impressed. Also terrified. And the look on his father's face didn't help any.

"Both urns were opened outside of this house?" Han said.

"Yes, Father," Bolin said.

"Didn't I tell you that you were NOT to do that."

Min and Bolin looked at each other. "I guess we kinda forgot," Min said and rushed to add, "It was only this once. And besides, it's been so long, they can't still be looking for us, can they?"

"Looking for us?" Jonny said. "Who's looking for us?"

"China," Han snapped. "And your actions just might have given them an opportunity to locate us."

"How can that be possible?"

"You took them out where there is no shielding. Their radiation can be detected. There are lots of satellites up there. Even the U.S. could detect it if they have a satellite set to look for the specific type of radiation."

"I'm sorry, Father. What do you want us to do?" Bolin asked.

Han sagged, exhausted. "Put the Admiral and the Huli Jing back in the cabinet. Go to bed. I need to think." With that he turned and left the kitchen, Lei following close behind.

After a moment, Min spoke up, "I think that went pretty well."

Both brothers punched him.

Chapter 27

Kang dropped off a bag of dog food to Andrew, but there were still no further sightings. A week passed and the ghost story faded with the news of the confession of Frankie Liu, a gambling kingpin of San Francisco. The police were flabbergasted by the man's sudden overpowering need to come clean on all his crimes. They found the bodies of a rival gambler and his henchmen, so the stack of charges was lengthy.

Bored, Kang had just ordered another drink when his cellphone rang. It was the consul's office calling. He was to report there, immediately. He downed his drink and headed out.

When he arrived, they handed him a sealed envelope. Inside was a coded message:

Second transmission received from the noted location. *Satellite gone silent, declared lost. Orbit expected to decay. This is your last chance. Success is mandatory. Bring home items at all costs.*

Kang noted the longitude and latitude on the message and went to the consul's office. Although the consul was out of the office, his assistant assured Kang he would get the location right away and indeed produced the address within ten minutes. When Kang looked up the records of the building, he felt a moment of recognition, then it came to him, the news report. *Frankie Liu! Frankie Liu was a Guardian!*

Kang shook his head. Capitalism had corrupted even the honorable Guardians and made them gamblers and murderers. He had discounted the Liu family for just that reason. How stupid of him! Frankie was in police custody. He sat back. *Looks like I'll be making a visit to police headquarters.*

Contacting the assistant, Kang scheduled a meeting with the consul the next morning, then headed home for a good night's sleep. Tomorrow would be a big day.

***

"So... what exactly are your intentions?"

"I don't understand your question. What do you mean by that?"

"I mean...I won't let you hurt that boy."

"You pompous, overbearing...who do you think you are?"

The Admiral and Wei Zan went almost nose to nose until Chengli and Jin stepped between them. Lady Ji placed a hand on Wei Zan's shoulder and tried to get her to sit back down, while Physician Ho did the same to The Admiral.

"Please," Physician Ho said, "there is no need for this. We all have Jonny's best interest at heart." He turned to the Huli Jing. "Wei Zan, we know how much you care for him. The Admiral is just being stubborn, as he often is. He knows the truth. Pay him no mind." He followed that up with a stern glance at the Admiral that only he could give when it seemed The Admiral would protest his statement.

Looking away, the slighted warrior crossed his arms in a sulk so Lady Ji walked over and kissed his cheek, laughing, then returned to Wei Zan. "I'm so glad to finally meet you. I'm tired of being the only female around here."

"Thank you." Wei Zan bowed her head. She saw skepticism on the faces of the two brothers, but, following the physician's lead, they hadn't voiced any opposition to her being out of her urn.

Laughing again, Lady Ji said, "I'm like a house cat in a cave of bears."

"Now you have a fox as an ally." Wei Zan giggled.

The Admiral gave a small grin before he frowned again.

Physician Ho took his seat and motioned for the others to do the same. "We have some things to discuss and I feel there are decisions to be made," he began. "I see some changes happening that concern me as I am sure others of you see also. Our question is, what do we do about it?"

"Shouldn't we discuss this in the presence of the Guardians," Chengli said.

"No," The Admiral and Physician Ho said.

***

Kang showed up at Central Police Station in a three-piece suit and walked up to the front desk.

"I've been asked by counsel to see Frankie Liu," Kang said.

"You a shrink or a lawyer?" the desk sergeant asked.

"A lawyer," Kang said flashing his business card.

Not bothering to look, the desk sergeant motioned him back through and instructed an officer to take him to an open interrogation room. Kang took a seat and waited. Ten minutes later, a dazed, middle-aged man walked in and sat down.

"Mr. Frankie Liu?" Kang said.

"Yes," Frankie said looking at Kang. "Do I know you?"

"No. I'm here to ask you a few questions."

"I don't know what more you could want to know. I've told them everything I know, but they really don't believe." Frankie looked around the room. "I keep wondering how I got here. I can't quite figure it out." He rubbed his chin as his brow furrowed, then sighed. "But she'll come back, right?"

"Who is that?" Kang asked getting a strange vibe. *This didn't make sense.* This man didn't give the impression of being the confident warrior Kang considered the Guardians to be.

"I don't really know." Frankie placed his hands before him on the table. "Could you find her for me?" He leaned forward.

"Maybe," Kang said. "Tell me something about her. What does she look like?"

"She's the most beautiful woman I've ever seen." Frankie smiled and his face took on a glow.

Disgusted, Kang sighed. *He wasn't here for some love-struck, middle-aged man. He needed something more.* "Why is she so important?" he pressed.

"She saved me from the demon."

Now we're getting somewhere.

"What demon is that?"

"The Admiral. He wanted to eat my liver!" Frankie trembled.

Wait a minute. This isn't right. If he was a Guardian, why would he be threatened? "Mr. Liu, if you told me where the urns were, I could be of more assistance."

Frankie looked confused. "Urn? I don't seem to remember anything about any urn."

"But, what about the demon?" Kang repeated.

"Yes, yes! He wanted to eat my liver!" Frankie's mantra went on over and over whenever Kang asked about the Admiral. And the same words repeated whenever Frankie spoke of the woman. He was a broken record and Kang was getting nowhere.

Kang came to realize that this man was never a Guardian, but instead was a victim of them. "I wonder what you did to deserve this?" Kang mused out loud not expecting a response.

"I asked a question."

Kang sat up. He thought for a moment. What do I say next, to not send him back into his crazy loop. "Who told you to ask a question?"

"Jonny."

"Jonny who?"

"Jonny Chen."

***

Kang went back through his list and found the Chen family. Once again, he had made an error. He had discounted the Chen family based on his assumption of the young man's handling of a narcissistic woman. Foolish really, since the other brothers hadn't been in residence at the time.

Without bothering to change, he decided to visit the shop and see what kind of a feel he got now that he knew they were the Guardians.

When he walked into the shop, he found it busier than on his first excursion. The sign outside announced "inventory reduction sale" and evidently, these capitalists liked their sales. He walked around the bustling shop trying to identify who was who.

Jonny caught his attention immediately, but he looked different. He smiled a lot as he entertained the children while the parents shopped, but he'd changed somehow. A slightly older less handsome version of Jonny stood behind the cash register and rang up sales chatting with people and laughing. That one had the face of someone who liked to laugh—a useless talent really. The one that caught Kang's particular notice was the oldest looking brother. He stood the tallest, had a direct watchful gaze, and his confident stance bespoke of training. This man would be an honorable adversary. At present, he was speaking to a customer about a valuable piece and by the time he was done, he'd made another sale.

Kang turned away to leave, then he heard a voice say, "May I help you?"

Turning back, he saw an old man, the assistant he remembered from his first visit.

"I'm just browsing," Kang said.

"Do you have any particular interests?" Ting-a-Ling asked.

Kang couldn't help himself. "I have an interest in ancient funerary receptacles."

"Let me get Mister Bolin over here. He's, our expert." With that Ting signaled the oldest brother who approached with a slight smile. Ting-a-Ling told him Kang's interest.

"Any particular materials?" Bolin asked.

"I'm open. Everything from clay, to bronze, or even, say, gold." Kang smiled. "Do you carry such items?"

"I do have a 17th century bronze urn from the Han Dynasty circa 1600-1650 listing for $9,000. The only other I have available at this time is an antique cloisonne covered urn circa 1900. It is a set of two, and the list price is $4,000. Would you care to see either of those?" Bolin smiled.

Kang returned the smile, but shook his head. "I'm afraid both are a bit out of my price range at this time. You and your family seem to do very good business here." Kang waved his hand around the store.

"Thank you." Bolin gave a slight bow.

"How long have you been at this location?"

"A long time."

"I see." Kang nodded. "Has your family always lived in San Francisco?"

"Why do you ask?"

"Oh, just curious. San Francisco is such a unique city. I often wonder what brought people here."

"Well, what brought you here?" Bolin asked.

"Business."

"And what business is that?"

"Well, I guess you could say I find things."

"Just things or people."

"Sometimes both."

"That must be challenging work."

"It can be."

Bolin nodded, then turned when the brother at the cash register called out his name. "Sorry, I'm being summoned. It's been—interesting—talking with you." With that, Bolin walked away.

Kang watched as the two brothers talked. Bolin never looked back, but he caught the younger brother looking in his direction once. Kang smiled. These were the Guardians, no doubt at all. And he had just thrown down the gauntlet.

Chapter 28

Jonny and Wei Zan walked through Golden Gate Park until they got to an area where she wanted to lay on the grass. "I don't feel a strong energy anywhere around here, but this spot is better than most. Is all of your land like this?"

"I don't know," Jonny said. "Since I can't feel what you feel, how could I know?"

"I think there's too much concrete all around. The earth can't breathe," Wei Zan sulked.

Jonny lay down beside her and took her hand. "I know."

"Did they give me a name yet?" Wei Zan asked with a giggle.

"Lady GiGi for Golden Gate." Jonny laughed.

"Did you tell everyone that you were taking me out tonight?"

"No."

"Are you going to get into trouble?"

"I don't care. You've been locked up long enough. Besides, I think you've proved you can be trusted. Don't you?" Jonny rolled on his side and looked down at her. "Why? You're not planning on doing anything crazy, are you?"

Wei Zan gazed up into his eyes and smiled. He was so lovely, just like her Jianyu, how could she not love him? She reached up and pulled him down for a kiss, careful not to use her power. This was just him and her.

When Jonny finally pulled back, he started to speak, "Wei Zan..."

"Shh," Wei Zan stopped him with another kiss. She didn't want to think about anything but being with him. The air seemed to hum about them as the breeze rustled leaves and carried the scent of the forest to her. It may not have been her forest, but it was welcoming her all the same. For a moment, her memories overcame her. Jianyu filled her thoughts as her heart strained towards him.

A memory flashed once again. Wei Zan went hunting for dinner while I gathered wood for the fire. Sweaty and dirty, I go to the pool and strip down to wash. The water is cool and clear, relaxing my tired muscles and soothing my spirit. I lay back to float. A laugh sounds from the rock above me and I'm submerged by a splash as my Wei Zan lands in the water. Sputtering, I come up to see her, still smiling. Her playfulness disarms me and war is declared. We splash and dodge until she yells "surrender". With that, she leaps forward to wrap her arms and legs about me. Wet skin slides across wet skin as our lips meet. Passion burns through me. I must have her. We find ourselves on the grass by the pool, arms and legs entwined. The forest sings about us.

My little fox.

"My little fox."

Jonny's murmur of passion brought Wei Zan to her senses. She heard Physician Ho's warning. Jianyu is too strong, his love too great. Jonny was never meant to remember. Your Jianyu is gone; this is Jonny's life. Let him live it.

She broke away and smiled up at Jonny. "Don't be foolish and fall for my tricks," she teased. "I am sorry."

Dazed, Jonny shook his head to clear his head. "Oh, yeah, right." He stood up and offered his hand. *What just happened? What did I do?* "I'm sorry, I didn't mean..."

Wei Zan took his hand and when she stood, kissed his cheek. "It's okay. Thank you for understanding."

The walk back took longer than they thought, but they didn't care. The dawn light peaked over the bay as they walked up the back steps at home to find Han waiting.

"Where have you been?" Han said.

"Golden Gate Park," Jonny said standing tall and looking his father in the eye.

Han sighed. "You're being foolish. You know this cannot be."

"Leave it for now, Dad." Jonny pulled on Wei Zan's hand and they walked towards the stairs, but Wei Zan turned back to look at Han and nodded.

***

The next morning, Min walked beside Lady Ji as she strolled down the street. His escort duty today was to see her safely out and about then return her within the two-hour time limit. He still felt somewhat intimidated—not just by her beauty, but by her grace and gentleness. Yet, this was all on the outside. Inside, he sensed, she had a strength he might never understand. He kept thinking about the old saying 'never judge a book by its cover'. Knowing her story, she must have been clever and strong enough to make the famous journey. But he was curious. He knew how all the others died, but not Lady Ji.

Today, Lady Ji wanted to go to the playground. They sat and chatted while watching the children play, often laughing at some of the antics they witnessed. After a while, she looked sad and said she was ready to return.

"You still have some time left," Min said.

"That's fine. I am ready to go back."

Min noticed a tear. "What is it? Is something wrong? Are you okay?" He felt frantic. This was his first time out on solo duty with one of the spirits.

"No, my dear boy. I am just a little sad today. It is something you could never understand—a woman's inner desires. You see, I got to have a son for a few short weeks, and even though he was not my blood, I came to love him very much."

"But didn't you get to see him after you got back to the palace?"

"Very little. The Empress was a jealous woman, and he was the Crown Prince. She took him immediately to her palace rooms to raise him there. And though she had to call on me for help at times, she hated me for it. Besides, I died soon after and didn't have the chance to see him grow."

"But you were so young. How did you die?" Min blurted out. "Oh, sorry, you don't have to say if you don't want to."

"I will tell you if you really want to know, but you won't like it." Lady Ji stopped walking and faced Min. He was a special and tenderhearted young man—very sweet, really. She felt a bond with him that she hadn't felt in a very long time. With what was happening now, she wanted someone in the real world to know her story. She sat and patted the seat next to her. "Please, sit."

Min did and turned to her with an open expectant face. Lady Ji held back a smile. He'll make some woman very happy. She'd only really spoken about her death with Physician Ho because, knowing imperial court politics, he'd suspected the truth. None of the spirits really wanted to speak of their deaths. She took a breath and started her story.

"You know about my journey with little Wu Ming?" Lady Ji paused waiting for Min's nod. "Well, when I arrived at Ting Won Sun's tavern and told him my story, we had a bit of a problem on how to sneak me into the palace. Uncle Won Sun approached a young captain who came from our area and frequented his tavern. When he heard of my plight, he agreed to meet with me. We spoke, and met a few times trying to come up with a plan that would not endanger either of us.

"We found we had much in common and I was drawn to him and he admitted he was drawn to me. It was all very innocent as I belonged to the Emperor, but my heart truly beat for the first time. I now understood the meaning of the words I sang at court. The plan we settled on broke my heart, but I had to think of Wu Ming and his safety.

"I put a warrior's uniform and armor over my peasant clothes. One night as the soldiers returned from night duty, I reported back to the captain as if I was returning late from leave. Wu Ming cooperated and slept in the bottom of my pack. I pretended to be tipsy, so the captain pulled me aside to his office to be reprimanded. There I slipped out of the uniform and he guided me to the kitchen area where I placed a sleeping Wu Ming in the bottom of a basket of cabbages. From there we worked our way up to the Emperor's palace where he was able to sneak me into the eunuch's supply rooms. I hid inside until the captain located the First Eunuch and turned me over to his care."

Min sat enthralled by Lady Ji's tale. "Weren't you frightened?"

"Very much so. If Lady Bao's spies had caught us, we would have died. However, the gods were with us. You know that I presented Wu Ming to the Emperor and Lady Bao was taken away. I often wonder what became of her." Lady Ji paused for a moment.

"You don't know?" Min said.

"No. We never heard a word about her. She just disappeared. Rumor said she paid for her sins with a long painful death. It was even said that it wasn't the Emperor's order for the manner of her death, but his mother, the Dowager's."

"Well, then, what happened next?"

"As you can imagine, the Emperor was very grateful and showered me with many gifts, but my unhappy heart was very apparent. A few weeks later, he called me before him and I feared that he had finally called me to duty. I was wrong. Instead, he very kindly asked me what was wrong. Of course, I said "nothing, your highness". He said I had given him his heart's desire so he wished to give me mine. Then he asked, 'what is your heart's desire'? And here I made my big mistake. I asked to be allowed to retire and return to my family. In my heart, I hoped my Captain would follow me and ask for my hand in marriage. I could then have a family of my own.

"The Emperor acted as if I had slapped him. His face turned red and he glared at me. He had never looked at me in anger before. I became very frightened. He said nothing for a moment, then waved to the First Eunuch and said, 'Take her away'."

"Why was he angry?"

"He felt humiliated that I would want to leave his service. He may not have wanted me, but I guess I was supposed to want him. Men!"

"Then what happened?"

"Two days later, I received a message to visit the Empress Dowager in her rooms the following day. I was told to dress in my finest robes. I was sure she was going to tell me I was to be set free. My heart was racing. I sent a message to my Captain that I would let him know the date of my release. When I arrived at her rooms, I was shocked to see two of her personal guards were present and a formal tea before her. After all, the Empress Dowager had always been kind to me, so why were her guards present?

"When I was seated, the Dowager pulled out my letter to the captain and my heart sank. She accused me of having a lover and betraying his majesty. Though I protested my innocence, even begged them to send for the doctor to verify my virginity, she refused. I knew then that the Empress had decided my fate as well. You see, she was jealous. The Crown Prince preferred me to her. He quieted for me—he cooed for me. Now that the Emperor was angry with me, she wanted to act quickly."

"But why have the Empress Dowager handle it?" Min asked.

"Because the Emperor would never countermand his mother nor take revenge should he change his mind. It was the Empress who intercepted my letter and gave it to the Dowager telling her it was sent to my lover."

"How do you know that?"

"Because my Captain was killed also."

"So, what did you do?"

"I drank the poison."'

Min sat in shock. "After all you had done for them, they made you drink poison?"

"Yes. It was actually considered quite honorable. No public humiliation, no retribution to my family and relatively painless."

Min swore under his breath. "Then how did you get into an urn?"

"Imperial remorse and guilt. You see, after the Emperor calmed down, he called for me and they had to tell him I was dead. When the Dowager told him what she had done, he called for the physician and when he was informed that I was still a virgin, he was furious. Since the captain was also dead, he had no one to question. My letter took on a different meaning and now looked like someone asking for a safe escort home from a trusted Captain."

"So, he put you into an urn," Min stated the obvious. "Imperial politics sure were deadly."

Lady Ji could only nod. "Politics are always deadly."

Chapter 29

THE SALE WAS OVER. Bolin looked around the shop and considered what he wanted to do next. His father had turned everything over to him, but the knot in Bolin's gut made it difficult to make a decision. Jonny came down the stairs in a rush and walked over.

"Did you decide?" Jonny asked.

"No." Bolin said.

"Want my two cents?"

"Not particularly."

Jonny started to bristle, then he saw the expression on his brother's usually stoic face, and he took a breath. "You'll do fine, you know."

Startled, Bolin looked at his little brother. "Don't you start being nice to me, or I'll have to call a shaman."

The two brothers smiled.

"I'd like to open up a little space and not have things so crowded," Bolin said.

"That's what I was going to suggest." Jonny smirked.

"I want to get new shelves and replace those old ones on the back wall."

"Ditto." Jonny smirked again.

"I want to punch you right now."

"You have to catch me first," Jonny laughed, "and I promised Mom I'd run to the drug store for her this morning." With that, Jonny took off out the front door.

Min came down and the two brothers spent the morning moving the remaining inventory to one area where the shelving was solid, and they started dismantling the old shelving they wanted to trash. The store would be closed as the family did a reorganization. New stock would be brought in as it arrived. The upstairs storage area would be reevaluated and the stock brought down to be sold or auctioned off.

While the boys worked, Han and Lei watched from the top of the stairs. Han had had a rough night and he knew Lei hadn't slept either. But standing here and watching his boys working together with a long-range plan for their business, brought a smile to the dying man's face.

"They're good boys, aren't they?" Han said so only Lei could hear.

"Yes, dear, they are."

Han sagged against Lei. She took his arm and they turned back, returning to the living room where Han sat in his recliner with his feet up. "I need some water, please."

Jonny returned with the medication, then went back downstairs to help his brothers. He pretended not to notice his father's condition since that only increased his father's distress.

After taking the narcotic, Han fell asleep while Lei sat beside him and soon followed suit.

***

Meanwhile, upstairs the residents were restless. The television played in the background, but no one really watched it. Chengli and Physician Ho played chess, but neither seemed to be able to concentrate. Jin played Candy Crush on the computer with his chin on his fist, sighing every few minutes. The Admiral just sat staring into space.

Lady Ji and Wei Zan looked at each other, then at the men.

"What should we do?" Lady Ji said.

"Is immortality always this boring?" Wei Zan replied.

"Pretty much." Lady Ji sighed.

"Can't we go out on our own?" Wei Zan asked.

"We're not supposed to," Jin muttered.

"Why not?" Wei Zan said. "I'm a powerful Huli Jing. Nobody better mess with us when I'm around. I'm also old enough to take care of myself, so are all of you. I say if we want to go out, we should go out!"

With a bellow, The Admiral stood up and changed into a strapping young man. "I say we get out of here." He looked around for agreement.

Jin jumped up laughing, and soon the image of his younger self spun around. He pointed at his brother. "C'mon, Chengli, once more. We gotta go out and have a drink, meet a girl, play a few games. Do something crazy."

Chengli sighed as he changed. "That's the reason they never let you out in the first place. But, for today, I'm with you, brother." He accepted Jin's slap on the back and hurrah with a big smile.

The entire group now turned to face the physician who sat quietly watching the group's antics.

In all the centuries, none of them had ever seen the elderly man's younger self.

Lady Ji walked over and took his hand to raise him up. "Just for today, can't you let us see the young Ming Chou Ho?"

The physician seemed dazed. "I don't know if I even remember what it's like to be young and foolish."

"I remember," Jin called out, "I'll coach you along."

As the others laughed their encouragement, the physician began to change, slow at first, with his hair growing darker. Then a few wrinkles disappeared. The slight curve in his back straightened, and the bow in his legs followed. Within minutes, a handsome young man stood before them.

"Why Ming Chou Ho," Wei Zan said flirting shamelessly, "I would have visited your shelter any night."

There was a moment of shocked silence, then the room erupted in laughter as the poor physician blushed bright red.

Lady Ji kissed his cheek. "Don't pay her any attention. You know these Huli Jings. Today you belong to me." She hooked her arm through the physician's and said, "Thank you for granting my wish. Let's go."

Feeling rowdy, the group raided the money jar before tiptoeing past the sleeping couple and down the backstairs to the alley.

"Where do we go first?" Chengli said.

"I vote for the casino," Jin chimed in.

"Of course you would," his brother complained.

"No, really. We could do some gambling, then go over to the Great Star Theater, and see what's playing, or there's supposed to be an open-air market at Golden Gate Park."

To Jin's disappointment, no one else voted for the casino. They all headed over to Golden Gate Park where the troupe wandered around the open-air market and mixed in with all kinds of people. As always, Lady Ji gravitated to the children. Ming Chou Ho stayed by her side, once or twice taking her hand for a brief moment before self-consciously breaking contact.

Jin and Chengli found the games of chance and sleight-of-hand. Jin won more often than he lost. Chengli had to try all the food trucks and fell in love with churros before pulling Jin away from his seventh attempt at the wheel of fortune or should one say, misfortune.

Wei Zan found herself paired with The Admiral and the first half hour felt cautious at best. Then they hit an area of games where he could show some of his prowess. First came archery, where after four rounds of bulls-eyes, the vendor asked him to move along to give others a chance. She *oohed* and *aahed* appropriately so The Admiral decided she wasn't all bad. He did the same at the shooting gallery, the basketball booth and darts.

"Don't you want to try anything?" he asked her.

"Not really," Wei Zan munched on the last of her ice cream cone. "I'm having fun just watching you have fun. You humans are so funny."

"We humans?"

Wei Zan nodded and smiled with a face full of chocolate. "This is the best thing I've ever tasted," she said.

The Admiral laughed. "You do know that none of us are human any more, right?"

"You still act like a human. I, on the other hand, have never been human. And, I've only been one of you spirits for a matter of days. I'm just an apprentice, really."

The group reunited to eat at a large tent. Chengli grabbed Wei Zan and took her up to the ordering counter and read off the list. "You have to try a cheeseburger and French fries. It's an American staple."

"I will try that if you say so. What should I drink? The only thing I recognize is water and tea."

"Try Pepsi. It's my favorite. I think you will be surprised at how it tastes and how it makes you feel."

"Will I get drunk?"

"Oh, no, no. But, well, just try it."

Chengli proved to be right. Wei Zan laughed at the fizzy sensations in her mouth. "This is wonderful. It bites and tingles at the same time." Ketchup was also a hit and poured over everything. The group was impressed that, for a small woman, she kept up with Chengli in the quantity of calories consumed.

"We foxes have good appetites," Wei Zan bragged. "You have to eat when the food is there. Who knows when the next meal may present itself."

The group pretended not to consider the meaning of 'the next meal'. Wei Zan noticed the silence and had to smile. "What shall we do next?" she asked.

"I want to see a show," The Admiral said. "Do we all feel strong enough to go for a few more hours?" He looked around at everybody and got nods so they headed to the Great Star Theater. They didn't really care what was playing, they just wanted to go see something together.

Enthralled, Wei Zan sat wide-eyed throughout the performance. She didn't understand most of the comedy acts, so she just laughed when the others did. The musicians played all different types of instruments she'd never dreamed of and were astounding to watch. The lights flashed prettily but the volume sometimes hurt her sensitive ears. However, the dancers, they were her favorite. She never dreamed that the human body could move like those bodies moved. In one performance, they stood on their toes! Poetry. Power. Grace. By the end of the performance, she had tears in her eyes.

"Oh, it was wonderful." She turned to see Ming Chou Ho watching her and smiling.

"We had nothing like this in our time, did we?" he said.

"I could never go into the towns," Wei Zan said, "so I never saw anything like this. Even the traveling fairs I had to stay away from because they all had dogs with them." She shrugged. "If for nothing else, I'm so glad I got to see these miraculous things I never knew existed."

As the group left the theater, Chengli and Jin both started to fade for a moment. They firmed up again, but the group realized it was time to return home. Grabbing two cabs, they climbed in and headed back to the store. They exited asking the driver to wait at the front.

Turning to his fellow spirits, Physician Ho said, "Today means a great deal to me. I shall treasure this memory."

With a nod of agreement, The Admiral ran around back and up the stairs to find three angry, anxious brothers waiting in the kitchen.

"I know you're mad, but I've used all the money. Please pay the taxis, and we'll tell you everything."

Bolin grabbed his wallet and went down the stairs and out the front door. After paying the drivers, he turned to find himself alone. By the time he got to the kitchen, no one was there either. He rushed up to the room to find his brothers with only The Admiral and Physician Ho, both once again old men.

"Where have you all been?" Bolin demanded.

"We went out for the afternoon," The Admiral said.

"You were out too long. You know what could have happened."

"But it didn't. We were back in time," Physician Ho said. "I was watching, Bolin."

"Why didn't you tell us you wanted to go out." Min sounded hurt. "That's part of our job. We would have taken you out."

The Admiral sighed. "I'm tired." With that he returned to his urn and the lid snapped shut.

Physician Ho looked at the boys. "He commanded fleets of ships and armies of men, and you want him to ask for permission?" Then he, too, returned to his urn.

***

Kang continued his surveillance of the store as the sale kept the brothers busy. The sign said they would close for business to prepare a grand reopening. He wondered if something more was happening. Had he tipped his hand? Were they preparing to run? But he could detect no sign of that. So, the eldest brother hadn't caught on. Perhaps he'd given the young man too much credit.

Kang had selected his men for the assault and chosen the night. With the plan in place, he only watched. And, it paid off. One afternoon, a group of people left the shop by way of the alley; four young men and two young women. He'd never seen them before and he hadn't seen them enter the home. He pondered for a few seconds if he should continue to watch the brothers or follow the group, then decided to follow the group.

He ended up spending the afternoon trailing along behind what appeared to be some carefree young friends enjoying a day at the park. They didn't meet up with anyone suspicious, nor do anything out of the ordinary. When they entered the theater, he thought for a moment "this was it", but nothing happened there either. Then, they returned back to the shop and the Chen boy came out to pay for the taxis.

Were they family? When did they arrive? If they were staying at the house that could only mean they were Guardians as well. There must be a secret entrance that he hadn't discovered. Thinking this, Kang would need to reconsider his plans.

Chapter 30

TING AND WU ZHANG finished dinner, their throats dry from all the talking they'd done. Wu Zhang felt a small spark rekindled just looking at his warm brown eyes. Those eyes were still sharp. She knew he had to realize something was going on at the Chen's. He never used to miss a thing.

"How much longer do you plan to work for Han Chen?" she asked.

"Till I'm too old to move or too senile to care." Ting took the last bite of the cake they'd agreed to share. His sweet tooth hadn't changed.

"I'd still like to talk to Jonny again if you'd remind him."

"About what? Do I need to get jealous again?" Ting smiled. "He's too young for you. You need someone your own age."

"Are you volunteering?"

Silence. "And if I were?" Ting looked into her eyes and she saw he was no longer smiling.

Oh, my. I didn't know my heart could still flutter. It must be indigestion. Wu Zhang stared back. "Um, my life hasn't changed, Ting. I still do all that hoodoo stuff you complained about."

"Maybe I can put up with it now that I'm older. Besides, maybe there is something to what you do after all." Ting paused. "I had the weirdest dream the other night. You and I were tied up and inside a big warehouse. I was all beat up and that guy Frankie was there threatening everybody."

"Why did he beat you up? You owe him money?" Wu Zhang said trying to play along.

"No, but he's been to the store a few times pressuring Jonny. Guess that's why he's been on my mind." Ting signaled for the check.

"So. what happens in your dream?" I thought that Huli Jing erased his memories.

"I'm not sure. After that, everything gets fuzzy and I can't decide what's going on. But somehow, I seem to think about a snake. Does that mean anything?"

"Do you think it was Nuwa, the snake goddess, or Bashe?"

"You know I don't follow all of that, right?"

"Then I'll put on my Madam Zin persona and tell you. Nuwa would have the head of a human with the body of a serpent. She's the creative life force. The myth is that she created China when she separated the heavens and the earth. She's also the symbol for fertility, rebirth, immortality, and healing. "Bashe, on the other hand, is an evil spirit most often symbolizing greed. His snake form is large enough to devour elephants. So, what did your snake look like? Nuwa or Bashe?"

Ting started to laugh. "No human head. Besides, fertility is out of the question, as is immortality. Maybe, the healing."

"Why do you say that?"

"Well, in my dream I was in a lot of pain from being beat up. When I woke up, I felt fine, except I had some bruises I can't remember how I got." Ting rubbed his shoulder. "It's confusing."

"No elephants got devoured?'

"Didn't see a single elephant and no one got eaten."

"Well, usually, serpents mean good luck, so the spirits are telling you something good is going to happen to you."

"Like what?" The conversation paused as the waitress brought their check and Ting paid the bill. Ting reached over and took Wu Zhang's hand. "Like what?" he repeated.

"Like, maybe, an old love will return." Wu Zhang looked down at their entwined fingers. "And, perhaps, this time, things might work out."

"I guess it's possible." Ting stood up and offered his hand. The two walked out of the restaurant holding hands.

Wu Zhang resisted the urge to giggle. *I'm an old woman. Have some dignity.*

After a few minutes of walking, Wu Zhang decided to bring Jonny up again. "You will remember to ask Jonny to contact me?"

"What is going on between you two?"

"Nothing to be concerned about. I just need to ask him a few questions and he promised to answer them for me."

Ting-a-Ling waved down a taxi and the two sat close on the ride back to Madam Zin's red door. After she left, Ting gave the driver his address and lost himself in thoughts of the past. As they approached the shop, a movement caught Ting's eye.

A man dressed in black stood watching the store, at least that's what Ting thought. The cab stopped for a red-light, so Ting had a few moments to watch the man. He never moved. When the cab started to move, the headlights flashed for a second, long enough for Ting to get a look at his face. *Wait a minute! That man has been in the store. Why was he staring at it?*

Ting lost sight as the cab passed. *Maybe he's a thief! I'd better tell Mister Bolin!*

Kang looked at the store from the corner down the street. He'd noted all the local security cameras and marked the ones he wanted taken out. The neighborhood had a rhythm and this time of 0300 was when the streets were the emptiest, after the late-night crowd and before any early deliveries. He wanted to prevent civilian casualties. Keeping the battle within the store would be the best scenario. As he finished his plans, he was surprised when the front door to the store opened. A man walked out, looked straight at him, then marched right up to him.

"Do you think we don't know you've been watching us?" the man said.

Kang considered his answer. "So?"

"What do you want?"

"We want what was stolen."

"And if we don't want to give it back?"

"Then we will take it and kill everyone who gets in our way." Kang's eyes gleamed in anticipation.

"I see. You are very confident," the man said with a furrowed brow.

"Yes."

"Do you know who we are?"

"Again, yes."

"Then don't be too confident." The man now smiled. "But there may be a way we can avoid all the death and destruction of the last encounter."

"Oh?" Kang's eyes narrowed to slits. A traitor! He made no effort to disguise his disgust. "What is your offer?"

"Listen."

Chapter 31

BOLIN WATCHED THE COMPUTER screen trying to identify the number of watchers tonight. The man returned and stood statue-still just down the block, his eyes focused on the shop. A bead of sweat traced a crooked path down Bolin's face. *Are we going to have to fight?*

Min entered. "What's up?"

"Those men are back. I only see three tonight."

"Then I doubt they'll attack. I would think they'd use more men if tonight was it." Min sat next to his brother. "Are you going to tell Father?"

"I'll have to, but he can't fight in his condition. We must find a way to get he and Mother out of here."

"You know that won't happen." Min shook his head. "Father won't leave the urns and Mother won't leave him."

"Go get Jonny. We need to come up with a plan."

"I didn't need sleep anyways."

***

Jonny kept dreaming. They were getting stronger, and every morning when he woke, this world felt more unreal and disjointed. Yesterday morning when he went to the kitchen for breakfast, he couldn't remember how to start the coffee-maker. Where's my tea? Fo He's wife usually had it made first thing in the morning. Then he shook his head.

"What the…?" Jonny mumbled, confused. "Who the hell is Fo He?"

Snapping out of it, Jonny tried to laugh it off. "Maybe I need a shrink."

However, tonight his sleep was not disturbed by a dream, but when Min came into his room and pulled his pillow out from under his head.

"Wake up," Min commanded. "Bolin wants you in his room for a meeting."

"Go away," Jonny mumbled. "It's the middle of the night."

"It's important. We've got trouble."

"We've always got trouble," Jonny grumbled as he rolled out of bed. His head cleared when he looked at Min. "Oh."

The three brothers sat in front of the computer screen and watched the watchers.

"Who do you think they are?" Jonny asked.

Bolin shook his head. "I can't be sure, but that man was in the shop saying he 'finds things'. I can't help but speculate that the MSS has found us. Remember, the urns were opened out of the house. We may have given ourselves away."

"You're talking about more than seventy years!" Jonny said. "How could they still be looking for us?"

"They still want the urns." Bolin sat back. "It'll be harder to run nowadays with technology working against us. Also, I don't think Father has any backup plan. I think we've become complacent because of the lapse of time."

"You're right," Han said from the doorway. "I haven't made any contingency plans. Your mother and I can stay here as decoys. Besides, we'd only slow you down. You boys can get away with the urns and start somewhere new."

"We're not leaving you behind to face Chinese agents," Min said. "Forget that."

"The residents are what's important," Han said. "Remember your oath."

"Sorry, Dad," Jonny spoke up. "I didn't sign the oath, so I won't go along with that."

"You are committed simply because you know. In times past, you would have been killed just for knowing of their existence."

"Yeah, well, it isn't times past, is it?" Jonny scowled at his father. "I know about them, so deal with it."

The two glared at each other for a few tense moments until Min swore under his breath.

"We have enough problems already without you two fighting." Min pointed at the computer screen. "Remember? Bad guys?"

Han relented. Looking at his eldest, he asked, "So what do you want to do?"

"We're going to have to fight, but maybe not the way they think."

Chapter 32

JACKIE LING SAT AT the safe house ruminating over the turn of events that had decimated his life. The police closed down the casino, took every computer and ledger they could find and froze bank accounts. As far as he could tell, Frankie was still spilling his guts about every law he'd ever broken, including parking tickets. *Now, I'm stuck here until I can figure out what the hell I should do.*

He didn't know what happened at the warehouse after he'd left. After questioning the old man, he returned to the casino to meet with the fence for Frankie since Frankie wanted to handle Jonny in person. Jackie expected that Jonny might lose a body part. But the news said nothing about Jonny Chen and there was no one left for him to question. They were either in jail or in the hospital, all babbling nonsense.

"Wait a minute," Jackie spoke out loud. "What about the old man and Madam Zin?" He pulled out the paper and reread the articles. *Did they escape before the cops got there? How?*

Jackie stewed about this for a long time before he decided it was time to find out. The two of them had to know what went on and they'd tell him or else.

***

"Why don't you come in for a cup of my special tea?" Wu Zhang said smiling.

"I'd like that," Ting-a-Ling answered taking her hand. "I'm really not ready to go home and face my apartment."

Wu Zhang turned, opened her red door and they entered. They walked through the hanging bead curtains and through the door back to her private rooms. She walked to the kitchen and began heating the water leaving Ting to look around her space.

Ting wasn't sure what he expected, but this room looked too normal. There were no tokens or talismans, no bells or drums, just ordinary comfortable-looking furniture. Ting elected to sit on the couch so Wu Zhang would be able to sit next to him. He watched her preparing the tea and still appreciated her graceful economical movements. His heart did a flip. Rising, he walked over to where she stood with her back to him and put his arms around her.

"What?" Wu Zhang said, startled by his actions.

"I needed to hold you. Please, just let me."

After a moment, Wu Zhang gave a laugh. "You foolish old man." But she let him.

"Isn't this sweet," a rough voice growled from behind.

The two separated and spun around to see Jackie Ling standing in the room with an evil glint in his eye and a smirk on his face.

"What are you doing here?" Wu Zhang demanded. "Do you want to end up like the others?" she bluffed.

"I don't believe all that crap. I'm not like Frankie." Jackie walked to the couch and sat down. "Since you went to the trouble of making tea, I think I'll take a cup. Put it right here." He tapped the coffee table.

Ting took a step forward. "What do you want from us?"

"I want to know what happened at the warehouse. I want to know why my life has turned to shit."

"I don't know what you're talking about," Ting said confused as he looked back and forth between the two.

"Yeah, maybe, but she does." Jackie pointed at Wu Zhang who walked forward to put the cup of tea on the table.

She stood before Jackie and looked down at him as he picked up the tea and sipped looking over the rim at her. "The demon must have done something to all of us. I don't remember anything either."

"Then how come you're not babbling like the others?"

"I don't know."

"Isn't this your job—to know about these things? You wouldn't have set us up, right?" He took another sip, watching her.

"Of course not. How could I have? Your men kidnapped us!"

"How come the newspaper doesn't mention Jonny?"

Wu Zhang tried to think up some plausible reason, but she couldn't think straight under his cold gaze. The man just sat there sipping tea and his aura chilled her to her old bones. She'd prefer anger to this.

"I-I don't know."

"Seems like you don't know a lot." Jackie Ling put down his teacup. "Here I thought you were a professional." He stood up and reached behind his back. "I really don't like being lied to." The gun appeared. "Maybe your memory needs a little jolt." He fired. Ting crumbled to the floor.

"Ting!" Wu Zhang screamed and started to move forward.

"Stay," Jackie commanded, "or I repeat the performance."

Wu Zhang tried to think. If she told this man what had happened, the entire Chen family could die and the urns could be lost. "Please," she begged, "let me go to him."

Jackie looked at the old man lying on the floor. Blood seeped out of his belly and pooled beside him. *What would make her talk?*

"Go."

Wu Zhang rushed to Ting's side. Pulling off her scarf, she pressed against his wound to try and stop the bleeding. *Ting's still breathing. Spirits, please help me!*

"I'll do whatever you want if you just let me call 911." She looked up with tears in her eyes. "Please."

"I'll tell you what, you call Jonny and tell him to get over here. Then—I'll let you call for help."

Frantic, Wu Zhang reached into Ting's pocket and pulled out his cellphone. The phone rang and rang, but there was no answer. She called again. This time a sleepy voice answered.

"Hey, Ting. It's late. What's up?" a drowsy voice said.

"Jonny, this is Madam Zin. Can you get over here right away? Something has happened."

"What? Is Ting okay?" Jonny's voice became urgent.

Wu Zhang looked up at Jackie. He shook his head.

"Ting's been hurt. I need help," her voice shook.

"How bad? Do we need to call 911?"

At Jackie's prompting, she said, "No, I need your help to get him to go to the hospital to get checked."

There was a slight pause. "I'll be there as fast as I can." The line went dead.

"There," Wu Zhang said, "I did what you asked. Let me call for help."

"Tsk, tsk," Jackie said smiling, "did you really think I'd let you? You played us. There's a price."

Jackie Ling raised his gun.

Wu Zhang wrapped her arms around Ting. "I love you," she whispered in his ear hoping he could hear her. "I always have."

Chapter 33

Jonny ran to his brother's room.

"Bolin!" he shouted opening the door.

"What?" Bolin sat straight up in bed, awake in an instant.

"Madam Zin and Ting are in trouble," Jonny threw Bolin's clothes on the bed. "We need to get over there. I don't know what's going on, but we need to be ready."

"Get the Admiral," Bolin said slipping on his pants and shirt.

"What about Min?"

"He needs to stay here. This may be a diversion. We can't leave Mom and Dad on their own."

Jonny ran up to get the Admiral while Bolin woke Min to tell him what was happening. When Jonny reappeared, the Admiral was by his side in his young, warrior persona.

"Let's go," Jonny said. "Be careful, Min."

At Min's nod, the three of them left, running down the stairs and out to the Enclave. On the way, Jonny filled them in on the short conversation.

"Madam Zin's voice was shaking. It didn't really sound like her. I've seen her handle meeting the Admiral, getting kidnapped and seeing Wei Zan's serpent, and her voice never shook. Do you think it's that Chinese guy?"

"I don't know, but it doesn't seem like it's his style. Otherwise, why come into the store to let us see him? I don't see him using an old man."

"He's a spy!" Jonny said. "Doesn't that mean he'd do anything?"

Bolin shrugged. "You might be right, but my gut says it's not him."

"Then who?"

"Who else would have a grudge?" The Admiral asked. "I'd put my wager on that casino man."

"He's in jail along with his crew," Jonny said.

"All of his men?"

Jonny thought back to the warehouse. Kong and Godzilla were there along with other faces he recognized. He thought again. Who? A face flashed before his eyes.

"Jackie Ling!" Jonny gritted out.

"Who's that?" Bolin asked.

"Frankie's lieutenant. I don't remember seeing him at the warehouse. How could I be that dumb?" Jonny hung his head. "I never gave him a thought. He must still be free."

"What kind of man is he?" The Admiral said.

"He's a cold SOB that Frankie uses to do his dirty work. He keeps to the background, but he carries out the orders to break legs when Frankie says to." Jonny covered his face with his hands. "Damn, I should have known he'd be involved since they kidnapped Madam Zin and Ting."

"We will rescue them," The Admiral put his hand on Jonny's shoulder. "I will make him pay for any harm he does."

Jonny's hands shook. "Hurry."

The Enclave parked in front of the red door. The three approached the front door and since the lock was broken, they entered. The Admiral went incorporeal. They went to the back of the room and through the bead curtain.

"What do we do?" Jonny asked.

"He's expecting you, Jonny," Bolin said. "Just knock. I'll stay behind the doorjamb. The Admiral will follow you in."

"Come in," a male voice said from behind the door in response to the knock.

Jonny opened the door and took a cautious step inside. He felt a swish of air behind him as The Admiral slipped past. What he saw next sent him rushing forward, his eyes widened with horror.

"No!" he screamed in anguish. "No!"

Laying at his feet were the bodies of Madam Zin and Ting-a-Ling. Tears filled his eyes as he knelt. Madam Zin's arms encircled his friend, her blood mingling with his. He shook Ting's body. "Ting, Ting! Answer me!" But there was no answer.

"This is rather touching," the voice said from behind him.

Jonny looked up to see Jackie Ling standing over him with gun in hand. "How could you do this?" Jonny shouted. "Ting never hurt anybody in his entire life. He has no part in any of this."

"It got you here. That's all I needed."

"What do you want that's worth killing two innocent people?"

"I want to know what happened in that warehouse. I want to know what happened to Frankie. I want to know why you aren't babbling like the rest of them." Jackie smiled. "Then, I want to kill you."

"I'm not going to tell you anything. If you're going to kill me, just do it. Don't talk me to death."

Jackie's face flushed with anger at Jonny's cool demeanor in the face of death. "You're really pissing me off," he growled. "I can really hurt you, so you better be afraid."

"No," a deep voice boomed, "you better be afraid."

Jackie spun around to see the Admiral's form materialize. He fired. He saw the bullet hit the large man, but the man stood tall and unmoved. No blood appeared. Eyes opening wider in panic, Jackie fired again. Then as he watched, the large man held out his right hand and a huge curved sword appeared.

"What are you?" Jackie screamed, firing again and again.

The Admiral's eye began to glow a dark red and his body took on a brightness that burned the eyes. Jonny looked away. He didn't want to watch this.

The Admiral stepped forward, "Coward, you'll pay for your sins." The sword flashed.

Jonny heard a scream that ended with an abrupt gurgle, then silence. He kept his eyes closed until he felt a hand on his shoulder.

"Jonny, it's over," Bolin said. He knelt beside his brother. The two mourned their friend and his lady.

Jonny felt the presence of The Admiral behind him and looked up. The Admiral's face was calm and composed.

"I'm sorry for your friend's death," The Admiral said. "The man has paid for his crime. Now it's up to the gods. That man will surely return as a slug."

"What do we do now?" Jonny said looking up at his brother.

"I'm sorry, Jonny, but we have to leave. We can call the police from Ting's phone before we go."

"Can't we do..."

"Don't touch anything. We have to leave everything the way it is." Bolin stood up and tried not to look at the man lying on the floor in two pieces. "Let's go."

Jonny sat silent on the way home, images flashed through his mind, images he would never forget. "It's all my fault," he murmured as tears rolled down his cheeks.

"No," The Admiral spoke up. "Murder is always the fault of the perpetrator. That man chose his path a long time ago. He chose to live his life that way. Evil always ends badly."

"But he took others with him!" Jonny wailed.

"Yes, but he will pay the price for an eternity. Your friends, however, are together. Perhaps, in the next life, they will get to spend their entire lives together.

Chapter 34

"Poor Jonny," Lady Ji sighed the next day as the residents sat together.

"The entire family is grieving," Physician Ho said.

"Is there anything we can do?" Wei Zan asked.

"I'm afraid not. The boys are going to have to face this death and learn to deal with it." The Admiral paced back and forth. "I'm concerned about how this loss will affect Han's health. Physician?"

"He is doing as well as we can hope."

"Han?" Wei Zan said. "What's the concern with Jonny's father?"

"He is dying," Physician Ho said to the Huli Jing. "He doesn't have much time left."

Wei Zan looked around the room at the other spirits. *Jonny knows this? He didn't tell me.* "Who will be the head guardian then? Bolin?"

"Yes," Jin spoke up. "He's a strong and good man. He will do well in whatever he chooses."

The other residents looked at each other and Wei Zan felt left out. "Why do you all look at each other like that? Is there something I don't know?"

"Let me explain," Jin said. "You see, there is this man..."

Han was restless and couldn't sleep. The pain in his gut was now unrelenting. He left Lei asleep and walked to the bathroom and took two pain pills. He checked on his boys then walked about the living room looking at a lifetime of photos he and Lei had set out.

There were pictures of Bolin, age 6, getting his blue belt—his stance full of pride. Min got his a little younger, but Min excelled at all sports. His picture showed his trademark big grin. No one could ever seem to stay mad at the perpetually happy boy. Then, there was Jonny scowling at the camera, but his competitive nature made him excel as well. He just had to work harder.

Family outings, school plays and awards, birthday parties, childhood friends, and a prom picture or two all brought warmth to Han's heart. *I've had a good life. If I have to leave it early, at least I know it was lived well.*

"Father?" a female voice spoke.

Startled, Han turned to see the Huli Jing standing there, tentative, as if to ask permission to enter the room.

"Yes, what is it?" Han said trying to be courteous in response to her giving him the respectful title of "Father".

"Are you well?" Wei Zan asked.

"I'm fine. What are you doing down here?"

"I wanted to check on Jonny. He's so sad." Wei Zan bowed. "I am sorry for the death of your friend."

"Thank you." Han sighed. "Jonny is asleep, finally. I just peeked in on all the boys."

"Very well, thank you." Wei Zan turned to leave then stopped. "Father, may I give you a hug?"

"What?" startled, Han realized how rude he sounded when he saw her face flush. "I'm sorry. Of course, you may."

Wei Zan walked over and put her arms about the man. "Please accept my condolences." She felt the energy drain and smiled. "I shall go back upstairs now." She stepped back and walked away.

Perhaps Jonny is right about her. She seemed very sweet just now. Physician Ho says she's trustworthy, and I trust his judgment. Feeling reassured, Han decided he should go back to bed. The pain pills were working and he thought he'd be able to sleep now.

***

Jonny wasn't asleep. He heard his father check on him, the soft voices in the living room, and the tick of the old grandfather clock out in the hall. He lay curled up in bed, his mind and body a mass of confused thoughts and feelings.

First, his grandparents are lost to a senseless accident. Then, the news he will lose his father—and now Ting—this was too much. Jonny laid back and looked at the ceiling trying to decipher what he was feeling,

I wasn't close to grandfather. He was just like Dad. But I did respect him. He was a taskmaster. Grandmother was kind and

sweet. I wonder how such stern men manage to marry such wonderful women. I miss her smells. She always smelled like lavender. And, she laughed at my stupid jokes. I miss her cooking and the way she put flowers around everywhere.

Then, Dad drops his bomb. I can see him weaken almost by the day. He tries to hide it, but we all can see it. What will Mom do without him?

Now, Ting-a-Ling's gone. He was more of a grandfather to me than Grandfather was. I shoulda told him how much I cared. Now, it's too late.

Jonny's eyes closed as exhaustion claimed him. The clouds of the past circled around in his head until pictures began to form.

***

Chang Jianyu wandered, aimless—banished, shunned by his family, his heart broken. Life held little purpose except survival now that he wasn't a guardian. Taking a few odd jobs here and there put food in his stomach. He'd sent another petition to his family stating his case and asking them to reconsider. He needed to see Wei Zan again. He had to know if she made the transition into the urn. *Did her spirit survive intact?*

Chang Jianyu collapsed down on his blanket. It had been a long day of manual labor, but his belly was full. Sweaty and dirty, he thought about a bath, but fatigue won and he slept.

A sound woke him from his sleep. Exiting his shelter, he saw four men by the ashes of his fire-pit. The full moon shone on their shapes and he recognized them. Hope swelled.

"Father," Jianyu said with a bow to an imposing figure at the center. "Uncles, brother, please sit and I will light a fire."

"No," his father said. "We are not here to talk."

Jianyu stepped back. Hope died. "Then...why?"

"You have broken your oath. You have disgraced our family. The others may have been lenient, but you are my son, and I shall be the final judge."

"Did you even bring my petition to the family elders?" Jianyu looked at his brother, Fo He.

"No."

Jianyu hung his head. "What will happen to Wei Zan?"

"You dare to ask?" his father gritted out. His sword appeared in his hand as if by magic.

"Yes. You owe me that."

Fo He couldn't stay silent. This was his brother! They had fought and played together. Tears gathered at what was to come. He could at least give his brother this answer. "She is within the urn, but she will never be let out. She will sleep forever."

Tears filled Jianyu's eyes. He had condemned them both by his reckless action. He fell to his knees. "So be it."

His father's sword flashed.

***

Jonny woke in a sweat grabbing at his chest. It hurt. He tried to slow his breathing and felt the pain begin to subside. He felt muddled, his spirit deeply saddened. *I'm lost.*

Rolling out of bed, Jonny went to the kitchen. *I need a drink.*

Lei was busy preparing breakfast. "Good morning, my son," she said, "did you get any rest?"

"I'm fine, Mom. I just need something to drink. My throat is dry."

"The tea is ready."

"Thanks." Jonny poured a cup and sat at the table. *Not what I needed.*

"What's the matter? You're so pale this morning. I know Ting Wang's death is hard for you, but he wouldn't want you to become ill. Please talk to me." Lei sat at the table with her cup of tea. "Let us say a toast to our dear friend." She held up her cup and they touched. In silence, they each took a sip saying a prayer for Ting's soul.

When he put the cup down, Jonny looked at his mother. "I had a strange dream again last night."

"Really? What about?"

"My death."

"Jonny! How horrible. You must have been frightened."

"No, I wasn't scared, Mom, just very sad. I think I was so sad I was ready to die. But, Mom, what made it even worse was that it was my father who killed me."

"Jonny, your father would never do that!" Lei's hand went up to her chest before reaching out to take Jonny's hand. "You know that, don't you? I know you two have had your differences, but your father loves you."

"I know." Jonny paused, his brow furrowed. "It was only a dream, but it felt so real. It felt like I was living it."

Their conversation stopped when Han walked into the room. Lei turned and rose to give him a kiss. "Did you sleep well, dear?"

"Actually, I slept very well. In fact, I'm a little hungry this morning."

Lei's face lit up. "Oh, Han, I will make you whatever your heart desires."

Han laughed, and Lei's face glowed in response, her smile broadening. "I think I'd like some rice porridge and maybe a few of your dumplings?"

"Wonderful. I'll have them ready in a few minutes. Jonny?"

"A few dumplings will be fine, Mom. I'll take them upstairs."

For a moment Jonny thought his father was going to say "no", but he didn't. The two sipped on their tea and watched Lei bustle about the kitchen. When she put a bowl of dumplings on the table, Jonny murmured his "thanks" and headed upstairs.

Chapter 35

KANG SAT AT THE bar and sipped his drink. The last few days had been frustrating since the night he caught a glimpse of three young guardians rushing from the store. Something wasn't right. He followed.

He watched as the three men went through a red door that announced the residence of a local shaman. Not too long after, the three exited in obvious distress. Kang considered for a moment, then decided to enter the building.

Cautious, Kang went through the door, then the bead curtain. Pushing open the second door, he entered and stopped, shocked for one of the few times in his life. Carnage of a truly bizarre nature confronted him. He recognized the old man from the store. He approached to see who the woman was. *Must be the shaman.* The position of the bodies showed they were close.

Kang turned to look at the other body. A shiver passed through him. He'd seen a lot of death, he'd caused a lot of death, but this was one he wouldn't forget. Blood pooled thick and dark soaking the carpet. The man had been cleaved in two from the right shoulder to the left chest.

What kind of weapon? What kind of strength was needed to do this? He felt a touch of fear and awe. Who were these Guardians?

He did a quick scan of the scene until he heard the sound of distant sirens. Time to get out.

Now, Kang sat in the bar thinking about his next step. *Three Guardians took out that man despite his gun.* Kang wondered if they wore bullet proof vests. Thinking back, they didn't look like they were wearing any protection. Nor did he remember seeing any weapons. *Where did they hide a sword?*

And that third Guardian. Where did he come from? I haven't seen him come or go since that day. Despite searching city records for underground tunnels or sewer lines, he could find no underground entrance into Chen's building. *What am I missing?*

Irritated, Kang threw some money on the bar, and headed out. He hailed a cab and said, "Haight Street entrance, Golden Gate, and hit the drive-through at Kentucky Fried."

After being dropped off, Kang walked through the park until he found Andrew's campsite. As usual, Andrew was snoring, but his dogs, Shadow and Buster, woke with tails wagging. Their barks of greeting roused Andrew.

"Hey, man, you here again?" Andrew rubbed his blurry eyes.

"Yeah. Here." Kang dropped the bag at Andrew's side.

"What's this?"

Kang shrugged and sat by the dogs who scurried to him for attention.

"Chicken! Hey, man, thanks." Andrew pulled out a chicken leg and bit into it. "Oh, man, this is delicious." Pulling out a biscuit, he almost swallowed it whole. Then he threw one to each of his dogs.

"There's nothing to drink in this bag." Andrew looked up, hopeful.

"Sorry, get your own. There's a bottle of water. That's something to drink."

"You're a hard man, Kang." Andrew pulled out another piece of chicken. Pulling off pieces of meat, he fed them to Buster and Shadow, then poured some water into their dish.

"How's Shadow's wound?" Kang asked.

"It's healing pretty good. I've been trying to keep him quiet."

"That's good." Kang reached over and scratched Buster's ear. The dog laid his head next to Kang's leg. "Any more ghost sightings lately?"

"Nah. And the stupid TV broadcaster never came back for my interview."

Kang looked at the bedraggled and malodorous man as he stuffed food into his mouth and had to smile. "Too bad. You still got dog food left?"

"Yeah, thanks." After a moment of silence, Andrew felt compelled to ask, "Hey, Kang, why are you being so nice to me?"

Kang looked at the man. *I really don't know.* "Because your dogs were hurt. I like dogs." Kang stood up, walking away without another word.

For the next hour Kang wandered around the park. *Stupid waste of time. Would they really come back here after that video?*

Deciding he was tired, Kang headed back to the entrance and caught a cab back to his hotel. He stripped and showered, walking naked to the bed. *I need sleep. I'm too tired to think.* He put on clean briefs and laid down with his arms behind his head, his thoughts swirling about. *Enough. Sleep. Maybe I should consider the deal. I'll decide tomorrow.*

Jonny sat in the room munching on a few of his mother's dumpling. It was his turn today to let the residents out. He found himself sitting and staring at the urns. *Ting's dead because of those urns. Because of secrets. Because, I took one.*

He brushed the tears away and stuffed a few more dumplings into his mouth. *Ting loved Mom's dumplings.*

Early that morning the detectives had come with their questions. The family felt like they were betraying Ting, but Ting was past caring. Gang violence was being blamed for Jackie Ling, but the detectives wanted a reason for Ting and Madame Zin's death. The family could only shrug and claim ignorance.

Standing up, Jonny went to the cabinet and asked a question to release all the residents. However, it was a somber group that appeared. Lady Ji placed a hand on his arm, leaned forward to kiss his cheek and said, "We are all very sorry, Jonny."

"Thanks," Jonny gave a weak smile, then went back to sit on the couch. "Is there anything I need to do for you all today?"

Wei Zan was the last to exit her urn and had stayed in the background. She was desperate to touch Jonny, but something held her back. Finally, she stepped forward and sat next to him. A strange sensation passed through her. She looked over at Jonny and watched as his eyes darkened, his facial expression changed, subtle, but noticeable.

"No, Jonny," Chengli answered Jonny's question. "We're fine. Why don't you do whatever you want to do. We'll stay here."

Jonny looked at Wei Zan. "Will you go outside with me today? Perhaps a trip to that park. We'll get you away from all the concrete." Jonny smiled as he reached towards her. His touch sent a current across her skin.

What is this I'm feeling? Curious, Wei Zan nodded and stood.

Jonny joined her and the two left the room, heading down the stairs. The living room was empty as the family were all working in the store, so they left without telling them. Jonny flagged down a cab for a silent ride to the park.

"Let's walk the Oakland Trail. I think you'll find it relatively close to how some areas of your forest must have looked."

Wei Zan nodded agreement. After a while, Jonny reached over and took her hand. Once again, she felt the sensation. The urge to touch him grew stronger. Her heart began to race, her breath to quicken.

They'd entered an isolated area when Jonny pulled her off the trail and into a thick copse of trees. Before she realized what was happening, he'd taken her by the shoulders and pushed her back against a large Oak tree. His kiss took her by surprise.

"My little fox," he murmured pressing against her.

Jianyu! I knew it.

Wei Zan's arms rose of their own accord and clasped him to her. The present disappeared as she went back to the time when she could love him without fear or worry. It had been so long! Jianyu's arms picked her up and he carried her to a small patch of grass. Kneeling, he laid her down and followed, pinning her beneath him. She looked up into his eyes. *Jianyu! I shouldn't be doing this. Spirits, brothers and sisters, please forgive me!*

An hour later, the two lay side-by-side. Wei Zan found herself not knowing what to do. She turned her head to gaze at his profile. He looked so young laying there with his eyes closed, younger than her Jianyu, more innocent and vulnerable. Confused, feeling guilty, she needed to escape. Her form flickered and a nine-tailed fox rose to leap into the treetops.

"Wei Zan," Jianyu called out reaching upwards. "Don't leave!"

***

Andrew was walking Shadow and Buster through the trees. His boys loved these outings with a chance to explore and search for new and exciting smells. Shadow trotted easily alongside his buddy reassuring Andrew that the wound had healed enough for him to relax.

As they rounded a curve in the trail, Buster let out a bark and took off, Shadow close on his heels.

"Boys! Slow down! Get back here," Andrew yelled running after them. He found them at the base of a large Oak, jumping and barking, looking up into the tree. Andrew caught up to them and glanced up to see what critter they had treed.

There, looking down at him, was one of the most beautiful creatures he'd ever seen—a fox—a glowing white fox. *With how many tails?*

"It's you," Andrew said in wonder. "You're not a hallucination."

Excited, Andrew pulled out his cellphone and snapped a picture. Then he dialed that TV lady.

"She's here at the park," Andrew yelled into the phone. "We got her trapped up a tree. You can see her for yourself."

Opening his eyes, Jonny felt disoriented. When he heard the dogs barking, he knew a moment of panic. His gut said Wei Zan was in trouble. Jumping up, he started to run, but had to straighten his clothes first. *What?* Following the sound, he arrived to see a bum with two dogs and Wei Zan trapped up in the tree.

"What are you doing?" Jonny shouted.

The man turned and still holding his phone to his ear, pointed up the tree. "You see the fox, right?" He spoke into the phone again, "There's someone else here. He can swear to you that he sees it, too." The bum pushed the phone at Jonny. "Tell them what you see up there."

Jonny took the phone, raised up his arm and smashed it on the ground, stomping it with his foot.

"Hey, man, what are you doing? That's my phone!" The bum knelt down and tried to save it. "Why'd you do that?"

Jonny didn't answer. He looked up at Wei Zan and yelled, "Change back and come down. We gotta get out of here."

Wei Zan nodded and transformed back to her human form. The dogs yelped in fear as she took a graceful leap and landed beside Jonny. Backing up, they put themselves between Jonny and the bum in an obvious attempt to protect the man from this strange woman. Both growled a warning.

"Good dogs," Jonny said trying to placate the frightened animals. He looked at the man. "I don't want to hurt you. Just forget what you saw." Jonny took Wei Zan's arm and began to back away. "We're leaving now."

Turning, the Guardian and his love ran back through the woods.

Andrew sat on the ground, frightened and angry. That man had taken his evidence and smashed his new phone, a phone given to him by the TV station so he could report any further sightings. *I coulda proved my story. People woulda had to believe me. I needed that money.*

Picking up the pieces, Andrew headed back to his campsite.

***

Jonny pulled Wei Zan through the woods and back onto the trail. They walked in silence for a few minutes before Jonny stopped and turned to her.

"How did I get here?" Jonny asked.

***

Kang received a call from Andrew who was using a borrowed phone and went to see him.

"You keep asking about what I saw. Well, I saw them again today and it was broad daylight and I was stone-cold sober." Andrew looked up at Kang. "How much is it worth to you?" At Kang's look, he added, "I know you've been good to me, but a man has needs."

Kang took out his wallet and pulled off two hundred dollars. "Will that do?"

"Sure, sure," Andrew said grabbing the money. He then proceeded to tell Kang his story.

"Are the TV people coming?" Kang asked.

"Haven't heard a word from them."

"Give me your phone. I may be able to get the picture back. Then you'd have proof."

"Really? You'd do that for me? You're the best." Andrew gave the pieces to Kang, who nodded and left.

Kang went back to the consulate and gave the phone to the tech lab with a rush order. Not much later he had a picture that amazed him. Sure, the file had a list of who was in the urn provided by the traitor Chang, but this was hard to believe. The traitor said there was a supernatural being called a Huli Jing in one of the urns, but Kang hadn't believed it. He was sure it was just a way of scaring the Guardians so they wouldn't open that urn.

Curious, Kang went online and researched the creature. *Amazing. Maybe that creature was responsible for what happened at the shaman's house.* The news had been full of the horrendous murder scene at Madam Zin's. So, perhaps the Huli Jing was the third man Kang witnessed going into the red door.

Kang sat back from the computer contemplating his next move. His fingers tapped the desk with a staccato beat as he weighed his options. He prided himself on strategy. Taking the life of an enemy never caused him a moment of hesitation, however, he was never rash. Good planning made his missions successful and right now, he needed a plan.

Guess I'll take the meeting.

Chapter 36

THE FAMILY SPENT THE day in the store with a spirit of cooperation that was rare. After a small but tasty breakfast, Han felt able to spend some time alongside his sons. He looked at his boys as they joked and worked. They argued set-ups, displays and selected objects they wanted to feature. For today, his heart felt light and his pain negligible.

Lei ran upstairs to grab some drinks for a break. She rushed back down with a pitcher of lemonade and some cups. The boys all gathered around taking a cup.

"Ting would have loved the new set-up," Jonny said with a sigh. "I miss him."

Han grabbed a cup and raised it up. "To Ting."

In silence, the family sipped.

"Did the residents need anything this morning?" Han asked.

"No, Father," Min said. "Actually, only Lady Ji and Physician Ho stayed out. They were online when I came down. The others went back inside their urns. I think the Admiral's energy was still low."

"What makes you say that?"

"I don't know. He seemed quiet, kinda depressed really. Anyway, he wasn't himself."

"Well, he did have to..." Lei's voice broke.

"I doubt that would bother him," Bolin said. "After all, he's a warrior. He's fought many battles against others that were way better men than Jackie Ling."

The family nodded agreement, then went back to work finishing up. Later, Lei called down that dinner was ready. After dinner, Min ran upstairs to check on the residents. All the residents, except for the physician who was reading a treatise on pancreatic cancer, were back inside their urns. When he came back down, he found everyone around the table with a deck of cards.

"Poker?" Min said.

"No," Jonny spoke up. "I've given it up. Let's do Hand and Foot."

The rest of the evening passed with the family enjoying each other's company and trying to forget that their time together was limited.

***

The clock struck midnight. Physician Ho had been waiting. "Chulai," he said and the residents joined him in their young personas.

"Does everyone know what they are to do?" The Admiral looked at his fellow spirits.

They all nodded.

"Did you finish your task?" Physician Ho asked the brothers.

"Yes," Jin said. "We took the Dremel's and made the cuts. The Guardians never check the lids." With that, he gathered up the lids and brought them to the table. He and Chengli pried open the gold lining inside of the lids to expose what was inside.

"They're beautiful," Lady Ji said in awe.

Inside of the lids lay amulets of red jade. The brilliant red of the stone almost looked like red glass showing imperfections and variations of color that were dazzling. Symbols carved on each in an intricate pattern seemed to glow from within. Power radiated upward. This was the stone revered for its metaphysical ability to allow access to the spiritual realm and to help achieve divine knowledge.

"So, this is where the magic began," Jin said.

***

Kang waited for the signal.

So, this is how it would end. After a millennium, a traitor would once again cause the fall of the Guardians. He didn't want to admit it, but Kang felt a deep sadness. He shook his head and imagined what the other Guardians would feel in the morning.

"Huh," Kang muttered to himself, "are there no real men left?"

The meeting had been simple. One of the young men came out and told him to be here at 0400. He would let Kang into the shop and hand over the urns on the guarantee that no Chen would be harmed. The Guardian swore that the others would be asleep—he'd see to it.

True to his word, the young Guardian opened the shop door and signaled Kang. Scanning the surroundings, Kang looked for any sign of ambush. *Can't trust a traitor.* Seeing nothing, he crossed the street and entered the store. The slender young man pulled down a newly installed security screen that blocked the view into the store. Kang felt a moment of unease.

"Come on in," the young man said.

Kang looked around at the remodeled store. His glance took note of any areas where a Guardian could come out and attempt to take him down. He didn't see anything, so he followed after the man toward the back of the store. There stood the same six he had followed that day.

A plump young man stepped forward holding a case. He put it on a table that had been cleared off, dialed in a code and opened the lid.

"Come see," the young man said. "I kept my word."

Kang walked over and looked down. He couldn't help but catch his breath—there lay six shining gold urns, each in its own pocket. Not sure what he was really expecting, Kang was surprised that they weren't larger. He reached forward and touched one of them and looked up at the man.

"They're solid gold?"

"Yes."

"How do I know they're the real thing?"

"Seriously? You think we have enough money and know-how to fake them?"

"I see your point." Kang would have sworn he felt a slight tingle when he touched them so he knew these had to be real.

"What about the Chens?"

"That's none of your business. We kept our part of the bargain. You keep yours and disappear," the slender man said.

"Very well." Kang closed the case and heard the lock click. "What's the combination?"

The chubby man handed him a piece of paper with the code written on it.

"How do I open the urns?"

"We've done all we're going to do. You'll have to figure the rest out for yourselves." The man turned away.

Kang grabbed his arm. "My superiors will want to know."

"That's not our problem. I'm sure your leaders have the necessary information. If they didn't give it to you, you're not supposed to know."

"What the hell is going on?" a voice yelled out from the upstairs doorway.

The group spun around to see Jonny rush to the stair railing. "Go!" the slender man urged Kang.

"We'll take care of this."

"Stop!" Jonny shouted and almost tumbled down the stairs in his haste.

Kang stayed rooted in place, not sure why he did, but he did. He watched as the young Guardian came down to stand between him and the front door. The shock on Jonny's face registered deeply with Kang—betrayal, confusion, anger—all flashed across his young face.

"Sorry, Mr. Chen," Kang said, "but, I had a deal."

"You're not taking those out of here." Jonny braced himself.

"Jonny," a young Zheng He stepped forward, "we decided to send the urns back to China where they belong."

"But, Admiral…"

"The Admiral agrees with our decision," Zheng He interrupted.

"Jonny," a young Physician Ho said, "the residents want to go home."

That simple statement stopped Jonny. He looked at all the resident's faces and saw the deep sadness living there. Jonny understood. They weren't going with the urns!

"Jonny," Wei Zan stepped up to him and laid her hand on his chest, "please honor the decision." Her beautiful eyes implored him to say no more.

Jonny knew then that Kang didn't realize the residents were in front of him and not within the urns. "Are you doing this to save us?"

"No," Wei Zan whispered against his cheek.

Jonny hung his head as Wei Zan stepped back and joined the others.

"Looks like your democracy at work," Kang said smiling. "I gave my word I wouldn't harm any of you and I keep my word. You should feel honored because my orders were to kill all of you."

"Why aren't you?" Jonny said.

Kang thought for a moment then shrugged. "I don't want to. You didn't steal the urns, your ancestor did. Your family had this task before my China was even a thought, so somehow, I don't see a purpose in killing all of you."

"But I can't just let you walk out of here with those urns," Jonny said bracing himself to attack.

Kang looked at the young man's bravado and almost smiled. Before Jonny could take a breath, Kang kicked out, catching Jonny in the crotch and sending him to the floor in a huddled mass.

When Kang stepped forward, a noise from behind caused him to spin around in response. While he watched, a long, curved sword seemed to grow from out of one man's outstretched hand. Stunned for a moment, Kang felt a thrill of fear clutch at him. *What am I seeing?*

Kang looked into the eyes of the man and saw an unrelenting warrior. He knew if he made one move towards the boy, he would end up cleaved in two like the man at the shaman's home. This was magic—magic that he couldn't believe even though it stood facing him in deadly earnest. *Guardians! Who or what are they?*

"We had a deal," the warrior said.

"I will honor our deal," Kang replied with a nod. Still holding the case, Kang stood over the boy and looked down. "You'll live. My superiors will be told you're dead. Stay that way and don't do anything stupid."

With that, Kang walked to the front screen, lifted it and left.

Chapter 37

THEY ALL STOOD IN the store and looked at one another. With a shake of his head, the Admiral walked over to Jonny. "Always thought that would hurt." Smiling, he offered his hand.

Jonny accepted the offer. "What now?" he asked, still gasping. He tried to stand up straight, but found it a little difficult.

Physician Ho pulled up another small case from behind the desk and opened it. He motioned to Jonny to come forward and when he stood next to the physician, Jonny looked down to see six beautiful red jade amulets shining within.

"What are they?"

"That's what gave the urns their power. Without them, the urns will just be urns. Sure, they will radiate residual energy long enough to fool the MSS, but that's all."

"Will Kang come back for us?"

"I don't know, but I doubt it. He'd have to admit he let you all live. As far as he's concerned, he can say he brought the urns back. That was his mission." Physician Ho closed the lid.

"How can we keep you safe then?" Jonny frowned then smiled. "Oh, I get it. I need to get you different urns. They don't have to be golden urns, right? A covered vase would do nicely." Jonny rushed to the shelves. "Let's see what we got. Do you each want to pick your own? That'd be cool." He looked back over his shoulder.

"Why don't you pick something," Chengli said.

"I think you should wake the family now," the Admiral said looking at Lady Ji and Wei Zan.

"Very well," Lady Ji said. "We'll meet in the kitchen?"

"Yes."

The two women headed up the stairs to gather the family together. Jonny felt relief at the idea he wouldn't have to explain everything by himself. He wasn't sure he could.

While the other residents followed the women, Jonny searched for substitute urns he could take up for when the residents needed to rest. Gathering together a selection, he placed them in a shipping box and carried them up. Let the residents pick which one they liked. Jonny smiled. *But they'll never beat solid gold.*

When he got up to the kitchen, he found his family sitting around the table in their pajamas looking dazed. Lady Ji and Wei Zan stood to the side. The smell of tea was in the air. Lei rose and filled cups for the family.

"Okay," Han said after a sip, "what's going on?" He watched as Jonny placed the box on the floor. "How come you're up already? What's in the box?"

The rest of the residents entered, filling the room. Han looked nervous. "Something happened."

Physician Ho stepped to the table. "My dear friends and Guardians, we have a confession to make. Please let me speak before you say anything." He looked around the table to get everyone's nod, sighed and began to speak.

"A little while ago we came to a decision. Please don't think it was made in haste for we have been considering this for a long time now. You all know what our purpose is, but for many decades now we have not performed our duties. Indeed, we feel there is nothing left for us to do. We are a computer that has outlived its function. These modern times have no need for us.

"We are tired. The time has come for us to leave. None of us chose this existence, but we feel we have fulfilled our given task with honor."

The family sat stunned. Han looked up at his friend. "You can't mean what I think you mean." Saying that, Han looked from resident to resident and after receiving their nods yelled, "No!"

"We plan to go watch the sunrise together," Jin said. "So, after the sun has risen, we ask that you destroy the jade."

"I can't do that," Han said. "My oath!"

"Your oath was to serve us. You will be doing that." Jin laid his hand on Han's shoulder.

"But..."

"I want a child," Lady Ji blurted out.

"What?"

"I want to hold my very own baby. My hope is that in the next life, I can do that. Right now, I'm a prisoner forever as are all of us. Physician Ho's dream was to have another family as well. We just want a real life!"

"I'll admit that it would be nice to be a complete man," The Admiral murmured.

"I thought it might be interesting to come back as a woman," Jin said with a smirk.

Chengli rolled his eyes. "The heavens will decide. You might come back as an ass."

Everyone looked at Wei Zan. Her eyes opened wide. "Do not look at me! I liked being a Huli Jing." Her glance flitted to Jonny. "Besides, I can't be human unless I earn it."

"Being a celestial fox wouldn't be bad," Jin said. "I'd pray to you."

"Stop!" Han cried out. "How can you joke?" He clutched at his chest.

"Han," Lei leaned forward to comfort her husband, "please, calm yourself. Do I need to get your medicine?"

Han brushed her words aside. "I don't need medicine. I need to not have my whole life negated!"

Silence fell.

"My dear friend," Physician Ho said, "we do not wish to do that. You have served us long and well, but all this must end. Your sons shouldn't have to continue caring for us. They have their own wishes. Bolin has already sacrificed for us. Now he will be free to pursue his dream. The same for your other sons."

Han slumped in his chair.

The three boys watched as their father struggled to come to terms with what the residents were saying.

"So, my last act will be to destroy what I've cared for my entire life." Han reached for Lei.

"You have a loving family and a good business. These things are more than most people have. You've had a good life." Physician Ho put the case on the kitchen table. "You have only one more task to perform as our Guardian. We ask you to honor our request."

Tears slid down Han's face. Unable to speak, he gave a nod and lay his hand on the case.

"Thank you." The physician bowed to Han then turned to the boys and did the same.

"Sunrise will be soon," Chengli said looking up at the kitchen clock. "We best say our goodbyes."

"We want to go with you," Min said standing up.

Lady Ji stepped forward and smiled. She reached up to place her hand on the young man's cheek. "You are a good man, Min, but no. I believe you will make some young woman a fine husband. Love her well."

Bolin stood and faced the residents. "It has been an honor. I would have served you my entire life if that is what you wanted. But I understand what you are saying, and I can't say that I don't agree with your decision. May the fates be kind." He bowed to the residents.

Han managed to stand and embraced all the residents except Wei Zan, tears flowing and still unable to speak. Lei followed after him then collapsed back into the chair.

Wei Zan stayed apart watching the family and her heart felt strange. She'd had her forest, her fellow creatures, but she'd always been alone. This scene made her heart hurt.

Jonny stood to the side watching as well. His head began to spin and anger surfaced. They were going to leave forever!

"Jonny!"

At the sound of his name, Jonny snapped back to the now.

"You will come with us," The Admiral said.

Chapter 38

Jonny sat on the blanket surrounded by the residents. A glow rose over the Eastern horizon from their Battery Spencer viewpoint signaling the coming sunrise. His head continued to throb as flashes of memories and feelings cascaded through him. *Am I going insane?*

"Why did you want me here?" Jonny asked. "I don't want to see this."

"Your family won't be able to believe we're gone without there being a witness." Physician Ho sat next to him. "You know that. Just as you know you wouldn't be able to accept that we're gone. The world of the supernatural works that way."

"We drew straws and you lost," Jin said smiling.

"Isn't it beautiful?" Lady Ji said with a sigh. "Are there sunrises in the afterlife?" She looked at her fellow residents. No one answered.

The Admiral stood to walk to the edge of the viewpoint and look out over the bridge as the colors blossomed in a blaze of yellows, oranges and reds. "Yes, my dear Lady, the sunrise is beautiful."

The other residents joined him in silence, each thinking their own private thoughts as Jonny watched. He found he couldn't catch his breath. His heart pounded. Tears gathered.

What will I do for the rest of my life? I'll never be able to feel like this again! Wei Zan, don't leave me!

The sun cleared the horizon, the blue of the sky spreading out to erase the dark.

"My dear friends," Physician Ho said, "it has been an honor to serve with you." He hugged Lady Ji, then the brothers, and finally Zheng He. "Maybe we'll meet again in a future life."

Almost as if on cue, there was a burst of red light. It surrounded the good physician and with a smile, he faded away.

The brothers were the next to fade, together as they had always been, Jin giving a wink and a wave. Then, after a quick hug to the Admiral, Lady Ji crossed over.

"Take care of our boy," The Admiral said to Wei Zan, and with another burst of light, he too, was gone.

Wei Zan offered her hand to Jonny to help him stand. Tears streamed down his face and his fierce grip would have pained a human. "Please, stay, my little fox," he choked out.

Wei Zan wrapped her arms around her Jianyu. "I can't. If I stay, Jonny will disappear. Please, be happy and live YOUR life." With that, Wei Zan exerted her power and pushed Jianyu away, walling him back where he belonged. "Maybe the fates will be kind in our next life."

The burst of red swallowed her and a million stars spread out fading until only the morning sunlight remained.

Chapter 39

Han gathered up the fragments of red jade and placed them in a small locked chest. His hands continued to shake, faint, but noticeable. Lei stood beside him not really knowing what she should do. When Han placed a hand over his heart, she grew more concerned.

"Do you need your pain medication?" Lei said putting a hand on his arm.

"No medicine will cure this pain. I'm sorry, Lei, but I need to be alone." With those words, he left the room.

Min looked at the two empty shelves of the urn cabinet, then walked over to straightened the piles of books on the remaining ones. He'd only read a handful, but already knew he wouldn't stop until he'd read them all. His heart felt empty.

Bolin walked over to the fridge and pulled out a couple of beers. He placed one on the table and opened the other. After taking a long pull, he motioned Min over. The two drank in silence.

"You should find Jonny," Lei murmured. "Do you think he's okay?"

Bolin looked at his mother. "I know he is. He's a lot stronger than any of us ever thought. He'll come home when he's ready."

"I hope you're right." Listless, she wandered around the room.

One by one the family left the resident's room, each going to their respective bedrooms to grieve in their own way.

The day passed and Lei decided it was time to make dinner. She fussed around the kitchen, trying to make something that would appeal to the men in her life. When finished, she knocked on their respective doors and ordered everyone to the kitchen.

Han was the first to come out. He went to Jonny's door. When there was no answer, he walked to the kitchen. Not seeing his youngest there, he asked, "Where's Jonny?"

"He hasn't returned, yet," Lei said putting the rice on the table. "Please eat something. If he doesn't come home soon, I'll send the boys out to look for him."

Han took his seat when Bolin and Min walked in. Dinner was quiet as each of them contemplated what the future would hold. Lei stood and cleared the table. When she checked her phone, she listened to a voicemail left earlier that day, then turned to Han.

"I have a message that you're not answering your phone. The doctor's office wants to remind you that you have an appointment tomorrow."

"I don't think I need to go," Han said. "I don't need anything."

"They won't refill your prescription for pain medication if you don't go in."

"I haven't taken any today." Han paused for a moment. "Come to think of it, I didn't take any yesterday."

"Oh, Han, they told you not to worry about becoming addicted. I don't want you to be in pain."

Han shook his head. "I'm not. Guess I've been so focused on what happened that I didn't give my cancer a thought." His sons pretended not to see the tears in his eyes.

"Isn't that a good thing?" Min asked looking around the table.

"Yeah, but Father, you will need it in the future so you'd better have some on hand." Bolin stood up. "I want to go with you. I'd like to talk with your doctor."

"Very well. I'll go."

***

"Are you okay?" a woman asked.

Jonny woke up lying on the ground and for a moment, wondered how he got there. Clarity returned slowly. The sun was up, the clouds heavy with moisture. Rain? A sob escaped.

"Do you need help?" another voice said. "Can we call someone for you?"

Gathering himself together, he stood up and looked around to get his bearings. "No," Jonny finally managed to answer. "I'm fine. Just fell asleep." With that he picked up the blanket and started to walk away. He could hear curious murmurs behind him, but chose to ignore them. They'd never believe the truth anyway.

Jonny found the SUV in the parking lot and headed toward Golden Gate Park. He didn't want to go home yet.

Once there, Jonny found himself wandering around the park retracing every step he'd taken with Wei Zan. He found the field where she first lay down to gather energy. He lay in what he thought was the same place hoping to feel a trace of her. Nothing. He looked up at the clouds again and noted the gathering darkness. It fit his mood. Putting his hands behind his head, he waited for the storm.

"Hey, Mister," a gruff voice called out. "You better get a move on or you'll get soaked for sure."

Jonny ignored the man until two dogs ran over and began to sniff—in pretty private places. "Hey! Go away!" Jonny pushed at the dogs.

"Sorry about that," the man gave a silly laugh as he approached. "They're just curious. They won't hurt ya none." The man scratched the ear of one dog. "Could you spare some change?"

Jonny took out his wallet and handed a twenty to the man. "Only if you leave me in peace."

"Sure thing." With a nod of his head, the man grabbed the money. "Thanks." He whistled to his dogs and turned to leave. His brow furrowed and he looked back. "Don't I know you?"

"No."

"Oh, okay." The man shook his head. "Thanks, again."

Jonny closed his eyes for a moment—a deep sadness filled him. When the first raindrops hit, he snapped out of it. A rumble of thunder echoed around the park. He stood and walked over to the canopy of a large tree. Sitting once again, he watched the rain fall. The temperature dropped and Jonny became aware of the chill. *Shoulda worn a better jacket.*

Common sense reasserted itself. Putting the hood of his jacket up, he sprinted back towards the parking lot. He made it just as the lightening announced the arrival of the main storm.

Rain started to fall in buckets while he sat and watched. *This is her nature. This is how she lived. Did the rain even bother her?*

These were questions he'd never know the answer to. Time passed and the storm waned. Hunger finally motivated him to move. He started the engine and drove to the nearest fast-food place. *I should go home, but I don't want to answer their questions. I don't want to talk about it.*

He drove back up to the Spencer Battery viewpoint, parked to eat and watched the sun set. Trying to recapture his time with Wei Zan, Jonny noticed gaps in his memory. Try as he might, the memory wouldn't return. He hadn't known the Huli Jing for long so why were his feelings so strong? *I don't get it.*

The time came where he knew he had to go home. His family would be worried and he knew they needed to hear what happened. The residents told him they would and he understood that now.

He started the car.

Chapter 40

THE FAMILY SAT IN the clinic waiting room. Jonny could tell his father felt uncomfortable having all of them there, but he'd been outvoted.

"Mr. Han Chen," the nurse called out.

On cue, they all stood and followed the woman back to the exam rooms. No one spoke while they waited, even Min had nothing to say. The doctor entered and sat down.

"I see the entire family came with you today. I'm glad. My name is Dr. Dean Haskell and I'm your father's oncologist. I'm assuming you all have some questions?"

The next few minutes were spent going over Han's diagnosis and prognosis. Dr. Haskell pulled up the MRI pictures to show the family the location and size of the primary tumor. They were able to see the secondary sites of metastasis throughout his abdomen, pelvis and up into his lungs.

"Is it really too late to try?" Bolin asked.

"Your father's tumor is aggressive and was very advanced by the time he came to see us," Dr. Haskell said. "Even if we had started treatment that same day, his prognosis was bleak. I understood his thoughts about not trying radiation and chemo. We can try to keep him as comfortable as possible. I think today we should get you signed up with hospice.

"You'll need a new prescription. Are the pain pills working or do I need to increase the dosage?"

"I don't think I need another prescription," Han said. "I haven't been feeling any pain for two days now."

"What?"

"That's true, Doctor," Lei said. "And his appetite is better. He hasn't thrown up in the last few days that I know of."

The doctor looked at Han and he nodded agreement.

"This is very strange," the doctor said. "I thought you looked pretty good when I first came into the room, but..." The doctor paused. "Please, get up on the table."

When Han lay down, the doctor began to palpate his upper abdomen. His brow furrowed. "This is unbelievable," he muttered. "I can't feel the primary tumor." After another few minutes, he motioned Han to get up and follow him.

"I'm going to ask all of you to wait here." With that, the two men left the room.

Lei and her sons looked at each other. "What do you think is going on?" Lei asked.

The boys shrugged. Bolin reached over and put his arm around his mother's shoulders. Lei clasped her hands to say a prayer.

An hour later, Han returned. "The doctor is looking at the films. He'll be here in a little bit. He asks that we wait."

And wait they did. Another hour passed before the door opened. Dr. Haskell walked in followed by a middle-aged female doctor. "This is Dr. Julia Jackson, my associate. I called her over to view the scan as well. I needed to confirm what I was seeing."

Lei started to shake, so Han grabbed her hand. "Tell me, Doctor. What is it?"

"Simply put, the tumors are gone."

"I-I'm sorry. What did you say?"

"We can't find any of the secondary tumors and the primary is the size of a penny. We think you're going into spontaneous remission."

"H-How is that possible?" Han asked stunned.

"We really don't know. It's rare, maybe about 1 in 100,000 patients. But the statistics are argued as both over and under re-ported. All I can tell you is that it appears your cancer will soon be totally gone. I'll want to see you in a month to repeat the scan and verify that the primary tumor is totally gone."

"Will it come back?" Lei's voice shook.

"I can't answer that. I've never seen a remission like this. Especially a case as advanced as your husband's was. This is a mir-acle." Dr. Haskell held out his hand and shook Han's. "Congratu-lations." Dr. Jackson did the same.

Lei broke down in sobs, so Han pulled her into his arms. The boys sat wide-eyed and tried not to follow her example.

"I guess you won't need that prescription," Dr. Haskell laughed. "Please call me if anything happens. Remember, I want to see you in a month." With that, the two doctors left the room.

The family sat stunned and disbelieving. Han looked at his boys over Lei's head and smiled.

"Let's go home."

***

By unspoken agreement, the family gathered in the residents' room. Han and Lei collapsed on the recliners, while the boys paced the room.

"What do you think happened?" Bolin said.

"This is wild," Min agreed. "I'm still pinching myself."

Jonny thought for a moment and walked over to the computer. He opened it up and checked his email. There it was.

Dear Jonny,

I hope by the time you read this; you and your family will know about the gift I left you. You lost your family once because of me—because I loved you. In this life and this time, I want to return them to you as best I can.

Goodbye,

Wei Zan

A fist squeezed Jonny's heart. Once again, Wei Zan had saved him. This time through his family.

"It was Wei Zan's doing," Jonny murmured.

"What did you say?" Bolin asked.

"Wei Zan cured Dad."

"What? But how..."

Stunned, Han spoke up. "According to legend, Huli Jings have the power to heal. I never thought..."

"After we locked her up for generations, she still did this for us," Jonny said as grief welled up inside him. So many of his memories of Wei Zan were just misty remnants now. Jianyu was gone—locked away forever as he should be. But Jonny remembered Wei Zan's beauty, her smile, her kindness. He may have only been fascinated by her, maybe half in love, but now he'd never know. Tears slid down his face.

"Wei Zan says goodbye."

About the author

KL VanderJagt is a retired nurse, wife, mother, and grandmother. Born and raised in rural New Jersey, she later settled in Arizona after meeting and marrying her husband.

A lifelong reader, she turned her love of reading into a love of writing and has spent the past ten years developing her craft. Her work spans multiple genres, including mystery, fantasy, science fiction, and contemporary fiction.

I dedicate this book to my family. Their love, support, and patience helped me develop as a writer. In particular, for this story, I want to thank my son, Chase, who announced one day, "Mom, I had an interesting dream." From that sentence and the conversation that followed, this story came to be.

I hope this tale captures your imagination the way it captured mine.

KL VanderJagt